Lock Down Presents

Presents

CITY OF SMOKE

Opps In The Air

A Novel by Molotti

First Edition July 2023

Printed in the United States of America

Lock Down Publications
P.O. Box 944
Stockbridge, GA 30281
www.lockdownpublications.com

Like our page on Facebook: Lock Down Publications
www.facebook.com/lockdownpublications.ldp

Book interior design by: Dynasty's Cover Design
Edited by: Sunny

Stay Connected with Us!

Text LOCKDOWN to 22828 to stay up-to-date with new
releases, sneak peaks, contests and more...
Or CLICK HERE to sign up.

Like our page on Facebook:
Lock Down Publications: Facebook

Join Lock Down Publications/The New Era Reading Group

Visit our website:
www.lockdownpublications.com

Follow us on Instagram:
Lock Down Publications: Instagram

Email Us: We want to hear from you!

DEDICATION

This book is dedicated to my brother 4Buddy, the real King of the 100's and the rest of my brothers who not here anymore. BT, Risky, Mackey, Kese, Moe, B-Dub, 180, B-Moe, Lil Aaron, Myles, Reese, Domo, Rico, Pat, CB, Vic, Muggy, Marty, Moe Joe, Beezy, Zack C Money, J Rock, Lil Tommy, Serge, and Boom... Long Live The Kings.

ACKNOWLEDGEMENTS

First off, I wanna give thanks to the Most High. Nothing is possible without your blessings. Thanks to LDP's CEO Ca$h for giving me the opportunity to turn my dream into fruition. To my second mother, Big Red. I love you and I miss you. You left us too early and I hate that you weren't able to see what I accomplished. I remember everything you said to me and I know you would've been proud of me. To my family, friends and others who been supporting me, thank you. I appreciate all the support love y'all show to me.

Chapter 1

New To The Game
(Southside Chicago...The Wild 100s)

"Man, I gotta start high school off the right way, on Stone. I can't fall in that bitch broke. No sir," I told my younger cousin, Nutso and our lil homie, Bone while shaking my head. My short braids were nappy and rough. They were looking like I had them in for months instead of just a week and a half. I had on a wife beater and a pair of khaki cargo shorts that sagged off my ass. We were sitting in my junky bedroom at my mother's apartment in the Pullman Wheelworks Building known as The Condos on 104th Street. It was a huge low income building. The halls stayed packed with kids and older guys from the hood. The elevators smelled like piss, but they worked. Crime was heavy even though the building had security.

It was the summer of 2006 and Bone had just went through his creation and officially became a member of the Black P Stone Nation. Me and Nutso had already been members. I had just graduated from 8th grade and was about to start my freshman year at Corliss High School on 103rd and Corliss, right across the street from my building.

"I'm tryna go right in fuckin seniors but we all know that that shit dead if I'm broke," I said making Nutso and Bone erupt in laughter. They were laughing so hard that Nut had to pause their game of Madden 06.

"How you plan on making some money? Yo' black ass must be ready to cut grass for the rest of the summer," Nutso said not taking his eyes off the TV screen.

"On Stone, that shit dead," I replied reaching for his controller. "I'm about to see if Killa will let me sell some weed for him," I stated. I had been contemplating that move for well over a week now.

"Man, you gon' let somebody take yo' shit," Bone joked. For a 11-year-old, his voice was deep and raspy, and he spoke slowly.

"Not while I'm totin' this," I said upping a small gold and black .25 from my pocket.

"Auntie gone beat yo' charcoal black ass if she see you with that," Nutso said with a straight face. We all knew that he spoke nothing but the truth.

"Shut yo' scary ass up! Y'all can play the game all summer but I'm 'bout to go on the block and get some money," I said before walking out of the room and out of the apartment.

I left out the back entrance to the building and walked down 104th and Maryland until I seen Killa and Primo standing on the porch to one of their traps across the street. They were rotating a blunt of Dro. "What's up, big bro? Let me hit that shit," I said to Killa reaching for the blunt that he was holding.

Killa was a skinny, light skinned guy. He stood about 5'10 and wore his long hair in braids that hung past his shoulders. He was a well-known shooter and very respected throughout the hood. He was getting money selling weed. Killa and Primo were from the buildings too but they were GD. We had Black Stones, Four Corner Hustlers, and GDs in our building. We were different gangs but we all claimed the same hood so we didn't see stars or colors with each other. You could be a GD but if you fucked with me or one of the foes from the building, Killa and Primo would fuck you up for us. That's just how shit went in the hundreds. We set banged more than gang banged. Killa and Primo were a few years older than me but they fucked with me hard and I looked up to them.

"Yo' baby ass can't handle the shit I smoke. Where the rest of the lil guys at? I heard about y'all robbing that pizza man." Killa threw a quick jab that hit my chest and continued. "Fuck is wrong with y'all? I know y'all smarter than that."

"Nigga we was fucked up and hungry so we killed two birds with one stone. You know how that shit go but speaking of that, we can prevent it from ever happening again if you let me sell some weed for you," I said with a smile showing my big, white teeth. "I'm tryna step my shit up and you could help me do it," I added.

Primo stood there with his tall, lanky body slightly slouched. He looked at me, smirked and said, "Yo' lil ass ain't no trapper," He hit the blunt and blew out a cloud of smoke. "You so little that a nigga might try you," he added. Primo was known for putting in work. He was always on go. He was getting money too but everyone who knew him knew that he stood on business. Him and Killa were a dangerous duo.

"You got me fucked up. You know I keep my pocket rocket," I replied flashing my .25.

"Lil Dre, I'm not fuckin with you if you gon' smoke my shit up. I can put you on and show you the game but I can't make you an All Star," Killa told me.

"I understand all that big bro but the only way we'll know is if you give me a chance."

"Don't fuck up folk's paper or I'ma beat yo' lil ass," Primo cut in.

"Stop playin' with me before I beat yo' yellow ass till you turn blue like them niggas from up the hill did when they caught you at Popeyes," I said making Killa laugh. "And pass the blunt, you domin," I said reaching out for the blunt until Primo handed it to me.

"Come on, we in the trap," Killa said before leading us inside.

Killa's trap was a boarded up two flat apartments. We entered through the backdoor and went to the second-floor apartment. Inside of the apartment was much cleaner than I'd expected it to be.

In one of the bedrooms, Killa had a raggedy ass full sized bed with no sheets or blankets on it, a 19-inch TV, a PlayStation 2 and a few games scattered around on the floor. He reached under the mattress and grabbed his scale.

"Do you know how to bag up," he asked me and I shook my head.

"Aight first, I'ma teach you how to weigh and bag up," he told me leading me into the living room and taking a seat at the card table that sat in the middle of the room. The living room was basically empty besides the card table, three chairs and a lot of weed baggies scattered around.

"I'ma start you off with a quarter ounce. Bring me back fifty dollars and that's gone get you a half," Killa told me before showing me how to use the scale and bag up. He gave me a few tips on how to build up my clientele while we rotated a few blunts. I bagged up eleven nickel bags.

As I prepared to leave, I told Killa, "Tell Monie to hit my phone too, bro," talking about his younger sister who I'd had a crush on forever. He chased me out of the trap and down the block.

"I'm fuckin you up when I catch you," he yelled when he realized that he couldn't catch me.

"Open the window, you goofy ass nigga," I yelled to Nutso standing outside his bedroom window at his mother's house on 106th and Indiana.

"Chill, cuz," he mumbled opening the window." I was doing something nigga. Why didn't you come through the front door," he asked.

"Cause I didn't want to," I shot back while climbing through the window. "Look what I got, cuz," I said pulling the bundle of weed from under my nut sack.

"Who you steal this from?" Nutso asked, snatching the bag and putting his nose to it.

"I didn't steal shit. I told you that my boy Killa was gon' look out for me. Don't get to looking stupid now," I said. I was feeling myself.

"How many you giving me?"

"Man, I'm not giving you none of my weed so you can go smoke it up with that skinny ass bitch of yours. I'm tryna get this money, lil nigga," I said speaking as if I had a thousand pounds.

"Cuz, don't make me beat yo' black ass and take that shit," Nutso threatened, grabbing me by my throat. He was my younger cousin by a year, but we were close like brothers. We were about the same height, about 5'3. He was skinnier than me and while I was the same color as dark chocolate, he was golden brown. He had his hair cut into a shaped up afro. Even though he knew he couldn't beat me in a fight, he always tried and sometimes he got close.

"On Stone don't grab my neck," I said shoving him hard and almost making him fall. "You gone make me beat yo' ass. I only got eleven bags so I'ma give you five and you gotta bring me back the whole twenty-five dollars and next go around you'll get more. *Do. Not. Smoke. My. Shit!*" I stressed saying each word with emphasis.

"Cuz, have I ever let you down," Nutso asked with a smile.

"Hell yeah," I said a little too loud as my auntie Peaches walked into the room.

"Watch yo' damn mouth boy," she snapped, smacking me on the back of my head.

"When you get here anyways," she asked.

"I been here. I just forgot to come speak. How you doing today, Auntie?"

"Boy, take yo' ass home," she told me before leaving the room.

I felt my cell phone vibrating in my pocket. I pulled it out, looked at the screen and saw that it was my homie T Stone calling. "What's the demo, Law?" I answered.

"Where you at bro," he asked frantically.

"I'm at Nut crib. Why, what's up? You good?"

"Some niggas just jumped on Bucky. We at the White Castles on 103rd and Michigan. They outside posted, waiting for us to come out."

"Bet. We on our way up there," I said before hanging up.

"Come on, cuz," I told Nutso, heading for the door.

"What happened? Where we going," he asked.

"Some niggas just jumped on Bucky. They need us." I told him leading him out of the house.

When we got to the White Castle, there was a crowd of young niggas standing in front of the exit. I walked near the crowd and waved T Stone and Bucky out.

"I hope them ain't y'all homies because we beating they hook ass when they come out," A fat, brown-skinned kid wearing a dusty, bent up Cubs fitted cap said.

"You got us fucked up. Ain't nobody touching them. You better be cool," I warned sliding my hand near my waistline where my .25 rested.

"Who the fuck you telling to be cool? You must want to get did like yo' homie." The fat kid snarled.

"That shit dead," Nutso spat stepping in the fat kid's face.

"Damn, Big John, you gon' let dude skinny ass talk to you like that?" a bucktoothed dark-skinned, skinny kid asked, instigating.

"You know what," Big John said reaching in his pants pocket and pulling out a hunting knife. "I'm 'bout to cut this bitch ass nigga tongue out his mouth and see how crazy he talk then," he said.

When I saw the knife, I upped my gun.

'Click Clack'

I chambered a bullet. "Put that knife down before I smoke yo' fat ass," I told Big John pointing the gun at his face. He dropped the knife and threw his hands in the air. "Bring y'all scary ass out!" I yelled to T Stone and Bucky. When they came out, I saw that Bucky's left eye was black and swollen.

"Damn Bucks, look at yo' eye! We gotta fuck one of these niggas up," I said with my face balled up into a mug.

Nutso didn't hesitate to take off on Big John. He hit him in his mouth, drawing blood. T Stone threw a hard right hook that dropped the skinny kid. Another kid stepped up like he wanted to help so I shot a shot in the air.

"Next time we catch one of y'all ass over here, I'ma pop one of y'all ass!" I threatened but the group didn't give me a chance to finish my sentence before they fled the scene.

"Where you get that pipe from," T Stone asked as we marched to the building.

All of us besides Nutso lived in the building. T Stone was 13-years-old. He was light-skinned with a low cut and a big nose. He was a little taller than me and one of my closest friends.

"Nigga, you know we keep pipes," Nutso boasted.

"Me and Reesie stole it from one of the GDs off Corliss," I admitted. "Aw yea, and I got good green on deck," I added proudly.

"Good cause I need to get high. Where you get it from?" Bucky asked. His fat body moved slowly. He was always in his own world thinking of new raps. He always told us that he was going to be the one to get us out the hood with his music. Him and T Stone were cousins.

"It don't matter where I got it from. All you need to know is that I got it and it's some killa."

"Aight, let me get 3 for the $10 and that shit better be smoking or I'ma smack you in the mouth," Bucky replied, digging in his pocket, and pulling out a ten dollar bill.

"Can't do 3 for the $10, you can get 2 for that."

Bucky smacked his lips and shot me a look of disbelief."
Okay, you petty ass nigga. Don't ask to hit my blunts either,"
he said frowning.

"We just saved yo' fat ass so you gon' put that shit in the
air or I'ma close yo' other eye," Nutso threatened and
everybody burst out laughing.

"Don't move!" A voice gruffed from behind us. "The first
pussy that try to run gon' be the first one to die," the voice
said.

"Damn, man!" Nutso gruffed putting his hands in the air.
I thought about going for my gun but I didn't know if it
was the police or somebody trying to rob us. I'm not gon'
lie. I froze up. I looked back and saw a slim, brown skinned
kid with short dreads holding a .38. "Stop playin' so much
goofy ass nigga," I said to my close friend, Reesie.

"On the foe, you niggas was scared as hell," he said
laughing hard as hell. "It looked like Nut was about to shit
on his self!" Reesie grinned showing the gap between his
two front teeth. "Where y'all just come from? Y'all heard
that shot go off? I think somebody just got they ass popped,"
he said.

"On Stone that was us. We did that," Nutso bragged as if
we'd just murdered someone.

"What happened?"

"Some niggas whooped Bucky's ass, so me and Dre ran
up there with the pipe and we handled that business. I wish
you was there foe," Nutso said overexaggerating.

Reesie was a Four Corner Hustler. In the city, we called
them Foes for short.

"Stop lying. Y'all ain't pop nobody," he said. You could
see it all in his eyes that he was mad that he missed the
action.

"Naw," I cut in. "we didn't pop nobody. I shot in the air.
I could've popped one of they ass, doe."

"Where you just come from, foe?" T Stone asked Reesie.

"Tryna rob the delivery man from Tommy's Chinese food. He wasn't going doe," Reesie replied with a chuckle. He was always somewhere up to no good. Besides Lil Risky and B.T, he was the first one of us off the porch. "I Heard DeDe and Ayana supposed to be fighting in the hood. I gotta see that shit," he added.

"Them dumb ass hoes better not make the block hot," Bucky complained flaming up one of his blunts.

The next day, I was posted at the gas station on 103rd street right off Cottage Grove trying to sell my last three bags of weed. Nutso had already sold all five of his bags and given me the money he made.

"Damn, Dominique you gon' walk past like you don't know a nigga no more?" I asked a caramel skinned, petite girl that was walking past me. She lived down the hall from me.

"I don't have time to be playing with you," she replied pushing her blond and brown micro braids out of her face.

"I'm not playing. The only thing I'm tryna play with you is Catch a girl, Freak a girl," I told her grabbing her by her waist.

"Boy, you better let me go before my man see you," she replied giggling.

"Don't get yo' man fucked up."

"Smoke something with me."

"Hell naw," I said walking off. "You better ask yo' man to buy you some weed," I said over my shoulder.

"That's why I don't fuck with your black ass now. You think you the shit cause you selling that huff ass weed," Dominique said looking at me like I was crazy.

I stepped in Killa's trap with Nutso hot on my heels. I had sold all the weed and was ready to cop a half.

"Damn bro, I only made fifty five dollars and I gotta give you fifty dollars of it?" I asked with a frown. That didn't sit well with me. I did all that hustling for five funky ass dollars.

"Just trust the process lil bro," Killa replied bringing out the scale and the baggies. "The more you spend, the more you make. It's all about consistency and profit but most importantly you gotta stack yo' money. That's the only way you gon' see progression."

"I'm tryna progress and get like you," I shot back.

"Yeah, me too," Nutso said chiming in.

"On the G, you need to hurry up and progress so you can get outta that fake ass chain," Killa joked looking at Nut's silver chain with a big fake Superman S charm on it. "Just follow my lead and y'all gon' see some paper. I promise," Killa vowed as we bagged up my half.

***

By Spring 2007, I was in school showing out. I was now copping a few ounces at a time. Nutso was grabbing a ounce and a half for himself but we were still jugging as a team.

"Let me get four for the eighteen, lil bro," a bumpy-faced senior asked me as I walked through the hallways of Corliss High School. I rarely went to class. I spent my days roaming the hallways chasing girls and selling weed. I was very popular and everybody in the school fucked with me.

"Only because you always shop with me G but when is yo' lil ugly ass gon' come with the whole thang?" I asked slipping him the weed and grabbing the money.

"Don't do that to me you know I come correct sometimes," he lied as I counted the money before adding it to my thick wad of bills.

As I turned around, I felt somebody step on my Retro 11 Jordans. "Damn man, watch where you going!" I barked, checking my shoes for scuffs.

"My bad," a soft female voice said. I looked up and saw a fine ass sophomore. I only knew what grade she was in because of the color of her uniform shirt.

"I didn't mean to scuff yo' lil Jordans," she said.

"It ain't shit, shorty. I can buy another pair. I should've seen you coming. What's yo' name again?"

"Kahidijah, you would've known my name if you ever made it to eight period," she replied with a smile.

"I be chasing bread, shorty. Eighth period don't put no money in my pockets."

"Duh but it's teaching you things that could eventually lead to a job that'll put money in your pocket," she shot back.

I stood there admiring her almond brown skin tone, sexy smile, and shoulder length hair that she had in a style that I didn't know the name of. It was sexy though. The more I stared at her, the more I found myself wanting her. "Do you smoke?" I asked.

"Yes but I don't have money to spend on weed."

"Let's go to Gately Park and get high. I got you," I told her, leading her to one of the school's side exits.

Meanwhile, Nutso and a few of the bros were sitting behind the football field at Gately Park getting high.

"Them bitch ass MC's off Wentworth think they know how to hoop so good. We should go bust they ass," Big Lord said wiping sweat off his forehead. He was a Mafia Insane Vice Lord originally from the 4120 buildings, but he'd moved next door to Nutso a few years ago. The hood they grew up in was known as D Block. They were Black Stones and Four Corner Hustlers. Big Lord and his family were the only Mafias in the hood. All the bros from The Condos and D Block were real tight. We were clicked up. The older guys stayed on their own respective sides but us young niggas were locked in. We looked at each other as if we were all the same shit.

"Fuck them niggas I'm 'bout to go see if they want some weed though," Nutso said walking towards the basketball court where the MC's were hooping.

"Nickel weed, no sticks no seeds. Pass me by, you won't get high!" he screamed from the sideline.

A short, dirty looking dark skinned MC stopped playing ball and waltzed over to where he was standing. "Let me see how that shit look," he told Nutso who reached in his pants and pulled out his jab of weed. "This that kill right here," he told the guy passing him the whole jab. "Good looking. Charge that shit to the game," the guy said walking off with a mug.

"You got me fucked up. Nigga run my ·bread or run that weed," Nutso said, following after the kid.

"Or what," a smaller stockier kid asked stepping towards Nutso.

"Or I'ma beat his ass!" Nutso growled stepping in the middle of the court stopping the five on five basketball game that was going on. The group of Mickey Cobras all mugged him but that didn't scare him. They had a long way to go before they were in the safety of their own hood.

"Move around lil nigga," the dirty kid said.

Nutso threw two lightning fast jabs that connected with his chin. He followed with a uppercut, but the kid blocked it and countered with a nasty right hook that hit Nut behind his ear.

Before Nutso knew it, the whole court was punching and kicking on his ass.

"What the fuck going on over there?" Cello asked getting up from the bench he was sitting on and making his way towards the court.

"Somebody fighting," C Murder said taking off towards the fight knowing that Nut had just went towards the court to sell some weed.

As they got closer, they noticed that it was Nutso who was getting jumped. Cello threw a series of punches at the dusty kid's head dropping him. Big Lord was big for his age. At 15 years old, he stood 5'10 and weighed no less than 180 pounds. He easily went through the crowd of MCs punching and pushing until he made his way to Nutso who was balled up on the ground getting stomped out.

C Murder was a brown skinned kid from a hood on 115th called The Ville. Him and his brother Juicy fucked with D Block hard. He helped Nutso up after he received a punch to the eye that almost dropped him.

"Come on y'all, we gone!" Nutso screamed using his shirt to wipe blood from his face. He took off running and the rest of the guys followed. The MCs started to chase but thought against it. Gately Park was in our hood, and they knew soon the guys would be aware of what just went down so they ran to the bus stop. "It's on now!" Nutso yelled as he ran off.

I was sitting in the park smoking and vibing with Kahidijah when I saw the bros running our way. "What the fuck happened to you, cuz?" I asked Nutso when I saw his bloody mouth.

"The snakes off Wentworth jumped me and stole my weed," Nutso said. He was so mad that he was speaking louder than necessary.

"Them niggas been acting like they wanted smoke. We gotta fuck one of them up," Big Lord said.

Even though majority of the guys were Stones and Foes, we had a few BDs and GDs that hung out with us. C Murder was one of the main ones.

"I'm sorry that our lil vibe got rudely interrupted cause I was really enjoying your company but now I gotta go. Maybe you can call me later or something," I told Kahidijah before we exchanged numbers. "Maybe you could come over my house and braid my hair later," I said.

"Maybe, just call me," she told me before I ran off to catch up with the guys.

Around 8:30 that night, me and a gang of the guys were posted on 104th and Maryland waiting on Rock Solid and T Stone to come back with a steamer. Our plan was to go through Wentworth shooting at the MCs.

"Here," Primo handed me a heavy .357, "you better use that bitch. Who going with you?" He asked scanning the crowd.

"Me," Reesie said stepping up smiling devilishly. "I got a new pipe that I'm tryna test out," he added flashing a SD .40.

"Cello the best driver out of all of us so he gone drive," I said as a red Dodge Neon pulled up in front of us. T Stone and Rock Solid jumped out the car but kept it running. "What the fuck y'all waiting on?" Primo gruffed.

I climbed in the backseat of the Neon. "Damn, it stank in this bitch!" I said covering my nose from the smell of Newports and vomit. "Let's hurry up and get this shit over with," I added trying to mask my nervousness.

We drove through 106th and Wentworth and then 106th Place and street but didn't see anyone outside. "They probably up at Lavizzo with BD nem," Cello said while driving up Wentworth again. We spotted a crowd of guys in the gated area around Lavizzo Elementary School.

"Park on the side block and let us out," Reesie told Cello.

I adjusted my Coogi hoodie to cover my face as we walked towards the crowd of men and women. I saw the dusty kid that Nutso described to me. I knew his name but couldn't remember it at the time. He was standing in the middle of the crowd holding a smoldering blunt. "Y'all got some weed?" I asked the crowd as I approached.

"Lil Snake got it. What you tryna get?" An older guy with a raspy voice asked before the dusty snake pushed him to the side.

"I got it, too, what you need?" Dusty snake asked looking down at me.

"Five for the dub," I replied. He went in his pocket, and that's when I upped the .357 I had and started shooting. The crowd broke up running in every direction trying to avoid a bullet. Reesie ran towards the crowd shooting while I stood there shooting wildly, trying to hit anybody I could. People were dropping. I didn't know if they'd gotten hit or just hitting the ground to dodge a bullet.

"Come on!" I yelled to Reesie before taking off and running to the car.

As we pulled off, Reesie couldn't stop cheesing. He was looking out of his window.

"Why you smiling like that?" Cello asked curiously, taking little peeps over at Reesie who was sitting in the passenger's seat.

"On the foe, I seen a lot of they ass dropping. I think we hit something," Reesie replied, smiling even harder. "Them niggas ain't gon' play with us no more," he added excitedly. I just sat quietly in the backseat until we reached the hood. I didn't speak to anyone when we made it to the building. I went straight home.

Nutso came over early the next morning. He looked like he'd been awake all night.

"You saw the news, cuz?" he asked, pouring himself a cup of orange juice.

"Hell naw, why? What happened?" I asked dryly.

"Three people got shot at Lavizzo. One of them died. It was the dude who took my weed," he said, and my stomach started to turn. I never would've imagined that we'd killed someone. I really just wanted to show them that we weren't the ones to be fucked with.

"Let's slide in the back of the building and see who all out there," I said before grabbing my jab of weed and throwing on my Akademiks windbreaker.

We walked to the C Section's parking lot to see Reesie, Cello and Beezy sitting on Beezy's balcony. We were all close friends but Cello and Reesie were close like me and Nutso were. They stayed together and always had something going on. I was very close to Reesie too but I spent most of my time with Nutso, Bone and T Stone.

"What's up bro? What y'all on?" Cello asked as we shook up. His eyes were almost as red as blood.

"We ain't on shit. Y'all heard the news?" I asked quietly.

Reesie lit a blunt and hit it a couple times before speaking. "Hell yeah, I heard some hoes talking about that shit. I knew we hit something. Fuck them niggas," he said. His eyes didn't have the look of a ordinary 14 year old. They were dark and made you look away if you stared in them for too long. They told you that he'd been through a lot of shit in his young life.

"I'm glad we scored. I just hope them niggas don't snitch. That's all I'm worried about," I said.

Nutso grabbed my head and turned it towards the B Section entrance. "There go shorty you was at the park with the other day. She with Shabree. I bet they looking for some weed," he said as I jerked out of his grip.

"Let's go see what they on," I said hurriedly walking off.

"Kahidijah, what you on, baby?" I asked, admiring her frame in the red sweatpants she had on.

"Hey, Dre I was just looking for you. I need some weed," she replied with a smile while giving me a tight hug.

"How much you need?" I asked glancing over at Shabree. She was my homie, Lil 4's older sister. "What's up Shabree? Where Lil 4 at?" I asked letting my eyes roll over her nice ass. If I wasn't trying to fuck with Kahidijah, I would've most definitely shot my shot at *her*.

"He somewhere around here getting high with T Stone," she replied.

"How many you say you wanted again?" I asked turning my attention back to Kahidijah.

"Can I get five for the dub?" She asked flashing a pretty smile.

"Give me a nice hug and a kiss and you can have six for the dub," I said opening my arms until she fell into my embrace. "Damn, now I don't wanna let you go," I whispered in her ear. It was true. She smelled good and felt good in my arms.

"Girl, come on. Y'all irritating," Shabree complained.

"Yo' cock blocking ass," I grumbled to Shabree before pulling out my jab and giving Kahidijah the weed. I grabbed the crumbled up twenty dollar bill she was holding." Can I have some of your time later?" I asked before she could walk off.

"Maybe," was all she said before she went about her business.

"You tryna cuff that skinny ass bitch, ain't you?" Nutso asked while he broke down a Swisher.

"I don't know about cuffing her but I'm tryna fuck fasho," I said as we headed back to where Reesie, Cello and Beezy were.

Later that night while I was in the crib playing my PlayStation, I got a call from Kahidijah.

"What's up, baby?" I answered trying to deepen my voice.

"Hey Dre, what you doing?" she replied with a giggle.

"Shit in the crib high as hell, playing the game,"

"Why aren't you outside?"

"Because I'm waiting on you to come over," I said.

Kahidijah was quiet for a pause. "Boy yo' momma not about to treat me. I don't even play like that," she said making me chuckle.

"Shorty, I'm grown. I can have company. Plus, my momma at work anyways so you good."

"Whatever, if I come over, I'm not staying that long."

"Okay that's cool. As long as you come," I was *thirsty*. "Meet me on 105th and Corliss."

"Bet," I said hanging up and leaving out of the apartment.

By the time I made it to Corliss, Kahidijah was standing there waiting on me.

She wore a pair of white leggings, a small white leather jacket over a white tee and a pair of all white low top Air Force Ones.

"You looking this good just for me?" I asked giving her a hug and a peck on the lips. Once we made it back to my home, I led her to my bedroom. I turned on the music playlist on my laptop and 'Shawty' by Plies came on.

"I'm tryna make you my shawty. I wish you would stop playing games with me," I told Kahidijah, jumping onto my bed right next to her.

"I'm not playing games with you. I just don't want to get hurt by you. I know you're getting a little money so all them hoes be in your face. I just don't think it'll be a good idea to get into something serious with you," she said as I ran my fingers through her hair.

"I'm not tryna hurt you or play with your heart. I really like you. I'm not thinking about no other girl, just you," I said laying it on thick before planting a soft kiss on her cheek.

My words must've had some effect because Kahidijah said, "If I give you a chance you better not hurt me," while staring into my eyes.

"I won't, I promise. Now, give me a kiss," I said then leaned in and kissed her without waiting for a response. I kissed her long and passionately before reaching for her shirt and pulling it over her head revealing her pink bra. I started moving my kisses down to her neck and then to her breast before reaching her flat stomach. I stopped kissing to pull her leggings off then started kissing up and down her long legs. She was enjoying it. I could tell by how heavy she was breathing.

I quickly slipped out of my basketball shorts and boxers in one motion. I climbed on top of her and continued to kiss her, sticking my tongue in her mouth. She reached down and took off the pink panties she wore to match her bra. I reached down and slid a finger into her tight, wet pussy.

After a few minutes of fingering her, I slid my already hard, throbbing dick inside of her. She moaned loudly and dug her nails in my back as I forced myself deeper into her warm, juicy pussy. I slowly moved in and out of her as Trey Songz 'Gotta Go' played.

"Turn over," I ordered. She got on her knees and elbows with her ass tooted in the air. I went in from behind watching my big, black dick go in and out of her pretty pink pussy. I started stroking her faster and faster until she was screaming begging for me to slow down.

By the time I was slowing down, I was already bussing my nut deep inside her walls. I fell over next to her on the bed breathing heavily. "That was the best I ever had," I admitted complimenting her good pussy.

Kahidijah grabbed my still semi hard dick. "This is mine. Don't ever let another bitch get what belongs to me," she said with a light squeeze.

"You won't ever have to worry about that," I lied as my cell phone started ringing. I didn't recognize the number, but I still answered. "Talk to me." I answered cooly.

"What's good bro? This Donovan from London Towns. You think you could bring me a half to school tomorrow?" The caller asked. Donovan was my boy. We'd known each other since we were younger.

I thought about it for a second. I didn't really sell weight, but I wanted the money. I checked my stash to see that I had two and a half ounces already bagged up. "I got a half but it's already bagged up," I told him.

"That's cool as long as it's all there. How much you gon' tax me?"

"Sixty dollars," I said knowing that half ounces only went for fifty dollars but I had to put my tax on it.

"Aight, I'ma holla at you tomorrow at school," Donovan said before hanging up.

The next day me and Reesie were patrolling the halls of Corliss High School as usual. We rarely went to class and when we did go to class, it would be a class that we had no business in."

"These lame ass, hoe ass niggas fear me in this bitch," Reesie bragged, mean muggin' some senior who caught his glare and turned away.

25

"Ain't nobody scared of you nigga. They sacred of me for real. They just know you my homie so they stay out yo' way," I teased him, laughing. I considered Reesie to be one of my best friends. He lived in the apartment directly above mine. He was the unofficial leader of our crowd since Lil Risky and BT were locked up.

Before he could reply to my last statement, Donovan walked up.

"What's the word, Moe? I got that shit in my locker for you," I told him shaking up with him then leading him towards my locker.

Once we made it to my locker, I gave him the half and watched him count out sixty dollars. "Good looking out, bro. I'll be back for some more after I'm done smoking this," he told me tucking the weed and walking off.

On my way to my third period computer class, I bumped into Kahidijah coming from the senior side of the school. "What's up Bae?" I asked before giving her a hug and a kiss.

"Hey bae, I hope y'all wasn't just fighting," she said with a small frown. She knew that me and the bros stayed in the middle of something.

"Naw, why you say that though?"

"Because I just saw the police take some dude out in cuffs and I saw you with him before," she replied.

"Naw, we wasn't fighting, and I don't even know if anybody else was but I'm good. I'm about to go to class before they start accusing me of shit," I said walking off the opposite way.

Before I could make it to class, I bumped into my homie L.O.. He was a senior that I knew. He hung out on D Block, but he was a Black Stone from 87th and Wabash, a hood called Bash Town.

"Who just got booked?" I asked him while we shook up.

"They just booked one of the Moes from London Town. He got caught with some green," L.O. said, and Donovan immediately came to mind.

"D'Andre, come here!" A fat, light-skinned security guard yelled making his way towards me.

I started to walk in his direction but decided not to and took off running in the opposite direction. I ran out of the emergency side door on the freshman side of the school that lead to the bridge. As I hit the bridge, I ran past an officer that worked at the school and he joined the chase. I ran down the flight of stairs that lead to the school's side exit that would put me out right on Maryland Street. I hit the exit thinking that it was a hop, skip and a jump from being a free man but I was wrong. I didn't expect for it to be two more officers waiting outside for me. The bigger officer who had the body of a football player tackled me hard to the ground. After they roughed me up a bit, they cuffed me and threw me in the back of a CPD blue and white patrol car. The officers claimed that someone watched me serving Donovan on the school's cameras. They charged me with a delivery and that's how I landed in the Odie home.

Chapter 2

Lil D.O.C.

The juvenile correctional officer walked me onto the intake deck of the Juvenile Detention Center. "Make yourself at home," the big, black baldhead C.O. said pushing me into a dark cell before slamming the door shut.

"Bitch ass nigga!" I muttered to myself before hitting the light switch so I could get myself situated.

I looked around my cell and saw that my cell mate had pictures of a girl and posters of female musicians stuck to the wall.

"Where you from out there?" My celly asked me getting up from under his covers. He was a brown-skinned Juelz Santana-looking nigga with short plaits in his head.

"I'm from 104th and Maryland, the Condos. Where you from?" I shot back showing not even the slightest bit of fear.

"I'm from Moe Town, 54th and Laflin. What you is?"

"I'm Black Stone," I stated firmly.

"All Well," My celly said extending his hand for a shake letting me know that he was also a Black Stone.

"What you booked for?" He asked.

"A weak ass delivery. What about you?"

"An attempted murder," he replied nonchalantly.

My expression went from joyful to pitiful in a second. "Damn law, you fighting some real drama but every case can be beat so don't give up," I told him trying to sound confident with my advice.

"I been gone for a little over a year already. I'm preparing to go to trial though. I'm hoping I can come from under this shit," he replied looking down at the floor. "What's yo' name, law?" he asked me.

"Dre but you can call me Mo Money," I said already liking the new nickname I'd just given myself. I felt like I couldn't go by my government name in jail so I made up a name that sounded kind of cool to me. It was either that or Dre Moe.

"They call me Tone Bone," my celly said before climbing back onto his bunk.

My first two weeks went by extremely slow. Sometimes I would work out with Tone Bone but for the most part, I slept my time away. I got a letter from my moms letting me know how disappointed she was in me and that she wanted me to do better with myself while I still had the chance.

I wrote her back letting her know that I was okay and that I missed and loved her. I also wrote Kahidijah a letter but I hadn't gotten a reply.

"Williams, visit!" A female officer yelled inside my cell. I jumped from the top bunk and slid on my state issued karate shoes.

"Tell yo' OG I said I love her," Tone Bone joked looking up from the HipHop Weekly magazine that he was reading.

"Yeah, aight," I said waving him off as I left the room.

While walking through the halls with the C.O.. to the visiting room I saw the MC nigga, J.B. I remembered him from being out there the night Lil Snake had gotten killed. When we locked eyes, he threw up MC and screamed, "Ima catch yo' bitch ass!"

I entered the small visiting room and spotted the guys sitting at one of the tables. All of them looked higher than a kite.

"What's the demo, Ku?" I asked Nutso as I took a seat at the table. I had sent him a letter letting him know where I had three ounces of weed stashed. I told him to grab it and continue business without me.

"Same ol' shit, big cuz, you been all well in this bitch?" He asked me.

"Hell yea, one of these hoe ass niggas will try AIDS before he try me," I replied with my chest poked out.

"I just grabbed a QP from Killa. He said he got you as soon as you touchdown. Bucky been rapping his ass off out here—"

"And this nigga been goin' crazy shooting at everybody," T Stone cut in pointing at Reesie.

"I'm surprised niggas ain't in here talkin' about me," Reesie said with a grin.

"You need to chill out, foe before you end up in this bitch with me," I warned. "And I almost forgot to tell y'all that they call me Mo Money now," I told them.

"Man, who the fuck is Mo Money?" Cello asked laughing.

"Me, lil nigga!" I shot back trying not to laugh with him. He had me feeling like my new name was silly.

"Aye if you get into it with anybody in this bitch let me know and I'ma go fuck they block up," Reesie told me seriously.

"Aight good looking, foe. I just saw the Snake nigga JB off Wentworth. He was talkin' crazy when I walked past his wing," I told them.

"Man, buddy bitch ass not on a crumb. He in here for robbing an old lady in Roseland," T Stone said.

"I'ma give his bitch ass what he looking for," I said confidently.

"I'm already knowing. You better be able to manhandle his scary ass," T Stone said with a chuckle.

After twenty more minutes, the officer that walked me into the visiting room returned to let me know that my visit was over.

"Aight man. I love you niggas. Y'all be safe out there," I said getting up from the table and discreetly throwing the five up and coming across my chest before leaving out of the visiting room.

When I made it back to my cell, Tone Bone was writing a letter to his girl.

"Has shorty been holdin' you down this whole bid?" I asked.

"She do enough. I can't get no bitch to stop doing what she doing because I'm gone. She write me every now and then and come see me from time to time. Shit, she lie to me, I lie to her, but we make it feel real. That's all that count. I just need the company," he replied with a shrug. I was too young and naive to comprehend that it took a special, rare kind of woman to truly hold a nigga down while he did his time.

In my young mind, I thought that every woman was there for her man.

"I feel you, bro. As long as she here that's all that matter," I told him.

The next month, I went to court and the judge sentenced me to a year. In the bullpen, I saw one of the Stones that I knew from 93rd and King Drive named Lil Chicky.

"What's the demo, law?" he asked excitedly. He was a skinny, brown skinned kid who was a known shooter.

"Shit man, they just gave me a year for this weak ass delivery. I'm salty as hell," I replied not able to mask my bitterness.

"Damn they just offered me a deuce for this gun case and another year for this probation violation. This my second pipe case. I just got out. I'm not tryna do no more time. On Stone, they tweakin," he said brushing his wavy hair. "I'm on deck with one of the snakes. He said you came through his shit blowing and smoked one of his homies. I saw you walking past our wing one day but you ain't see me though. You want me to stand on that nigga?" he asked.

"Naw, broski I'ma bump heads with that goofy ass nigga. Tell him I said sign up for school."

"All well, law. Keep yo' head up," Lil Chicky told me when they called his name for him to leave the bullpen. We shook up and he left.

Behind me, I heard some Hispanic kid say,'' Fuck yo' hood nigga. I'm Two-Four 2-6." I looked back to see a tall, fat Big Worm looking kid cock back and give the shorter Mexican a heavy handed haymaker to the chin. The Mexican fell out cold landing on his face.

"On BD, on King David. That's what I do to goofy ass niggas!" Big Worm bragged after kicking the Mexican in his face.

"Damn," I chuckled to myself as I went on about my business.

***

School in the Juvenile Detention Center was decent. We watched movies and gangbanged most of the time, so time flew. We sat in a small ass classroom that held only about 15 students at the most. I always sat in the back of the class just in case some shit ever popped off.

"Aye celly," Tone Bone whispered leaning towards my desk. "I got a kite from some nigga that I bumped into at the dentist named Arab. He say he from 62nd and Kimbark. He mentioned yo' big cousin Panda or something. I go to court with him so write him back and I'ma get it to him when we go to court," he said passing me a folded up piece of paper. It only said that Panda told him I was locked up. He was in the hole and to keep in touch. I realized that Arab was my childhood friend, Amon. I guess he went by Arab now. I hadn't seen him in years. We went to elementary school together but I transferred after first grade. After that, I only saw him very rarely, mostly due to him always being in jail or me being in The Hundreds. I remembered me and him being very close when we were shorties, always getting into some bad shit. A small, long haired Mexican officer came into the classroom and yelled. "Rec!"

I walked onto the yard and removed my white tee. I looked around and saw a small crowd of Black Stones, Latin Kings, and Vice Lords. I approached the crowd and greeted a few of the brothers that I fucked with. While we were making small talk, I got snaked from behind. Whoever it was that snaked me, hit me with two more vicious jabs to the back of my head before I was able to turn around and scooped him up. After I slammed my attacker on his back I seen that it was JB.

"Bitch ass Nigga!" I snarled hitting him with four stiff jabs.

As we traded blows, another kid lifted me from the floor and threw me in a full nelson. Before JB could take advantage of me, a few of the Stones jumped in. At first, everybody was confused because Black Stones and Mickey Cobras were both under the Five pointed star. MCs branched off from Stones. We were once upon a time the same thing. JB had the MCs and the folks riding with him, and all the brothers were riding with me. A big brawl erupted on the yard.

I saw Tone Bone stomping JB's ears together and I joined him.

"Get the fuck off Snake!" A vaguely familiar voice roared then it felt as if the Incredible Hulk had punched me. I felt my legs buckle before I fell forward landing on my stomach. I rolled over and saw that it was the Big Worm looking nigga that I was in the bullpen with that day. Out of nowhere, he stumbled forward from someone landing powerful punches to the back of his head. I jumped up and started swinging my arms as hard as I could. I noticed that the guy who had come to my aid and assistance was my boy L.O. and he'd come just in the nick of time. The last thing I remembered was me and a few of the brothers stomping Big Worm out and a big

Ray Lewis looking ass C.O. running towards me at full speed. Those bitch ass C.O.s maced me and beat the fuck out of me before sending me to the hole.

My cell in the hole was dirty as fuck. A hundred different people had wrote their names and the name of their hood on the walls and ceiling. The floor was dusty as hell like it hadn't been swept or mopped in months and it had a rank odor to it. At first, I was in the cell alone but after about an hour, they threw L.O. in the cell with me.

"Damn Moe, how the fuck you get booked?" I asked while shaking up with him.

"I got caught with two poles on 88th and Michigan out there fuckin with Woo," L.O. replied stretching his long body. He stood about six feet even, had brown skin and a low cut. He was 17 years old. "Man, I haven't seen yo' lil ass since that day you got booked at school. What the fuck you do?" He asked while starting to unpack his property.

"They saw me serving Donovan on camera, so they charged me with a delivery. I just got a year for that goofy ass shit," I said starting to clean up a bit.

They gave me and L.O. both 45 days in the hole. He was a surprisingly quiet guy. I never expected that because on the streets he was always in the middle of some bullshit. During my time in the hole, I spent most of my days working out whenever I wasn't writing letters or joking with L.O.. We knew each other from the streets so we had a lot to talk about. Being cellies helped us grow closer and form a tighter bond.

"Williams, mail!" A baldhead white C.O. said dropping a envelope inside my cell.

"Bitch!" I yelled to him as I picked my mail up. To my surprise, it was a letter from Kahidijah. It said,

Dear Dre,

Hey Bae, I miss you and I wish you were here with me at home. I think about you all the time but I just can't bring myself to come see you locked inside a cage. I hope you're

not mad at me. If you write back, I'll send you some pictures. When do you come home? I hope we can pick up where we left off. I really have a lot of feelings for you and I know that you feel the same about me. I just got your info from T Stone. That's why it took so long for me to reach out. That and the fact that I've been going through a lot but that's another story. Anyways, write me back ASAP baby and keep your head up.

Love, Kahidijah.

I folded the letter and put it back in the envelope it came in before tossing it in my property box. "Man, this bitch probably got a whole 'nother nigga out there," I gruffed as I climbed onto the top bunk. I laid on my back and stared at the ceiling. I was all of a sudden missing Kahidijah like crazy.

"Man, Lil Dre, don't start stressing over no bitch. It don't make sense getting frustrated over shit you can't control," L.O. said. He had been through this before.

"My name Mo Money now, Law. Stop calling me Dre. I don't want niggas calling me by my government name."

"Who the fuck is Mo Money?" L.O.. asked bursting out laughing. "You funny as hell but if you like it I love it law," he said.

Whoever was in the cell next to us started beating loudly on the walls.

"Aye man, a mufucka over here tryna sleep. Cool down with all that mufuckin beating!" I screamed through the thin wall.

"Where you from, ku?"

"I'm one of the Moes from 104th and Maryland, the Condos. Where you from?" I shot back. By now, I was used to screening niggas.

"I'm from 72nd and Merrill. I'm one of the Moes too. All Well,"

"All Well," me and L.O.. said in unison.

"I'm Mo Money," I said before L.O. introduced himself.
"I'm from Bash Town, 87th and Wabash," he added.

"I'ma come see you brother's faces when I get out. I only got a few more days," Keem told us.

A few weeks later, me and L.O.. were chilling talking shit when I asked him, "What you gone be on when you touchdown law?"

"Ima be honest, lil bro. I'ma be on the same shit I was on when I was out there. My opps killed my right hand man. He was like a brother to me. I gotta get some type of get back. That's the only thing that'll make me sleep better," he paused and then continued. "This shit is all I know. If we don't kill them they gon' .. kill us. I know you know what I'm talking about," he said.

I understood where he was coming from but I didn't have anyone of my close friends get killed. I couldn't quite feel his passion but I knew all about being trapped in the streets with what seemed like no way out. Once you were stuck in a certain environment for so long, you learned how to adapt to that environment. You became a product of that environment. It was something that cursed black men all over America. Only a small few knew how to capitalize off that curse and turn it into a blessing." Hell yeah, you know I know, bro. I'm tryna run it up when I get out. We need to some do business together when we both get out.

"On Stone. I know how you coming lil bro. As long as you keep some of that good ass weed, I can see you running it all the way up with no problem," L.O. said.

We continued to plan and plot that whole night. We had so many ideas and shit we wanted to do when we got out. The next week they shipped L.O.. to the county because he turned eighteen.

The next six months flew by quick. My so-called girlfriend Kahidijah had broke bad on me and stopped responding to me. I didn't expect that and wasn't prepared for it at all. My heart was crushed.

January 2008

I had just turned sixteen and I only had a couple more months to do before I went home.

"Dre, what's good my nigga?" A light voice asked from behind me as I sat in the chow hall eating dinner.

"What's up?" I asked defensively looking back to see that it was only my boy, Arab. "My fuckin' boy! What the fuck you booked for nigga?" I asked excitedly as we embraced in a brotherly hug.

"An armed robbery that I caught in the beginning of '06. I took a nigga down for twenty-five hundred and a pound and the nigga told on me," Arab explained. He'd gotten way bigger since the last time we'd seen each other. His light brown skin looked a little lighter than I remembered it being and his long hair was braided to the back in five braids.

"You was tryna get good, huh?" I asked smiling.

"Hell yeah, I was robbing everybody. I get out later this year. What the fuck yo' black ass doing in here? You still short as hell man," Arab joked.

"I caught a delivery in school. I was selling weed making a lil money,"

"That's what's up. We need to exchange info so we can link up and make some real money when we both get out," Arab said and we exchanged info right there. "Keep yo' head up, Dre. I'ma see you around law," he told me giving me a half hug.

"They call me Mo Money now, law but keep yo' head up too. Love you bro," I said before turning back to my meal.

Chapter 3

Welcome Home

The day I got out of jail, I felt like a new man. I was free and able to do whatever I felt like doing. "No more locked doors and lame ass cellies!" I said climbing into the front seat of my mother's Chevy Tahoe.

"Boy, watch your mouth," my mom snapped playfully smacking me on the back of my head.

"Sorry ma, you just don't know how good it feel to be home after a year. Nut, what's good, cuz?" I said turning in my seat.

Nutso sat in the backseat next to Reesie and Bone. "Nothing much, lil nigga. I been waiting on you to come home," he replied.

I looked at Reesie. He looked even more rough than he did the last time I seen him. Not rough like fucked up rough but he looked hardened by the streets. His eyes were darker. His dreads now hung below his jawline. "What's good, Reesie? Shoot that money," I told him.

"You don't want these problems. You better ask Bucks how I did him the last time he ran up on me with some dice," Reesie replied.

Bone frowned his face up and said, "Man, Bucky sweet as hell on the dice. Everybody know that but that nigga be making some raw songs. I'll give him that,"

"Bone, how old you is now, like ten?" I asked joking.

"Nigga, I'm thirteen now," he clarified. The rest of the ride we made small talk while listening to Lil Wayne's *The*

Carter 3. I couldn't describe how good it felt to pull up to the buildings. I missed my hood so much.

When I got inside our apartment, I rushed to my room which looked like it'd went untouched since I'd been gone. Nutso walked in carrying various shopping bags.

"This for you, cuz. Welcome home," he said dropping the bags on my bed.

The first bag I went into was a Footlocker bag. He had me the new pair of Cool Grey retro 11 Jordans. Then, I went inside a DTLR bag and pulled out a Blac Label fit, and a grey and white Chicago White Sox fitted cap.

"Damn, good looking, cuz. Where you get the money to buy this shit from?" I asked curiously, causing Nut to smack his lips.

"Nigga, you thought I fell off or something," he said before getting down to reach under my bed and pull out two big Ziplock bags stuffed with weed.

"Damn!" I exclaimed snatching one of the bags from his hands. "How much is this?" I asked, staring at the weed as if it was a million dollars.

"This ain't shit but a pound and a half," Nutso said handing me the bigger bag and grabbing the one that I was holding. "You keep the pound and I'll take the half a pound. I been waiting for my partner in crime to come home. I missed you cuz," he said giving me a brotherly hug before dropping a gang sign with me.

That's when I noticed that he had grown a few inches taller than me. I was now about 5' 5 and he looked to be about 5'8. He had his hair cut into a Mohawk with designs cut into the sides. He was dressed in a crispy Jordan jogging suit with a pair of white, grey, and black retro 4 Jordans on his feet.

"I see you still wearing them fu' ass chains," I laughed looking at his big silver chain with a Transformers charm on it.

"You laughing now. My chain might be fu but my earrings real," he replied turning his head so I could see the medium sized screw ins he had in his ear. The diamonds glistened every time the light hit them from a different angle. "Okay, I see you, cuz," I smiled. I was happy to see my lil cousin on top of his shit and I was even happier to be back around him. I missed him and Bone the most out of everybody.

"Get dressed, cuz. We having a party for you at C Murder crib in about an hour. We gon' have that bitch turnt. Everybody waiting to see you."

Later that night when I stepped into my welcome home party, I felt like a celebrity. Everybody had showed up for me. With the money my moms gave me and the money my friends gave me, I had about $1,000 on me. To make my roll look like it was more than it actually was, I had my money in all five, ten and twenty dollar bills.

"Long time no see, lil nigga," Killa said to me walking up with Primo and Reesie.

I had heard that while I was gone Reesie spent a lot of time under them putting in work. Killa had a smile on his face as we shook up. He looked me up and down before saying, "It look like yo' lil ass tried to gain a lil weight. What you was doing pushups in that bitch?"

I nodded and Primo spoke up, "I stilla beat yo' lil ass," he said before throwing a playful jab at me. He had tattoos all over his arms and neck now.

"I think I got you now, bro. I was in there beating shit," I replied throwing a few jabs at his ribs. "I see you niggas lookin' like new money," I added checking both Killa and Primo out. They both wore spring Stall and Dean coats with the hats to match, Lacoste outfits and crispy all white low top Air Ones.

"Nigga we the plug now. Who you think supplying, Nutso?" Killa asked boastfully.

"Okay, that's what—"

I couldn't finish my sentence because somebody grabbed me from behind while another pair of hands patted my pockets.

"Welcome home, pussy!" Cello shouted releasing me from the chokehold he had me in.

"Dre, what's up bitch?" My homie, Smack yelled drunkenly. Smack was Bone's older brother. He was younger than me but way bigger than me in size. He was a real good fighter, and he knew that so he tended to act like a bully. He was always talking crazy or tryna fight somebody.

"Watch yo' mouth, bitch!" I shot back. "And my name Mo Money now," I added.

"This nigga go to jail and come home all tough with a new name?" A smooth voice said from behind me. I looked back and to my surprise it was my big cousin, Panda speaking.

"What's up big cuz?" I asked happily, shaking up with him. Him and our other cousin, Sheed, who was currently locked up, were the reasons why I became a Black Stone. I always looked up to them.

"I can't call it, lil cuz. Welcome home," he said while reaching in his pocket, pulling out a wad of bills and counting me out about five hundred dollars. Panda was a Black Stone from Crank Town, a hood on 62nd and Kimbark. He stood around 5'10, had a medium brown skin tone with short cut hair and was starting to grow a pudgy stomach. He had a twin brother that was doing life in prison for a triple murder.

"I see I need to start fuckin with Crack cause you winnin' cuz," I said still thinking about the thick wad of hundred and fifty dollar bills he had.

"Slow down, you not ready for the big leagues yet. Stay in yo' lane,"

"How you figure I'm not ready?" I asked with a frown.

"Because I know it. Just be patient one day. You'll be ready and I got you until then. I got some lil homies that need

41

a consistent plug on the weed. I heard y'all got that shit so I'ma put y'all in tune with them. Just don't tax my people."

"If they yo' peoples, then they my people. You should know I'm not gon' tax them."

"All well. Just slide through Kimbark whenever you get some free time so I can introduce y'all," Panda told me before giving me a half hug and leaving the party.

Everybody showed me love when they saw me. They acted as if I had been gone for years instead of just a year. The party was all good up until we started throwing money to Shawty Lo's *'Foolish'* and a hater punched Shody Shod in his mouth for throwing money in his face. I was pissy drunk off of different types of liquor.

I threw two sloppy hooks at the hater, but I missed, and he dropped me with a vicious uppercut. As I laid on the floor trying to recuperate, I heard multiple gunshots. Two females, my homie Thang and the hater had gotten shot. It turned out that Reesie started shooting after somebody went across T Stone's head with a Svedka bottle. Another nigga who was with the hater returned fire and that's how the party ended.

A few days later, I met up with Panda in front of the big court way building on 61st and Kimbark. I had Nutso and T Stone with me. He was with two young niggas, one was light brown skinned with dreads that hung to his shoulders and the other was a brown skinned, chubby guy with short wavy hair.

"50, Lil Mike, these my lil cousins, Mo Money and Nutso," Panda said introducing us. We were all Stones, so we all took turns shaking up with each other. "They need a new connect and y'all got it sooo..." He waved his hand to let us take over.

"How much y'all tryna spend?" I asked Lil Mike. He was the one with the dreads. They both pulled out there money and counted it.

"We got six-hundred-fifty-dollars," Lil Mike said.

"I'ma give y'all a half a pound for that and y'all can bring me back twelve hundred dollars and get a pound. The prices gone keep getting better," I said.

"That's cool," 50 said speaking for the first time before handing me his portion of the money.

"Look at my shorties looking like real hustlers," Panda said smiling proudly.

"I'ma need for you to hurry up and run yo' bag up so you can step yo' ice game up, lil cuz," he said to Nutso flashing his plain Jane Rolex wristwatch.

"Don't worry, I'm on my way," Nutso shot back flashing his Joe rodeo watch. We stood out there shit talking for a little while until I got a call from my homie, Five.

After we left Crank Town, we drove to the Parkway Gardens also known as WIC City on 64th and King Drive to serve my homie, Five. I met him through one of my exes. He was fucking her younger sister and would buy weed from me. He was the same age as me. He had brown skin and shoulder length dreads. He was a Black Disciple.

"What's the word, Skud?" Five asked climbing in the backseat of the hype rental that we were in. "My phone been ringing all day," he said in his usual slow slur. I handed him a half a pound that I had in a Ziplock bag inside a Burger King bag. While I was gone, he did business with Nut but now that I was back home, he was coppin' from me again.

"My bad it took so long. I had to stop in the Crank and holla at my peoples," I told him passing him the blunt I was smoking on.

"What y'all bout to get into?" he asked after taking a pull from the blunt.

"Shit really we 'bout to buss a few more moves and then we going to the hood to post up," I said before a fine ass chick with kinky twist in her hair caught my eye. "Who the fuck is that bitch with them white leggings on?" I asked pointing at the young lady.

"That's Mieysha. She probably looking for some weed or something."

"Call her over here," I told Five.

He turned his Nike backpack to the front and unzipped it a little before sticking his hand inside. "Aye Mieysha! Check it out," he shouted stepping away from the Grand Prix we were in.

"Boy, what?" Mieysha asked Five with a fake attitude as she headed our way.

When she got close enough, she took little peeks inside the car trying to see who we were. She was even prettier up close.

"What's the word Mieysha?" I asked hopping out the car dusting ashes off my white cargo shorts. She looked at me like I was crazy. She was the same color as peanut butter with a perfect smile and a nice ass.

"Do I know you?" She asked with a raised eyebrow.

"Naw, not yet. I'm from The Hundreds. I saw you over there and I told Five he had to get you over here so I could meet you," I said trying to pass her the smoldering blunt that I held in my fingertips.

She looked at me like I was crazy again. "Boy you tweaking. I don't know what you smoke. You might be tryna lace me," she said with a straight face. The more she spoke, the more I found myself attracted to her attitude. I couldn't help but to laugh at her last comment.

"Shorty, I smoke Kush. I don't know what you and yo' boyfriend be smoking on but I smoke the best," I bragged. "Matter of fact, where yo' man at anyway?" I asked.

"I'm single. Niggas not on shit these days," she replied.

I know she noticed how I was staring at her juicy thighs. In my mind, I was picturing myself fucking her in a hundred different positions.

"Yeah, you need to get that nappy shit braided," she said to me as I rubbed my nappy braids.

I passed her the blunt and asked, "You gone do it for me?"

She couldn't answer because she started coughing violently.

"Yeah, that's that good shit from The Hundreds. You gotta watch how you hit that," I joked.

"Boy, shut up. I inhaled it wrong," Mieysha lied. "Who car you driving?" she asked.

"This my shit," I lied quickly. I didn't even have to think about that lie.

"Can you drop me off at home?"

"Yeah, but you gone have to pay me," I said making her screw her face up.

"I thought you was getting money. I might as well take the bus if I'ma have to pay you," she snapped showing me that sexy ass attitude that I liked.

"Slow down shorty. I'm only charging you yo' phone number and a chance to take you out," I replied.

Mieysha smiled while thinking it over." Okay," she said finally. "But tell yo' homie to get his ass in the back. I'm not riding in the back like a buss down," she added. I quickly told Nutso to get in the backseat. All I needed was a bad bitch like Mieysha next to me to complete my image. Every nigga with money had a bad bitch by his side.

By July, me and Mieysha were locked in, bussing down pounds together. We did everything together. During the day, we rode around serving and we spent our nights going on dates or hanging with the guys in the hood. Whatever we did, we did it together. She was damn near living with me at my mom's crib. Her and my mom got along perfectly, and she fit in perfectly around my homies. I was in love without a doubt.

My clientele was rising, and I was going through pounds like they were dime bags. Nutso was too. We both had just bought our first cars. Mine was a silver Grand Prix and his was a black Monte Carlo SS. We would drive through every hood in The Hundreds so they could see that we were getting money. You couldn't tell us shit. We were feeling ourselves.

"Mo Money, what's good, law?" Reesie asked approaching me followed by a few of the guys. He was the hottest nigga in the hood at the moment. His name was ringing louder than ever. Whether it was a robbery or a shooting, his name was involved in something. He'd recently popped one of the big foes over a dice game.

"Shit, what's the word, Solid?" I asked before dropping a gang sign with him and the guys he were with.

"I'm tryna get some money with you bro. I see you and Nutso winning. Y'all got T Stone and Lil C in play. I need for you to look out for me," Reesie said.

"Man, you ain't tryna sell drugs. All you want to do is rob and shoot."

"I'm still gon' do that. I just need for you to front me something."

"Something like what?"

"A pound," Reesie said.

I'm sure my facial expression showed what I was thinking. He was out of his damn mind.

"A pound kind of steep to be fronting. I ain't got it like that but I can give you a half a pound and you can bring me back seven-hundred-fifty dollars," I said and it was his turn to screw his face up.

"Seven-fifty?" he asked and continued to speak before I could reply. "Damn, you taxing me like I'm not one of the guys. I see you want to be the only nigga getting money. That's some hoe ass shit. We come from the same mud and you actin like you can't look out for me. On the foe, you tweaking," he snapped.

"Nigga I'm tryna look out for you. You can take it or leave it," I said flatly. I was started to get irritated.

'You know what? You right bro," Reesie replied with a nod. "And let me get yo' cousin Panda number too. I need to holla at him."

"For what?" I asked. They didn't have anything in common. Panda sold crack and Reesie robbed niggas. That didn't mix.

"After I flip that weed, I'ma buy some work," Reesie said.

I gave him the number before leading him to my car and giving him a half pound. Lately, he'd been acting as if the guys weren't the guys. I brushed it off. Somewhere in my mind I charged it to the weed and X pills he'd been popping.

After leaving the gas station, I rode around listening to Bump J's 'New Niggas' My phone rang, and I answered without looking at who was calling me.

"Yooo," I answered smoothly.

"Where you at bro?" a voice asked frantically.

"Who is this?"

"This Beezy, nigga," he replied.

"Aw, what's the demo, law?"

"Shit, cooling with Shody Shod and Baby on 113th and Edbrooke. Come match a few blunts,"

"Bet, I'm on my way," I said and hung up.

Minutes later, I was pulling up on Edbrooke with my music playing loudly. Shody Shod hopped in my backseat. He was one of the foes from the building.

"You got yo' pipe?" Beezy asked jumping in my passenger's seat. He was sweating profusely.

"Hell naw, why? What happened?" I asked.

"I just beat Ramone ass," he huffed.

"Where Baby at?" I asked. Baby was one of the big foes from the buildings.

"Rayvon, Ramone, and a few other Vice Lords jumped him. That's why I beat Ramone ass,'' Beezy explained.

Before I could respond, gunshots went off and my back windshield shattered. I looked through my rearview mirror and saw one of the CVLs named Jerome blowing at us. I stomped the gas and peeled off.

"Them bitch ass niggas!" I shouted as I sped off. "Y'all well?" I asked.

CITY OF SMOKE | MOLOTTI

"Hell yeah," Beezy answered.

"Shody yo' hoe ass must be scared speechless cause you ain't never been this quiet," I joked until I looked over my shoulder and saw Shody Shod holding his neck. Blood gushed through his fingers.

"Damn, Shody hit!" I told Beezy.

I flew to 111th Street and made my way to Roseland Hospital.

"Hold on foe, I'm about to get you to some help," I assured Shody Shod as I passed State Street. In seconds, I was pulling into Roseland Hospital's emergency entrance.

I stayed at the hospital for a few hours. The only thing going through my mind was how I was going to shoot every CVL I caught on 113th Street. I let Beezy take my car to go pick up Mieysha and Bone to keep me company at the hospital because I planned on staying there until I found out what was going on with Shody Shod. It took another couple hours for a short Indian nurse to come out and inform us that Shody Shod was out of surgery and in stable condition. I wanted to speak to him, but she told me that he was sleep off of medication and it would be best for us to visit him tomorrow.

Later that night, me and Reesie were sitting in a stolen red Intrepid on 112th and Edbrooke.

"These niggas out here snoozing. This shit 'bout to be too easy," Reesie said grinning before chambering a bullet in his Mac 10.

"Let's do it," I said cocking back my P89 Ruger. We walked down to 113th and Edbrooke and saw Jerome and a few other Vice Lords standing on the porch of an abandoned house.

"Who that?" Ramone screamed sticking his hand inside his hoodie pocket.

"Nigga, who the fuck is you?" I replied.

Ramone pulled out a small pistol and moved down the stairs. Before I could say another word, he let off four quick shots in my direction. I ducked behind an old Ford Mustang and shot my gun over the hood. I saw Reesie creeping up on Ramone from behind. I heard his Mac go off shooting rapidly and I popped up to see Ramone lying face down. Another Vice Lord named Rayvon was crawling off the porch on which they were sitting. I ran up on him and aimed my gun at his head.

"I didn't have nothing to do with that shit," he cried.

"If you with 'em then you equal," I growled before pumping three shots into the top of his head and taking off running towards our car. We left three bodies dead on the scene.

CITY OF SMOKE | MOLOTTI

Chapter 4

No Loyalty

It was the beginning of September and me and Mieysha were looking like a real power couple. She had me head over hills in love and I knew she was the one. I was in love with spoiling her and showing her off. She was my trophy. I was young getting money with a bad ass bitch. I was content with where I was in life and honestly I was happy as I ever been.

I called Reesie's phone, and he answered after the fifth ring. "What's up bro?" he answered with an attitude.

I screwed my face up and looked at the phone as if he could see me. "What's up, solid? You got that bread for me?" I asked.

"What bread?"

"From that half a pound I threw you," I reminded him. It'd been months since I fronted that nigga and he hadn't given me shit.

"Man, you gon' get that shit when I give it to you bro. Don't be callin' my phone askin' about yo' money like I'm a goofy or something. On the Foe, you tweaking," Reesie snapped like I had did something wrong. "I see I'ma have to give you and Panda what y'all looking for if y'all keep playin me," he added, throwing me off. I didn't even know why he was mentioning Panda.

"What's that supposed to mean?"

"Find out," Reesie said, before hanging up in my face.

I was mad as hell. I really felt like he had just treated me like a goofy. He owed me some bread and I wanted my shit. Before I could call him back, Mieysha entered my bedroom.

"What's up baby?" I asked, giving her a kiss after she took a seat on my lap.

"Nothing, my cousin, Sosa wanna buy three pounds. He got four thousand dollars," she told me before giving me another kiss.

"Tell him to pull up," I replied grabbing her ass. I was thinking about getting a quick nut off before making the serve.

"He don't have traffic so I told him that you'd drop the pounds off to him."

I thought about it for a moment. I only had two pounds left but I knew that Nutso had at least one. I went under my bed and pulled out the X-Box 360 box that I had my money stashed in and counted out my re-up money. I planned on going straight to re-up after serving Mieysha's cousin. "Where he at?" I asked.

She gave me his address and phone number and I left out.

I met Nutso on D-Block,107th and Indiana and it was lit out there. Everybody was outside enjoying the good weather. He gave me his re-up money and a pound. We hustled off different lines, but we went to store together to get a better price.

"What's the demo, law?" One of the older Moes named Herron asked, jumping in the passenger seat of my car. He was a few years older than me. I fucked with him hard.

"Shit bout to slide out west to buss this serve. What you on?" I asked while dropping a gang sign with him.

"Ima ride with you,"

"All well,"

Herron looked at my broken back windshield and busted out laughing. "On Stone, Moe stop being so cheap and get that window fixed," he said as we pulled off.

We pulled up to Sosa's crib out west on Latrobe and Fulton.

"Come in with me bro," I told Herron, grabbing my Nike backpack that had the pounds in it. The only reason I asked him to come in was because I didn't have my pipe on me. I didn't like riding with my gun and I had a broken windshield. When we got on the porch to the crib, a short, cocky, brown skinned guy swung the door open for us without us having to knock.

"Slide in," he said.

I stepped in the crib and looked around the home. The living room was nice size but dirty as hell. The walls were beige, but they looked like they were white once upon a time. The grey carpet was stained and had burns all through it. It was a big 45' TV sitting on a raggedy ass entertainment center and a dusty black couch with three of the grimiest niggas I ever seen sitting on it eyeballing us. The 3 niggas on the couch matched the vibe of the house. Busted, disgusted and not to be trusted.

"Where that shit at?" the cocky guy who opened the door for us asked. I was assuming that he was Mieysha's cousin, Sosa.

"I got it. Where that bread at?" I asked.

"Let me see what I'm spending my money on first," A swole ass brown skinned dude with short dreads said from the couch.

"You Sosa?" I asked raising an eyebrow.

"Naw, I'm LC and one of them pounds for me," the swole guy said.

I saw a dirty ass table in the kitchen, so I went in there and sat my backpack on the table. I regretted that as soon as I did it because the kitchen was dirty as fuck with roaches everywhere. I opened my backpack, pulled out a pound and handed it to LC.

"This shit look decent," he said opening the Ziplock bag and thoroughly inspecting the weed. "SOSA!" he shouted.

I looked over at Herron who was looking at me. I'm sure he was thinking the same thing I was thinking. Something wasn't right.

"Aye bro I got another move to make. Where that bread at?" I asked growing impatient.

'Click Clack'

The sound made me look back to see Sosa holding some type of assault rifle. I thought about going for my gun but then I remembered that I didn't have it on me.

"Is you serious?" I asked myself under my breath. Before I could say anything else, Sosa hit me in the face with the butt of the rifle. When I hit the ground, LC was all over me smacking me with a .9. I heard a lot of movement in the background and then two gunshots went off. I was officially scared as hell.

"It's in the bookbag man!" I yelled from the floor. I wasn't trying to get shot. Fuck that. LC started running my pockets. I don't know why my mind told my body to resist but it did, and he smacked me with his gun two more times. That was enough to make me lay still as a statue for him to do whatever he wanted to do to me. I'd never been robbed before, and I was scared to death. I'm just being honest.

"Strip, bitch!" LC demanded.

Once I stripped, they made me lay on my stomach and count to five hundred. When I was done counting and I finally got up, I saw Herron stretched out in the living room with a bullet hole in the back of his head. I broke down crying and even though I was butt-booty-naked, I ran out of the house looking for help. An old white dope fiend stopped and let me use his cell phone to call for medical help. Aight, I called 9-1-1. I just wanted to make it sound good. They arrived and pronounced Herron dead on the scene. I had to go to the hospital because I needed stitches in my mouth.

All that night after getting out the hospital, I blew up Mieysha's phone, but she never answered. Even a blind man could see that she set me up. I knew it when I made it home and she wasn't there. Neither was the $4,500 that I had stashed in my X-Box box. I couldn't believe it. I was flat broke. No money, no car, and no drugs. I didn't know what to do.

Bucky was doing big things with his music. He had just dropped a mixtape and he was due to perform on Christmas day at my lil cousin, Ralph's birthday party. Even though it was only September, everybody was talking about Ralph's party.

Both me and Nutso were flat broke. I felt bad for not only losing all my money but I lost all of his too. Killa and Primo had both gotten locked up for a shooting that occurred in the hood.

When the police raided Killa's trap, they found both of them along with a bunch of pounds and some guns. They also found a half a brick of coke in a bookbag that Primo supposedly threw out of the window. Shit was all bad.

My cousin Panda had just gotten robbed for a half a brick of crack. It seemed like everybody on the south and east sides of the city were taking losses. It seemed like the only person who was doing good was Reesie. He had a new car and word on the street was that he was selling crack and weed. I hadn't spoken to him in a while due to me chasing money and him chasing bodies. We were still cool but distant. Regardless of how good or bad he was doing, I needed my backends that he owed.

Me, Bone and Juicy J were riding around through the hood in Juicy J's Nissan Maxima. We stopped at the G, the Citgo gas station in our hood, to grab some snacks and blunts. When I entered the G I saw Reesie.

"What's up Foe?" I asked walking up on him. He had Lil 4 and Beezy with him.

"What's up?" He shot back aggressively with a mug on his face.

"On Stone, I know you heard about me getting poked out west. I need that bread you owe me for that half a pound."

"Bro, on the Four Corner Hustler stop hounding me for seven hundred fifty dollars. I'ma pay you when I'm ready to pay you. Until then, move around," he snapped. I looked at the new 8732 fit he had on, his black ACG boots and the new leather Pelle he had on. It was obvious that he had some money. That pissed me off. Not to mention he was talking crazy like I wasn't one of the guys or better yet like I was just some random bitch ass nigga.

"Bro, why you coming at me like that? You tweaking," I replied.

Reesie cracked a smile, showing his gap. "Look lil bro, I'ma be honest with you," he said pulling out a wad of money. "I ain't giving you shit. That shit dead," he said stuffing the money back in his pocket. "I'm supposed to be yo' homie. You was supposed to throw me that shit on GP so I could get on my feet. Instead, you played me like I was a goofy. Now that shit dead, on the foe. I'm not paying you shit," he told me. Lil 4 and Beezy were chuckling and that made me even madder.

I didn't know what to do or how to respond so I took off on Reesie and hit him with a hard, stiff jab that made him stumble backwards. He threw a two piece combo that landed on my forehead. Before he could land another punch, I ducked and scooped him up by his legs. Once I slammed him I towered over him and only got the chance to throw two punches before Lil 4 and Beezy jumped in. When they stopped stomping me, I looked up to see Reesie and Lil 4 both had their guns out aimed at me.

"Tell Panda stain ass I said I should have been robbed him. I'm mad I waited so long," Reesie said before he smacked me upside the head with his gun. "Stay in yo' lane, Moe. Don't make me fuck you up," he said before leading Lil 4 and Beezy out of the gas station.

I stumbled out of the G holding my face. I had a big gash over my left eye.

"What happened?" Bone yelled jumping out the car.

"Reesie nem just jumped me," I mumbled. ·

"Why?" Juicy J asked.

"Because he owe me some paper. I asked him about it and the nigga started tweaking."

"Damn, he wild as hell but y'all need to squash that shit."

"I'm not squashing shit. That nigga just pistol whipped me!"

"Both of y'all the guys so I can't get involved in that."

I smacked my lips. "Come on, Bone, we walking," I told Bone jumping out of Juicy J's car.

"Damn, now you mad at me?" he asked through the window.

"I ain't mad at you. I just don't fuck with no in-the-middle ass niggas," I said storming off, never looking back.

When I made it in the crib, I called Panda to let him know what was going on.

"He told me earlier after him and a couple of the guys jumped me," I said to Panda over the phone.

"Cuz, I hope you telling me everything because this some serious shit. I'ma kill that lil nigga, on Stone," he growled.

"Yeah, he said he should have been robbed yo' stain ass."

"All well. I'ma hit you back in a minute, cuz," Panda said before hanging up on me.

"DRE!" My mom yelled my name from the living room.

"Yeah?"

"Your friends at the door!"

"Send them in," I replied and seconds later Nutso followed by a few of the guys entered my room.

"What the fuck happened cuz?" Nutso asked flopping down on my full sized bed.

"Reesie, Lil 4 and Beezy jumped me at the G," I said keeping it brief.

"I just saw them niggas riding around in a black Cadillac."

"That's Reesie new whip. That nigga super up all of a sudden," T Stone said.

"He robbed our big cousin, Panda," I said.

"What?" Nutso roared. "I'ma fuck that nigga up," he said moving all animated and shit.

"Man, Reesie my fuckin homie. Y'all tweaking talking about what y'all gon' do to him. If anything, y'all gone let that shit go," one of the foes named Big Malc said.

"Man, it's family over any and everything. I don't know what you stand for but I'm riding with mines till the end," Nutso replied standing in front of my mirror picking his Mohawk.

"Fuck all that shit y'all talking about. Me and Reesie ain't friends. We not the guys. We not none of that shit. That nigga an opp in my eyes and that's how I'ma carry him when I catch him," I said, shooting a look at Cello who was sitting in the corner of my room quiet as a church mouse. I knew out of all the guys, he was the closest to Reesie. I was surprised that he was even there with us. "Cello, what's up with you?" I asked.

"I don't know what's going on. I'm tryna figure everything out. It really sound like both of y'all tweaking," he replied flatly.

"You know I'm on whatever you on you. Don't even gotta ask me," Bone stated. For him to only be 13 years old, he acted like he was my age. Plus, he was big and stocky, so you would've never guessed that he was so young.

"Man sit yo' lil ass down. Don't you got a bedtime or something?" I joked breaking the tension in the room.

"Yeah, yo' momma want me to come lay down right now, ''Bone shot back.

"Man, you D Block niggas need to stay out of this and let us handle it," Cello said mugging Bone. I guess his statement about being on whatever I'm on didn't sit right with him.

"What that supposed to mean?" Nutso asked.

''Mo Money and Reesie both from the building. Y'all not so y'all really don't have nothing to do with this. Unless y'all on some Stone shit."

"Man, Mo Money my blood fuckin cousin. He is my business!" Nutso snapped.

"Man, them niggas jumped me like they was on some Foe shit," I stated

"That shit was bogus, Moe," T Stone agreed. "You know I'm with you 100% but that nigga Reesie got a lot of guns. That Lil ass .380 you got ain't gon' cut it. We need some more pipes," he said.

"What is y'all talking about pipes and shit for?" Cello asked, getting up from where he was seated. "Y'all gon' make this shit deeper than what it already is. I'm telling y'all,'' he said before storming out followed by Big Malc. I didn't understand how they didn't see that I wasn't the one in the wrong. I was the victim but at this point I didn't give a fuck how they felt. If they were riding with Reesie, then it was what it was. All the guys who stayed were Stones, so it did look like we were on some Black Stone shit. We didn't care though. For the rest of the night, we plotted on getting my lick back on the Foes.

My phone ringing loudly on a Friday night woke me up from a deep slumber.

***

"Yooo," I answered groggily. My throat was dry, and my voice sounded raspier than it normally did.

"Man, yo' cousin Panda just got shot up on the side block," a voice said on the other end of the phone. I wasn't sure if I'd heard right but my heart had dropped to my stomach and my chest got tight.

"Who is this?" I asked, confused.

"This Cello. I'm on 105th. We was out here coolin', and Panda pulled up woofin' at Reesie. Him and Lil 4 did him dirty."

"I'm on my way over there!" I said cutting him off.

"You might as well stay where you at cause it's on for real now," Cello said. His voice was solid, not loud but not quiet either. I couldn't help but catch the subtle threat behind his words.

"What you mean by that?" I asked just to be sure.

"Reesie my right hand. What I look like letting the Stones get down on him? You got all them other niggas riding with you I don't care if y'all family or not," he replied.

I wasn't surprised at all I knew he would side with Reesie before me any day. They'd known each other since they were a few months old and had met me and Nutso years later. Cello wouldn't admit it but it really pained him to choose sides.

"I know what you thinking, Moe," he said. "Just leave that shit alone bro. We don't gotta do this over seven hundred fifty dollars."

"It ain't even about the money foe. It's the principle. You know it don't suppose to be like this, but it is what it is," I said before hanging up on him. I was done talking.

I sat in my room in the dark contemplating my next move. I didn't expect for things to spiral this far out of control this fast. I thought I was doing the right thing by looking out for Reesie. If I would've known that fronting him would lead to all this, I would've never did it. I decided to call him.

"What's up?" he answered.

"So, this really what you wanna do?"

"Save that shit nigga. You know where I'm at. Get at me," he told me calmly before hanging up in my face. I never expected for us to ever be into it like this, but we were, and I was fully prepared to give him what he was looking for.

The next morning, me and T Stone were on 59th and Wabash trying to buy some guns from one of his cousins named Rakeem.

"Man cuz, I'm only selling y'all two pipes. We into it just like y'all into it," Rakeem said running a hand over his wavy head.

"Aight G, just don't sell us no broke ass pipes," T Stone replied only halfway joking. They were blood but that only meant so much when you were in the streets.

Rakeem made a phone call before leading us to the Wabash Market. Once inside, he led us to the back of the store where a midnight black guy with a full beard stood unloading a Taurus .45.

"Where them pipes at, Blackboy? I'm 'bout to sell my cousin a couple. They out there in The Hundreds getting fucked up," Rakeem said to the guy with a chuckle.

"They in that box on the top shelf," Blackboy gruffed nodding towards the utility closet. He mean mugged me and T Stone like he knew us or something. I trusted Rakeem just off the strength that he was T Stone's cousin but this Blackboy character was giving me a bad vibe.

"Y'all can buy this .45 Beretta and this Glock 19 for seven hundred fifty dollars," Rakeem said handing a gun to me and T Stone.

"Bet, but we gotta test them out first," I said when I noticed that neither of the guns were loaded.

"Hell naw, on folks nem, we not putting no loaded guns in y'all hands. Yo' ass must be crazy," Blackboy stated still holding his Taurus.

"Aight, well y'all shoot them," I suggested handing Rakeem the Glock. We watched him and Blackboy load each gun with five bullets apiece before they led us to the alley behind the Market. They shot both guns in the air. I gave Rakeem $750 in twenties and fifties.

"Good looking cuz," T Stone told him shaking his hand before we hopped in our hype rental and pulled off.

Later that day, T Stone called my cell phone.

"Aye, broski I just saw Reesie drop Lil E off at the YMCA on 111th Street," he said.

"You think Lil E with that shit?"

"Nigga, he a Foe, ain't he?" T Stone snapped. "Nigga it don't matter if he with that shit or not. He with Reesie so he guilty by association," he said.

"You right. Me and Nut bout to slide up there," I said and hung up before turning to Nutso who was playing the game.

"Lil E at the Y on 111th. T Stone just saw Reesie drop him off. Let's go get down on his ass," I told him. With that being said, I grabbed my Glock 19 and gave him the .45. We hopped in his Monte Carlo and headed to the Y.

I had on a black hoodie with the hood over my head to hide the braids that almost hung to my shoulder. We waited in the parking lot to the Wendy's across the street from the YMCA for almost a hour before Lil E came strolling out. We jumped out the car and made our way across the street.

"Lil E, what the fuck you doing up here boy?" I asked from behind, startling him.

"Damn bro, I didn't know who you was. I just finished hooping though," Lil E replied. "You rode the bus up here?" I asked just to see if he was going to lie.

"Naw, Reesie dropped me off," he said nonchalantly. I knew for a fact the he knew what was going on between me and Reesie.

"Tell that nigga I said fuck him," I said reaching for the Glock I had on my waistline. Lil E hit me with a uppercut before I could grab my gun and took off running. I recovered from the punch and started blowing him down. He ran as fast as he could using his strong athletic legs to easily outrun me. Little did he know, Nutso was already prepared for that. He lined Lil E up with his .45 and fired nine shots. One bullet hit Lil E in his leg causing him to fall. I caught up to where Lil E was laying, crying his eyes out. I ran up on him and pumped two shots in his chest.

"You hit like a bitch too, lil nigga," I snarled shooting him one more time before taking off running to Nutso's car.

Chapter 5

A New Hustle

A few days later I got a call from Arab. He was fresh out of jail and wanted to link up with me. We met up on 61st and Dorchester at Carnegie Park.

"I see you came home to some paper," I told him when he hopped out of a smoke grey Impala with tinted windows and 20-inch rims on it.

"This ain't shit. I got out and got right back to it. Law three stains paid for this," he bragged sitting on the hood of his car and flaming up a blunt.

"So, that stain money where it's at, huh, law?"

"Yes sir. On Stone, I'm addicted to hitting stains. I got one lined up for later. You tryna get involved?" Arab asked passing me the blunt.

I thought it over for a moment. The only thing I'd ever robbed was a few delivery men and, even with that, Reesie did all the work. But I was broke and I needed some bread in the worst way. "Hell yeah," I said.

"It's a party later on and it's gon' be a stunting ass nigga in that bitch, and I know for a fact he gon' be holding. I'ma give you all the details later just be ready by nine."

"All well," I replied thirsty to make some money.

"So, what's up with yo' homies shooting Panda up?" he asked. Panda was fucked up from the shooting. He had undergone multiple surgeries already and his condition changed every day.

"That shit got the hood into it with each other. Me and Nut just caught one of they ass and fucked him up."

"That shit crazy let me know if y'all need us," he said shaking his head.

"We good," I replied. We finished smoking the blunt we were rotating and then I left.

I went home and called my hair braider Ronda up to come over and braid my hair.

"Boy, this short shit be hurting my fingers," she complained while rubbing grease through my hair.

"Girl, stop it. You know you love playing in my head."

"No, I don't. I actually hate it. I deal with it because I like you so consider yourself lucky," she said playfully pulling my hair.

"I'm only lucky because I get to sit between these juicy ass thighs all day," I said squeezing one of her thighs.

"Stop before you start something you can't finish."

"As soon as you finish braiding my hair, I'ma show you how good I am at... finishing what I start."

Ronda must've been anxious to find out how well I finished things because it didn't take long for her to finish my hair.

"I always wondered how good yo' pussy was," I told her as she washed her hands in my bathroom sink. I stood behind her making sure my semi-hard dick rubbed against her ass. "Let me see what it feel like;" I said kissing the nape of her neck.

She reached back and grabbed my dick. "You a little happy ain't you?" she asked, taking a seat on the toilet and pulling my hard dick out of my pants. I cracked a slight smile as she put me inside her warm mouth. She sucked my dick hard and aggressively like it was the last one on earth. After fifteen minutes, I stood her up and bent her over the sink. I pulled her jogging pants and panties down in one motion and inserted two fingers in her wet pussy.

"Put it in," she begged as I finger fucked her. When I entered my rock-hard dick inside of her, she jumped, knocking the soap dish off the sink. I pounded her out with long, hard strokes while holding on to the back of her neck for leverage. Her pussy was so wet that her juices were running down her legs and had the bottom of my white tee moist.

After ten minutes, I slowed down a bit.

"Why you slowing down?" she asked throwing her ass back almost making me run. She had beads of sweat rolling down her forehead.

"I'm 'bout to buss," I told her as I continued to pump.

"You can keep it in. I'm on the shot," she said in between moans.

I picked up the pace of my strokes and within minutes I was exploding inside of her. When I pulled out, she dropped down on her knees and started to suck my now soft dick.

"Hold on! Hold on!" I said running from her tongue.

"I'm about to get you ready for round two," she said before slipping my dick back into her mouth.

"I got some business to handle so we gon' have to finish this la—" I was saying but stopped mid-sentence. She was using her tongue to massage the head of my dick and it felt too good. "You killing me," I told her, grabbing the back of her head and fucking her face. After another fifteen minutes I was busting a big nut and she swallowed every drop. "You make me wanna change plans but I can't. I gotta handle this business and you can come back over later," I told her. She left and I took a quick shower and got dressed. By the time I was finished tying up my wheat Timbs, Arab was calling my phone to let me know he was outside.

"The nigga name is SBE Randy. He be crackin' cards and shit. We gon chill and float through the party until I text you and let you know it's time to make our move," Arab told me, reaching for the blunt that I held in my hand. He passed me a little red pill with two naked ladies on it.

"What the fuck is this?" I asked looking at the pill like it was crack.

"It's an X pill, you stupid ass nigga," Arab said with a chuckle. "Pop it and you gon be high as hell," he told me before throwing the same type of pill in his mouth and chewing it before taking a sip out of the bottle of water he had.

I did the same thing he did and instantly regretted it. I wanted to rip my tongue out because the pill was so nasty. "This shit disgusting, Moe," I complained gulping down water trying to get the taste out of my mouth but that wasn't working at all. "Fuck is so funny?" I grumbled as we pulled up to where the party was.

"Nothing law," Arab chuckled.

When we walked into the party, I didn't know where to go first cause it was so many hoes scattered around the place and they were all looking good. They had an open bar so I went and poured myself a healthy cup of Remy. I needed something because my mouth was dry as hell. I peeped Arab immediately find a dark corner to post in. He subtly nodded towards a brown-skinned guy wearing a pair of Gucci shades. Even though it was a warm night, he had on a Gucci polo, a pair of black jeans and a leather Pelle. When Gucci Mane's 'Photoshoot' came on, I found out just how much of a flexing ass nigga SBE Randy was. He pulled out two big wads of money and held them in the air. When Lil Wayne's 'Bang Bang' came on, the whole party turnt up a notch. Everybody was jumping around throwing up gang signs. I felt somebody bump into me hard as hell. I turned around and grabbed an arm ready to check a nigga but then I realized that the arm I grabbed belonged to a young lady.

"I'm sorry," she said.

I looked at her big, round, brown eyes and her honey-colored skin and was caught off guard by her beauty. She looked like a skinny version of the singer Rihanna.

"It ain't shit shorty and for future references being sorry won't get you nowhere," I said smoothly looking at her from head to toe. Her long legs were sexy as hell to me. I only stood about 5'4. She had to stand at least 5'7. "I thought you was one of these lame ass niggas. I didn't mean to grab yo' arm like that. I didn't hurt you, did I?" I asked.

"No, I'm okay and it was one of them lame ass nigga that pushed me into you," she explained, flashing one of the prettiest smiles I'd ever seen.

"You might as well let a real nigga get a juke," I told the girl as Lil Corey's 'Say Yes' came on. She juked and grinded on me through the whole song. After the song went off, she tried to walk off, but I grabbed her by her wrist. "Damn shorty, you ain't gon' tell me yo' name?" I asked putting my sexy smile on.

"You didn't ask for it but it's Ashley," she replied flashing that smile again.

"It was nice to meet you, Ashley. I'm Mo Money."

"Boy, what kind of name is Mo Money?" she asked.

Her question caught me off guard, but I smoothly replied, "I got Mo Money than a lotta niggas my age." I know it was corny as hell, but it made her smile.

Me and Ashley made small talk and I became lost in her conversation. I hadn't even known her for twenty minutes and I was feeling her. She didn't talk like she was 15-years-old. She commanded my full attention.

"Where yo' boyfriend at? I don't want him to snake me and I have to shoot this party up," I half joked looking to my left and my right.

"I don't have a boyfriend. The only thing you boys want to do is have sex and go, so I'm cool with being single."

"First off, I'm a man not a boy. Secondly all niggas ain't the same. Maybe you just fucking with the wrong type of niggas."

"Naw, I think that all men are just dumb," Ashley replied and we shared a good laugh at that.

"If I was yo' man, I would appreciate you. I only knew you for a few minutes and I can already see that you special."

"Thank you, I see you think you got some game," Ashley said with a smile.

My phone vibrated. It was a text from Arab saying that it was time for us to handle our business.

"Look I got some business to handle so I'm 'bout to get up outta here. Let me get yo' number and maybe I could take you out or something," I said and handed her my phone.

Ashley saved her number and said, "Don't prove me right about all guys being the same. You better call me whenever you're free."

"Fasho, I got you," I said forcing myself to walk off.

I scanned the room and saw SBE Randy throwing money to Gucci Mane's 'Add it Up'. I made eye contact with Arab before making my way towards Randy. I slipped my Glock in the sleeve of my Coogi hoodie. When I got close enough to Randy, I pretended to trip and stumble into him, and I jammed my gun in his stomach.

"Don't say shit or I'ma blow yo' fuckin guts out," I said in his ear.

"What the fuck you on, fam," he asked, terrified.

"Walk to the bathroom. If you make any move, my homie over there," I nodded towards Arab, and he nodded back. "He gon' make sure you die," I said.

Once we got in the bathroom, I smacked Randy across the face with my gun. "You know what it is, bitch. I need everything!" I said snatching off his chain while he unscrewed his earrings. "Fuck this weak ass jewelry. Where the money at?" I asked.

SBE Randy went into his coat pocket and passed me a wad of bills. He must've thought I hadn't been watching him up multiple rolls. I smacked him with the gun.

"Where the rest of that shit at?" I asked and he emptied every pocket. He passed me two more thick wads of cash. "This everything?"

"Yeah, man," SBE Randy whined shooting a mean mug at me.

"Now if I search you and I find anything else, you know I'ma shoot you, right?" I asked seriously.

"Damn man, you a thirsty ass nigga!" Randy gruffed as he went into both of his socks and pulled out two more wads of money .This nigga was loaded! I pocketed the biggest wad for myself and put the rest of the money together. My pants pockets were stuffed.

"Yeah, funny guy. I am thirsty," I said punching SBE Randy in the jaw. "Now take off that coat and them glasses," I added before punching him again." Now stay yo' bitch ass in this bathroom until somebody come to get you," I told him putting on his Pelle and hurrying out the bathroom.

Arab was right outside of the bathroom's door waiting on me.

"We gone!" I said, speedwalking past him and out of the party. "On Stone, we hit the muthafuckin jackpot," I said once we were inside the car riding off. I counted the money out. "This eighty-six thirty-seven. On Stone, dude lame ass was loaded for real." I was amazed by how much money we got off just one person, and it was an easy job. He didn't even put up a fight. I split the money down the middle and had Arab drop me off at Nutso's house where I had been staying lately.

I stepped inside my Auntie Peaches house anxious to fill Nutso in on what I'd just done. He was in his bedroom playing his PlayStation 3."Why yo' eyes so buck?" He asked me after I entered his room.

I didn't know that the effects of the X pill had my eyes looking like they were ready to pop out of my head.

"Here, cuz, you can have this," I said passing him the Cuban link I snatched off Randy's neck.

"Good lookin' cuz. Where the fuck you get this from?" he asked, gazing at the diamond chain like a little kid. His eyes were big, and he was smiling hard. I knew how much he liked big jewelry so I knew I was going to give it to him as soon as I took it.

"Stop asking so many questions," I huffed as I emptied my pockets revealing my chop of the robbery money. I had a little over $4,300. That's when I remembered the wad of cash that I pocketed for myself. That turned out to be another $1,400.

"Damn Moe, where you get all that bread from?" Nutso asked

"Do you remember Amon from the Crank?" I asked, and he nodded in response.

"Me and him just hit a stain together. I made more money today than I did in two months selling weed. I think robbing mufuckas gon' be my new hustle."

"Shit, if we always gon' come up like this I'm finna start robbing too."

"That's cool but you know that ain't really our thing so we gon' follow Arab lead until we get that shit down pat, then we can branch off and do our own thang."

"All well, but next time y'all go to hit a stain, I wanna go too."

"All well, but first thing in the morning, I'ma need for you to take me to the lot to buy me a new whip," I said as Ashley popped into my mind. I sent her a text that read: *'Still handling business stay up for me'*.

I thought about her all night while kicking it with Nutso.

Chapter 6

Ashley

I woke up the next morning to a text from Ashley that read, 'I knew it.'

I called her immediately.

"What?" she answered, not masking her attitude. Her soft voice sounded cute tryna act all mad and shit.

"I'm sorry I didn't call you last night. I got caught up in some crazy shit that had me occupied until like four in the morning. I didn't want to call you that late like you was a hoe or something," I lied. The truth was I fell asleep.

"That's not a good enough excuse for me and if I remember correctly you told me that being sorry won't get you nowhere," she said recycling my game on me.

"You're absolutely right. How about you let me make it up to you by taking you out for breakfast?"

"I want to say that that'll be fine but I don't want you to send me off again."

"I promise I'm not. You just make sure you looking as sexy as you was last night," I replied. She gave me the address to her mother's apartment building on 112th Street and I told her that I'd call her when I was outside.

While I was getting dressed, I remembered that Nut was supposed to take me to the car lot to get a new whip. "Wake up pussy," I told him lightly smacking him on his cheek.

"Stop playing," he grumbled sleepily.

"I need for you to take me on 128th real quick," I told him.

When we made it to the car lot, Nutso whispered.

"Don't spend all our money."

"This my money," I clarified looking at him like he was crazy. I looked around the lot for a minute until I saw a white Buick Park Avenue that I liked.

"How much y'all want for this?" I asked a dealer whose name tag read, 'Zion.'

"Three thousand dollars," he stated.

"I got twenty five cash right now. Work something out for me," I said pulling out the wad that I already had prepared. The dealer agreed. We did all the paperwork and I told Nutso that I'd see him later before pulling off to go pick up Ashley.

Before going to pick Ashley up, I went to buy a bottle of cologne to spray on. I was looking good in a Red Lacoste polo, a pair of Black 501 Levi's and a pair of Wheat Timbs. The cologne added the extra emphasis to my good looks. When I pulled up to Ashley's apartment building, she came out looking gorgeous in a pair of blue jeans, a white turtleneck, and a pair of tan Ugg boots. She looked like she worked in somebody's office. She had her long hair flowing down past her shoulders.

"Damn you look even better in the sunlight," I joked touching one of her big hoop earrings after she climbed into the car and put on her seatbelt. "So how are you feeling today, Ms. Ashley?" I asked turning down the volume to the radio.

"I'm fine. Happy you didn't send me off again. Who car is this?" she asked.

"This my shit," I stated proudly before asking. "Where you tryna eat at?"

"It doesn't matter," she replied

"Don't worry, I got somewhere in mind," I said. We rode and made small talk just learning more about each other until we pulled up to Ms. Biscuits on 54th and Wabash. "This my favorite breakfast spot in the city," I told her as we walked into the restaurant. We ordered our food and chose to sit close to the windows.

"Why don't you have a girlfriend, Mo Money? Wait, before you answer that, what is your real name?" Ashley asked breaking the ice.

"My OG named me D'Andre. You can call me Dre if you want to. Now, as far as why don't I have a girlfriend, I was in a relationship, but I had gotten locked up and shorty broke bad on me. You know how that go. A female will see that you getting some money and she will be all in with you but as soon as you fall off or get locked up, all those feelings change.

Then, I jumped into another relationship once I got out of jail. I thought I was in love but once again she only saw me for my money, and she ended up setting me up to get robbed. I guess I don't have no luck when it comes to finding a good woman so now I'd rather put my energy towards chasing money than chasing a love that don't exist," I explained before putting a forkful of scrambled eggs in my mouth.

"It sounds like you just put too much faith in the wrong women. I hope you know that every woman is not like that. Loyalty is everything to me," Ashley said looking into my eyes.

"So, how deep is your loyalty?" I asked.

She held up a finger indicating for me to hold on while she chewed a piece of bacon. "Very deep. Once you earn my loyalty and prove that you're worth being loyal to, I'll move mountains and cross oceans for you."

"That sounds good, but I see I couldn't trust you around no bacon. You over there going crazy!" I joked before erupting in laughter. She couldn't help but to join me. She told me about her ex and how he couldn't stop cheating on her. She admitted that he really scarred her and that she was still getting herself together and over him.

I don't know why but it feels like I've known you forever. Like we already had a connection. It feels like we've been here before," Ashley told me and I couldn't disagree because I felt it too.

"Naw I think I would've remembered being here with a woman like you," I was saying, and just as I finished my sentence, I felt a presence behind me. I looked back to see Kahidijah.

"Hey Dre, I knew that was you. Give me a hug, boy," she said smiling standing there with her arms outstretched. She looked slightly different from how I remembered. Maybe because she gained a little weight and was wearing a lot of makeup.

"Naw, we ain't gon' do no huggin'. What's up doe?" I asked peeking over at Ashley, who was staring at Kahidijah with a blank expression.

"I haven't seen your chocolate ass in forever." She paused to check me out. "I see you still looking good and staying fresh, and your lil hair done grew," she added touching my braids. She didn't even know how much she was pissing me off.

First off, it was obvious that I was on a date. Secondly, I hadn't seen her since before I got locked up. Not to mention she broke bad on me and hurt my feelings.

"I ain't tryna kick it. You wasn't tryna kick it with me while I was locked up. I guess you couldn't paint yo' face and write me at the same time. It's cool doe. No love lost. But if you'd excuse me, I'm on a date and I'm tryna show my girl a good time," I said dismissing her.

Ashley smiled at that.

Kahidijah stood there looking shitty. "Niggas think they the shit because they getting a lil money. Boy, get yo' broke, ugly ass on," she mumbled as she stormed off.

"So, I'm your girl now?" Ashley asked.

"Yup, but you gotta promise to be the best I ever had."

"I *promise* to be the best you ever had and the best you'll ever experience," she replied cockily. "Don't worry, Baby Dre, I got you."

"Fasho," I said before stuffing a big piece of pancake in my mouth.

Chapter 7

War Time

It was the beginning of December and Ralph's party was in a few weeks. I had introduced Nutso and T Stone to hitting stains and that's what we had been doing for weeks to stack our money. It was easy and the thrill was indescribable.

"Aye law, drop me off at my bitch crib," Bone said to me in his usual slow drawl. It seemed like he grew bigger and bigger with every month that passed. He was already taller than me.

"Man, what bitch you got, lil nigga? I thought you was still a virgin," I joked as he climbed into my passenger's seat.

"Pinky. She live over east in Terror Town," he replied as we pulled off.

Bone slid a CD in the CD player and a raw ass beat boomed through my speakers.

"Who shit is this?" I asked, nodding my head.

"This Bucky new mixtape. He went crazy on every song. He got one song that say all the guy's names," Bone told me.

Bucky was putting his all into making music. He now went by the name King Bucky and his buzz was getting louder and louder. His music was getting recognized beyond the hood. He had even paid a radio station to put his song in rotation.

"You got some bread on you, lil bro?" I asked Bone.

He felt his pockets before saying, "Nope but if y'all would let me in on one of the licks y'all be hitting then I'd be straight."

Even though he was younger than the rest of us, Bone was mature way beyond his years. He was one of my best friends. If not my best friend and I didn't want him involved in that robbery shit.

"Naw, lil bro I can't have you out here like that but take this. "I pulled out a wad of money and peeled off $800 and passed it to him. "Grab two zips of loud with that. Start yoself a weed line and run it up. The block gon' be yours one day," I prophesized as I pulled up on 78th and Yates. The No Limit side of Terror Town. "Be safe lil bro. Call me later so I can come pick you up and don't give that money to yo' bitch either. I'ma keep this mixtape." I told Bone popping the locks so he could get out.

"Aight, good looking big bro," he told me closing the door. I turned up the volume of the radio to the max and rode off listening to Bucky rap about our younger days.

"Bitch, make another noise and I'ma kill yo' ass. And stop fucking moving!" I said to this Heavy named Cool's wife. He had a safe and some drugs that we needed so we had his bitch tied up waiting for him to walk in. They lived in a nice, big house in Oak Park. Nutso was waiting inside a small closet next to the front door holding a Mac 10. He got a adrenaline rush from hitting stains so did our homie Lil C. He was one of the Black Stones from the building. They both acted like they did this shit for fun. I was in it for the money. Fuck the thrill.

"On that door, Cool just hopped out his whip," Lil C yelled looking out the living room's window. He was a short, brown skinned, skinny kid with a big heart.

I flicked off the living room's light right before Cool put his key in the lock. He walked in to see his wife sitting on the couch. It looked as if she was just sitting there in the dark.

"Why are you in here sitting in the dark crazy woman?" Cool asked heading her way. He stopped in his tracks when he felt the cold metal of Nut's Mac press against the back of his neck.

77

"You know what time it is, big fella," Nutso growled. After successfully hitting a few licks, Nutso thought he was a pro now. Lil C walked up and gave Cool a quick pat down. He took his P94 Ruger off his waistline.

"Where that shit at?" Nutso asked.

"My wife don't have shit to do with this. Untie her and I'll let you know where everything is," Cool said.

I smacked his wife across the face with my gun before turning to him. "You not in a good position to be tryna compromise and shit," I told him.

Cool thought about it for a second before leading us to his safe. He opened it and Lil C emptied it. It was full of stacks of money but no drugs.

"Where the work at?" Nutso asked.

"I sold it all," Cool replied.

Nutso looked at me and then at Lil C. He nodded his head and with that notion, Lil C shot cool in his stomach. His wife shrieked. I grabbed her by her long hair and put my gun to her head.

"Last chance, nigga. Where that shit at?" I asked impatiently.

"The wall! The wall!" Cool shouted defeatedly.

"Which wall?" Lil C asked.

"My bedroom in the closet. Break the wall open."

"You should have been said that shit," I told him before shooting his wife in the head. Nutso followed suit and gave him a head shot. We broke down the wall in the closet and found eight keys of Heroin. When we made it back to Nutso's crib, we counted the money and it came out to $73,000. That was the most money either of us had ever seen. We split the money and the bricks.

Lil C took two while me and Nutso got three apiece since it was our stain. We all felt like we were rich.

The next day, me and a few of the bros were all on the side block, 105th Place, shooting dice.

"Shake and roll when I'm fading you," Smack told me knocking the dice from my hand. He was notorious for being a bully and as usual he was trying to use his bully tactics on the participants of the dice game.

"You can't tell me how to shoot my shot. Who the fuck you think you is?" I asked screwing my face up before throwing the dice and hitting my point. "Point! Nobody move!" I yelled excitedly picking up my money.

"Didn't I just tell you to shake and roll?" Smack asked stepping in my face.

He was at least three inches taller than me with the body of a football player. He always tried using his size to intimidate someone. We'd known each other since we were kids and he knew that I wasn't going for that shit. I was far from a hoe.

"And didn't I say you can't tell me how to shoot? If you don't like my shot, don't fade me," I gruffed.

Me and Smack had an intense stare down. I could tell he was thinking about trying me. Before he could say anything else, Reesie pulled up.

"What y'all on out here?" he asked climbing out of his car with a sly smirk on his face. His dreads now hung past his jawline. He had a couple of the foes with him.

"Shit, shootin' dice. I'm glad you pulled up. Now it's some real money out here," Smack said dick riding. I stood there mugging Reesie. He caught me looking and dug in his pocket.

"Here go that lil ass chump change I owe you," he said pulling out a wad of money and tossing it at the ground in front of me. He was trying to flex on me, but little did he know I was doing good.

"I don't need that shit," I spat.

"Give it to Panda then," Reesie said and that was all it took for me to lose control. I threw two ferocious jabs that landed on his nose.

"Bitch ass nigga!" I growled hitting him with a nasty uppercut that split his lip. I really wanted to kill him for shooting my cousin but I had love for him so I substituted bullets for the punches that I was hitting him with.

After taking so many punches, Reesie was able to up his gun. "You still wanna fight?" He pointed his .40 in my face.

"Whoa, whoa, whoa! Hold on!" I said throwing.my hands in the air. I thought he was about to shoot me all in my face. Instead, he hit me in the mouth with his gun. The first hit drew blood.

Bone stepped up only for Smack to push him back. "Stay out of this lil bro," he told Bone with a frown.

"Hell naw, he tweaking!" Bone yelled upping the .357 Sig Sauer that he was holding for me.

"Aye, Reesie, fight him head up or blow that bitch," Bone said.

By now, Reesie had already hit me with his gun more than a few times. We both were bleeding. He shot Bone a look that could kill. ''Shorty put that lil shit down before I let you feel this big mufucka," he said waving his .40.

"You heard what I said," Bone stated not backing down. Out of nowhere, shots rang out. I took off running and looked back to see that it was Nutso who was shooting towards Reesie's crowd. Reesie backpedaled towards his car while blowing his .40 at me. Bullets whizzed past my head. I stopped running and hid behind a parked Buick.

Reesie hopped in his car but his cousin, Jerry wasn't so lucky. Nutso had painted the side of Reesie's car with his brains. Watching Reesie screech off, I couldn't help but smile. He shot my cousin; my cousin shot his cousin. That was poetic justice. The only difference was that his cousin didn't make it, mine did. That get back felt good. I knew that now we were way beyond the point of no return and the war had truly begun.

***

"Man cuz, once you wake up I got something to tell you that's gon' have you proud of me. It's a lot I need to tell you. You just gotta wake up," I said to Panda. I was standing next to his hospital bed while Ashley watched us from the corner of the room. He had to undergo multiple surgeries after getting shot and at first it looked like he would come out okay but they were never able to stabilize his condition. He was now in a medically induced coma. My Auntie Lexas had to decide whether to pull the plug or not.

"I never told you this but I look up to you cuz. You and Sheed the reasons why I wanted to be a Stone. Ever since I was a kid I wanted to be like y'all. You was always the man in my eyes," I said. I felt a lump forming in my throat, but I continued to speak. "I got some money put up, like $25,000. You can have all that shit. Just wake up."

A tall, lanky Indian doctor entered the room holding a clipboard. "Sorry to interrupt but the patient's mother said she will be pulling the plug in ten minutes," the doctor said in broken English. And quickly left the room.

"Noooo!" I cried. Tears flowed from my eyes like a stream. I couldn't believe that my Auntie was deciding to pull the plug. She wasn't even giving him a chance to fight.

"See, Panda they giving up on you. You gotta get up and show them how strong you is," I said squeezing Panda's hand. I was hoping he would squeeze back. "Get up, cuz. I got some keys that you could have. I know you could get that shit off quicker than I could. We gon' run it up. You just gotta get the fuck up!" I urged him as if he could really hear me. I wasn't ready to lose my cousin. The pain I was feeling was quickly turning to anger. "Wake up!" I shouted startling Ashley, who was just standing there watching me break down. "Get the fuck up. They tryna kill you!" I said and started shaking Panda's body. "Wake up!" I screamed over and over again.

Ashley grabbed my shoulder, but I snatched away from her. "WAKE UP! WAKE UP! WAKE UP!" I continued to shout and shake Panda's body. I went on what could only be described as an emotional breakdown until family members and a few hospital staff members carried me out of the hospital crying, kicking, and screaming.

I thought I was up on Reesie, but we were even. I needed to get my lick back for Panda. I couldn't believe that one of my closest friends did this. A nigga that I had real love for, had murdered my blood. That shit had me feeling emotionally depleted.

"Baby, are you okay?" Ashley asked, lying next to me in my bed.

"Not at all," I replied sullenly. "A lot of the shit I know now I learned from my cousin, Panda. When they pulled the plug on him, it felt like I lost a part of myself." I added with a sigh.

"I'm here for you," was All Ashley said in response before placing a soft kiss on my cheek. She had been trying her best to comfort me, even though it was nothing she could do to make me feel better. I still appreciated the gesture.

Nutso entered my room without knocking on the door. "Aye, come buss this move with me cuz," he said.

I looked over at Ashley for her approval.

"Go. I'll watch a movie until you get back just be safe," she said.

When we left out of the building, I noticed that we didn't see Nutso's car.

"Where yo' whip at?" I asked.

"Lil C driving. We in a steamer. We 'bout to go slide on Reesie nem. We gotta make it count for Panda," Nutso replied.

I could tell that he was just as hurt as I was. He was just holding himself together better.

Once inside the stolen Jeep, I greeted Lil C with a nod. I pulled out my .357, put it on my lap, and stared out the window. All the love I had for Reesie had turned into hate. If you would've asked me this time yesterday could I kill him, my answer ·probably would've been no. We rode up Corliss until we got to 105th Street where we saw Reesie posted up with a group of Foes. We stopped right in front of the crowd. I quickly opened my door and hopped out shooting. Reesie returned fire after taking cover behind a tree.

"Damn," I grumbled jumping behind a parked Chevy. Lil C shot out of his window while Nutso chased the crowd down unloading his clip.

Reesie dumped his clip at the car I was hiding behind. I looked under the car trying to see where he was shooting from to see that he was way closer than I thought he was. I inched towards the hood of the car and popped up tapping my trigger. The first shot missed. Reesie stood there looking like a deer caught in some headlights as I squeezed my trigger trying to hit him all in his face. He flinched hard when he heard my gun click instead of *boom*. I kept pulling the trigger, but my gun was jammed. A wicked smile spread across Reesie's face as I tried to bolt for the steamer we came in. His gun was already aimed at the back of my head. The tables were turned now. I had fucked up.

Click! Click! Click! Click!

Reesie kept pulling his trigger but luckily he had no more bullets in the .40 that he was shooting. I jetted to the Jeep and jumped in the backseat. "Reesie just almost smoked my goofy ass! This weak ass Seven jammed up on me, luckily he ran out of bullets," I told Nutso and Lil C as Lil C sped off down Corliss.

"We just fucked them boys up," Lil C said boastfully. Neither me nor Nut responded. This was an act of justice for us. We were planning on making The Hundreds bleed because of Panda's death.

Chapter 8

Ralph's Birthday Bash

The night of Ralph's party came quick. After I showered it took me almost an hour to choose an outfit. I had been spending a lot of my money on clothes so I had a lot to choose from. I finally decided on a Black and Red Gucci crewneck sweater, a black, green, and red Gucci skully, a pair of jet black jeans and a pair of wheat Timbs.

Goddamn, I'm good looking! I said to myself, looking in the mirror as I topped my fit off with a red and white leather Pelle coat. I walked into the living room to see Ashley standing there looking absolutely perfect in a white Chanel dress, a pair of white Christian Louboutin pumps and her hair was in a bob that stopped at her shoulders.

"On Stone, me saying that you're beautiful would be an understatement," I said making her smile and blush." I got something for you." I grabbed her soft hand and leading her to my bedroom. "Close your eyes," I said. Once she did, I reached under my pillow, grabbed the jewelry box I had hidden there and handed it to her. "Open it," I urged her with a broad smile on my face.

Ashley opened the jewelry box and stared at the white gold diamond necklace that I bought for her. Once she pulled it out and saw the heart shaped pendant that had our initials engraved in it, her hand flew to her mouth.

"Thank you, Baby Dre. It's so beautiful," she said staring at the necklace. It was the first piece of jewelry that I'd ever bought for a woman and seeing how misty Ashley's eyes were getting, I knew I had hit a homerun with the gift.

"On Stone, I fuck with you the long way, baby girl. This just a token of my appreciation," I told her, and she gave me a tight hug and a kiss on the lips before I helped her put it on. She gave me another hug and an even more passionate kiss. Her soft, caramel colored skin felt so good on my hands that I didn't wanna let her go. "Come on," I finally said breaking our embrace." Let's go make our grand entrance."

The party was at a club called Mr. Ricky's on 142nd and Chicago Road. You could tell that the club was packed by the amount of cars that were parked in the parking lot and the line to get in the club was almost around the corner. I had VIP wristbands so I bypassed the long line.

Once inside the club, I was able to see just how lit it really was. T Pain's 'Can't Believe it' blared loudly throughout the club.

''Gon' head and have a good time baby," I told Ashley when she spotted a group of her friends. She walked off and I saw somebody grab her by her wrist. I instantly approached the dread head after I watched Ashley reject him and he continued to bother her.

"Aye fam," I said tapping his shoulder where the strap of his Louis Vuitton backpack was at.

"What up?" the guy gruffed turning around with a mug on his face.

"Five, what's the word broski?" I asked as we shook up.

"What's the word, my boy? You know I wasn't missing the party of the year for nothing in the world. I brought a few of the guys too," Five told me and I handed him four VIP wristbands.

"We bought the bar out so y'all use these to get free drinks," I told him.

"Bet but where shorty in that white dress just go? On King David, she was nice," Five asked, scanning the club.

"You gotta find somebody else skud, that's wifey," I replied seriously.

"Damnnnn that's crazy," Five said with a smile while shaking his head. He was dressed to impress in a white and black Prada shirt, a pair of black jeans, a pair of black Prada shoes and a black bubble Prada coat.

"I see you in this bitch looking like money too," I complimented him before walking off and running into Nutso.

"What's the demo, cuz? Why the fuck you got on them weak ass glasses?" I asked him with a smile as we shook up. He was wearing a pair of Rayban shades, a blue and red Burberry polo, a pair of light blue jeans and a pair of all white low top Air Ones.

"Merry Christmas, bitch. Don't worry about me!" Nutso replied and erupted in laughter. "Let's go grab a drink," he yelled over the music with Lil C right by his side wearing the same outfit just in a different color scheme. I could tell that they were high by the goofy smiles that they both wore. "Let me get a fifth of Remy, a fifth of Cîroc and what you want Money?"

"Patron," I said.

Nutso handed me my bottle and when the light hit the diamonds on his chain, it glistened in the dimly lit club. He had on the chain that I had given him. It was a diamond Cuban link with a nice sized diamond encrusted Five pointed star charm hanging from it.

"Look at Ralphy!" I said as our cousin Ralph approached wearing all white. He had a King's crown on his head. Ralph was younger than me but older than Nutso. We were all first cousins. He just wasn't as deep in the streets as we were so we tried to keep him away.

"Happy birthday, cuz. I love you my nigga," I told him giving him a half hug. I told the bartender to give us a bottle of Ace Of Spades just as Drake's 'Brand New' came on.

"Bucky performing in a minute and he want us all on stage so be ready," Ralph told us before grabbing the arm of a thick red boned woman and walking off trying to talk to her.

"I'm 'bout to slide in this bathroom," I told Nutso and Lil C before taking a swig of Patron.

As I entered the surprisingly clean bathroom, I heard somebody say," Take that chain off you bitch ass nigga!" I scanned the stalls and saw multiple feet in one stall.

Another voice said, "On Stone, pop his bitch ass since he think this shit a game!" I recognized that voice immediately. I walked over to the stall and opened the door to see Bone, T Stone and C Murder standing over a heavy set guy who was covered in blood.

"What the fuck is you niggas doing?" I asked.

"Fuck do it look like we doing?" Bone retorted snatching off the guy's shoes and checking his socks.

"Jackpot!" C Murder smiled when Bone found a large wad of money.

"I knew this goofy ass nigga had some bread on him," T Stone said taking off his belt. "Tie his fat ass up and leave him in here until the party over," he told C Murder handing him his belt. "And if yo' fat ass somehow make it out this bitch and I see you I'ma smoke yo' dumb ass," T Stone threatened coldly. He was addicted to hitting stains. That's all he did nowadays. He was vicious with it too. Some of the bros didn't like hitting licks with him because they felt like he always went overboard.

"Come on y'all, let's go fuck with these hoes," Bone suggested dancing his way out of the bathroom until C Murder grabbed his arm.

"We ain't going nowhere without splitting that bread," he said peeping that Bone was trying to slide away.

"Y'all hurry up. We going on stage in a minute," I said before leaving them alone to divide their earnings.

***

Reesie and a few of the niggas he ran with sat in Smack's Astrovan outside the club. Everybody in the car was dressed in dark clothing and everyone was strapped up.

"How many times I gotta tell you that you good?" Reesie asked the person who he was on the phone with. "Only thing I need for you to do is call me when Bucky starts performing. That's it That's all," Reesie said before hanging up on the caller.

"I can't wait to see how good this bitch blow," Cello said referring to the 30 shot Glock 19 he was holding.

"Don't go in that bitch tryna talk to hoes, party, or none of that extra shit," Reesie told his shooters looking at them one by one. "Go in that bitch blowing. I don't give a fuck who y'all hit," he added. Nobody replied. Everybody checked their clips and made sure that their guns were ready to shoot .

***

Back inside the club, we were all preparing to head onstage. "You got pipe on you?" Nutso asked me.

I looked at him like he was crazy. "Hell yeah," I said flashing my gun.

"Make sure you up yo' shit when Bucky say our names," he told me flashing the two guns he had on his waist. I couldn't do anything except laugh at him.

"Aye Five!" I yelled over the loud music. "Come on stage with us gang," I told him once I had his attention. I walked over to C Murder who was standing by the bar talking on his phone. He smiled as I approached and told whoever he was talking to, "Me and bro nem bout to hop on stage and act crazy. I'ma call you back later."

When he hung up, I gave him a half hug. "Merry Christmas my nigga, let's go show out," I told him before leading him to the stage. When I climbed on stage Bucky was performing his song 'Like Me' and all the guys were on stage going crazy. The Patron plus the X pill I had popped had me feeling groovy. By the time Bucky got done performing his song 'Wanna Bet' I was throwing five, ten and twenty dollar bills. I heard a loud boom like a speaker had popped or something. Then, out the corner of my eye I saw one of Five's homies fall face first off the stage and C Murder jump off the stage into the crowd of clubgoers ducking low. It was at that moment that I realized that we were getting shot at. Five must've realized it too because he pulled out his Glock 22 and started shooting. I pinpointed two shooters and sent a few shots their way. I scanned the club trying to find Ashley through the chaos. A glimpse of Bone shooting a 9mm over the DJ's booth caught my attention. I was stunned by the sight but quickly snapped back to my senses.

It was total pandemonium in the club and so many innocent people were catching bullets. I finally saw Ashley climbing over the bar. I never seen so much fear in her big, brown eyes. As I bolted in her direction, I saw one of the shooters watching me so I sent a few shots his way to throw him off.

I jumped over the bar and Ashley screamed at the top of her lungs. She stopped only when she realized that it was me.

"Calm down, baby. I got you, just be quiet," I told her wiping a few tears from her cheeks. Before I could figure out our next move, I felt cold steel being pressed to the back of my head.

"Drop that pipe, Moe," said a voice that I instantly recognized as my homie Eye.

"Damn G, I thought we was better than that," I said trying to play on his emotions and make him feel bad about getting in the mix. I did as I was told and dropped my gun. I looked over at Ashley and her eyes grew real big. Before I could turn around to see what she was looking at, four shots went off. As I fell forward, all I heard were Ashley's panicked screams. My neck and upper back were burning intensely. I just knew for sure that I was dead or dying at least. The burning was that bad. I managed to look up and I saw Bone holding a smoking gun. Eye was slumped over the bar with half of his head blown off.

"I-I Just K-k-killed bro," Bone stammered staring at Eye's dead body. I noticed that his body was slightly trembling.

"It's good, lil bro. He was tryna smoke me. You just saved my life but yo' goofy ass shot me in the process," I said with a crooked smile trying to hide the intense pain that I was in. "Shake that shit off bro and help me up. We gotta get the fuck out this club before twelve show up," I said. Bone helped me up and to the club's backdoor. On our way out we ran into Nutso and a few of the guys.

"You straight cuz?" Nutso asked rushing to my side checking me out. I was losing a lot of blood.

"I need to get to the hospital," I said feeling lightheaded.

"We gon' get you there cuz just be—" was all I remembered hearing Nut say before everything went black.

CITY OF SMOKE | MOLOTTI

Chapter 9

Still Alive

I woke up in the hospital with Ashley and Bone sitting by my bedside.

"What the fuck happened?" I asked through a dry, scratchy throat.

"You passed out from that backshot, my bad law," Bone stated sadly.

"It ain't shit Law you saved my life and I appreciate that," I said before turning my attention to Ashley who was sitting there with a small smile on her face. "Hey, Ashley. Baby, is you staring because of my good looks or is it something you wanna say?" I asked jokingly.

Ashley smacked her lips. "Boy you had me worried," she said with a smile. She shook her head then continued. "If that's how you and your guys party all the time then I'm not coming to no more of y'all parties."

"Naw, hoe ass niggas just do hoe ass shit," I spat angrily.

"I thought you died on me," she said softly. "I haven't left your side since you blacked out. Don't scare me like that again," she said playfully punching my arm.

"I'm sorry baby. I know who was behind that shit doe. I just can't believe that Eye was with that shit. I used to call that nigga my cousin. I see them hoe ass niggas mean business," I said.

"It's always the ones that we least expect. The ones who you love and trust the most be the ones that end up doing you the worst," Ashley said caressing my face with her soft touch.

"Fuck all them niggas!" I said angrily. "As long as I got you, my money, and a few real niggas by my side, then I'm straight. Unless y'all gon' end up snaking me too," I said looking back and forth from Ashley to Bone. I meant it as a joke but Ashley snatched her hand away from my face.

"Don't do that," she said frowning up. "I'll never turn on you. I'm with you through it all. I don't care how hard it gets or how scary it gets, I'm here. I'm in love with you," she admitted for the first time. Once she said that, I was at a loss for words. We had never said those words to each other. Plenty of times I wanted to, but I never did.

"I love you too," I said staring into her brown eyes .

A few days after I was released from the hospital, I was picking up Ashley from her mother's crib. "Damn, look at shorty looking all sexy and shit," I teased her as she got in my car. I took a deep drag off the Kush blunt that I was smoking and exhaled a lungful of smoke through my nostrils.

"Thank you," she replied with that smile that I loved so much. "Why are you smoking and you just got out of the hospital? You get on my nerves."

"This medical marijuana," I joked hitting the blunt again. "But what you tryna do tonight?" I asked turning down the Shorty Rome mixtape that I had playing. My homie Shorty Rome from Goon Town was taking off with his music career just like Bucky was. They both were hot on the streets.

"We can go out to eat or to the movies. It really doesn't matter to me," she replied while applying MAC lip gloss to her perfect lips.

"How about we order some Chinese food, go to my crib and we can cuddle up and watch a movie?"

"That'll be perfect."

I had convinced my OG to move out the building and into a small house on 125th and Wentworth. When we made it to my crib, we kicked back and ate orange chicken while watching 'Love & Basketball, one of Ashley's favorite movies.

"So, do you think that we got a love as deep as theirs?" I asked Ashley who was deep into the movie.

"Of course," she replied with a nod. "I feel like we do but instead of basketball I have to share your love with the streets. What made you ask that?" she asked taking her eyes off the TV.

"Because I wanted to know."

"Tell me how you feel," she said turning to me to give me her undivided attention.

"I feel like what we have is real. You my best friend and you the first woman who ever showed me real love. God know that the real niggas need love too and he sent you to me just in time."

"Aww, look at you tryna be sweet," Ashley teased me. "God most definitely did his shit when he crossed our paths. You're different from every other guy I've ever dealt with. I believe it when you say you're in love with me. That's why I'm going to forever be by your side. You won't ever have to worry about anything, Baby Dre. I got you," she said.

All I could do was smile at this point. I meant it when I said that I'd never felt this much love for a woman. I thought I was in love with Mieysha but how I felt for her isn't even close to how I feel for Ashley. I had been hurt a couple times so trusting was hard for me but for some odd reason, I trusted Ashley completely. She was perfect in my eyes. "I'm happy you feel that way," I told her, kissing her forehead.

"I told you that loyalty is everything and all we have is love and loyalty," she replied.

"Don't forget about trust issues. I think you been cheating," I joked, and she smacked me with a pillow.

"Boy, I am not cheating on you! Why would you even play like that?" she asked wearing a cute frown.

"I was joking baby," I told her as I got up and turned off the TV. "I trust you and I trust that you're all mines," I told her as I played Ace Hood's 'Ride or Die' on my laptop.

I climbed into the bed next to Ashley and started planting soft kisses on her neck and face. By the time 'Under' by Pleasure P' came on, that's exactly where I was headed. Under. I placed kisses all over Ashley's flat stomach before yanking off her Pajama pants. I then started kissing and nibbling around her inner thighs until goosebumps appeared on her legs. Her breathing sped up in anticipation of my next move.

Even though we had been dating for a couple months, we had never had sex. I slowly peeled off her panties and kissed my way back up her long legs until I was face to face with her pretty, bald pussy. Her scent was intoxicating. I inhaled her fragrance before I went in for the kill and started attacking her clit with my tongue. This was my first time eating pussy so I did what I saw men doing on porns I watched. I licked her clit real fast before sticking my tongue inside her pussy and tasting her sweet walls. I got up and climbed on top of her and we kissed for a long time. We touched each other like we had never experienced the opposite sex before.

"Don't hurt me," Ashley whispered before kissing and nibbling on my earlobe. I didn't respond. I just slowly entered the swollen head of my dick inside of her. "Ooohhhh," she moaned sounding angelic. She was so tight that I would've sworn that she was a virgin.

When I was fully inside of her, I almost came. I stroked her body slowly and it didn't take long for us to find a rhythm. I had to force myself not to moan as she clinched her vaginal walls around my dick. The love we made, made minutes seem like hours. We took our time and enjoyed every inch of each other's body. We tried every position of which we could think. Every muscle in my body was tired as I pumped in and out of her on our third round of passionate sex. She climaxed and squirted everywhere. Her juices wet my bedsheets.

"Don't stop," Ashley moaned in ecstasy. I bent her ass up so that her knees was damn near by her ears and hit her with long strokes. "I love you, DREEE!" she screamed and that must've did it because I came and shot my seed deep inside her womb. I didn't want to pull out so I laid on top of her breathing hard.

"Now I know what Drake was talking about," I said rolling off her.

"What you mean?" She asked confused.

"You the best I ever had," I joked making her laugh.

"You so corny," Ashley said still giggling.

For the rest of the night, we laid in each other's arms and fantasized about our future together.

Chapter 10

A Risky Road

A week later, I was back in the field heavy, sending shots at Reesie and the Foes every chance I could. We had hit a stain on a few bricks of coke and I was now selling weight of that shit. My money was stacking and I was enjoying the fruits of my labor. The smoke I had with Reesie was spilling over forcing more and more of the guys to pick sides. All the Moes from the hood and from

D Block were riding with me and all the Foes from the hood were with Reesie but now a few of the GDs from the hood were picking sides. I needed more guns so I had gotten up with my boy Shody Shod, who had told me that his cousin from the west side had a lot of guns for sell. We were making that trip on 290 to see what he had.

As we pulled up to his cousin's crib, Shody Shod made a call and his cousin came to open the door for us.

"Mo Money, this my cousin Fox. Fox this my homie, Mo Money," Shody Shod said introducing us.

Fox was a cut up, light brown skinned guy with wavy hair and a light mustache. He had a big red five pointed star wit LB inside of it tatted on his face. Shody Shod had already told me he was a 4 Corner Hustler from a hood called Lo Block. Fox led us to his basement which looked like a game room and then into a back room that had guns everywhere, literally. The floor, the dresser, the bed, and the entertainment center had guns scattered around.

"Damn, you got all these guns laying around like you not worried about twelve running in this bitch," Shody Shod said to bro.

"I'm not." Fox screwed his face up. "When you moving a certain way, you don't gotta worry about shit like that," he added before lighting up a thick blunt of Kush that he had hanging from his lips. "What type of poles y'all looking for doe? I got automatics, revolvers, pumps, choppas," Fox said using his fingers to count off. "Man on the Foe, I got whatever y'all need," he said after blowing a cloud of smoke in the air.

We ended up buying three Macs, an automatic Malzberg pump, a Russian Ak-47, a Colt.45 with the lemon squeeze, a 30 shot Tech and two 30 shot Glocks. Fox taxed us but to make us feel like he didn't ,he gave us a box of shells for each gun we bought.

"On the foe, who y'all into it with? Iraq?" Fox laughed as we packed the guns up. He had a funny ass laugh that made me laugh with him. We left and made our way to the hood to pass out our new toys.

***

Spring 2009

I had cuffed Bone and took him under my wing. He was by my side picking up game and absorbing knowledge while I made moves. He was still young so I didn't let him indulge in the war that we had going on. Plus, his brother, Smack was riding with Reesie so I didn't want to put him in a fucked up position. Nutso had Lil C by his side 24/7. T Stone hung with all of us whenever he wasn't somewhere robbing someone or putting in work. He was something like our muscle cause he was always anxious to get busy. The coke we had was actually good and we were establishing a name for ourselves as hustlers. We let Bone, Lil C, and a few of the lil guys sell bags while we sold weight. Reesie and everybody who was riding with him played the building while me and my crowd played 105th Place, the side block. Because we were all from the same hood, it was hard for us to actually keep our distance so it was always somebody getting shot at.

Reesie's name was ringing loudly throughout the city, not just for having some good ass crack but also because he was robbing everybody. He was instilling fear in the streets. He was our main competition. Considering our age a lot of older guys tried to pull it with us by either trying to get over on us of trying to muscle us out of a cheaper price but we wanted all the smoke so after we had to make a few examples niggas started to show us our respect. We were known to fuck niggas up and that kept nigga honest when doing business.

I recently upgraded my whip I was now pushing a navy blue BMW and Nutso had traded in his Monte Carlo and bought himself a '04' Porsche. I had some white boys I was serving hook my shit up with a stash so I could ride around comfortably with a nice amount of drugs on me.

Me and Bone rode around listening to 'Gorgeous' By Gucci Mane when a private caller called my cell phone.

"Yooo," I answered cooly before taking a hit off the blunt I was smoking.

"Mo Money, what's the demo, Ku?" Reesie asked. I could picture him wearing that sneaky ass smile of his.

"Fuck is you calling me for, goofy ass nigga?" I snarled feeling my anger star to rise.

"I was just smoking and thinking and shit right?" He paused for a second. "And I feel like instead of us waring we supposed to be getting this money together, you feel me?"

"Hell naw, I don't feel yo' weird ass," I spat stubbornly.

"I know you in yo' feelings about that shit with Panda but that's slight shit. This shit bigger than me and you. The big guys not feeling what we got going on so they're calling a sit down,"

"What kind of goofy do you think I am?" I said cutting him off. "The only place we can sit down together at is hell."

"I feel the exact same way goofy, but this came from Big Risky," Reesie said. I knew it was real if Big Risky was calling a sit down. He was one of the big Foes from the hood and had a slot for the 4 Corner Hustler's in The Hundreds, His sons lil Risky and BT were our two main hitters. They were both locked up for a robbery that went bad and turned into a double homicide. Out of the bros our age, they were the first two off the porch and we all wanted to be like them in one way or another. I knew that if Big Risky was calling a sit down then I had no other choice but to sit down.

"So, where we supposed to be meeting at?" I asked Reesie.

"In the back of the buildings at 8 P.M.," Reesie replied. "Maybe after we sit down me and you could talk business and run that bag up together."

"Get the fuck outta here!" I gruffed hanging up in his face. I didn't want to sit down with him but after I reached out to Wooski D and he confirmed that Big Risky indeed wanted to have a sit down, I knew it wasn't no way around going. I knew that Big Risky only wanted to squash what we had going on. He was a man who lived by the old codes and he frowned at how we were moving. I still didn't trust Reesie, doe. I knew he had something up his sleeve. Something told me to follow my intuition and say fuck that sit down but I couldn't disrespect Big Risky like that. I called up T Stone and told him to tell all the bros to meet us at our spot.

We all met up on 104th and State at Bone's step brother Rico's house. We decided to go to the sit down about four cars deep but only our main shooters would have pipe on them. We didn't want to make it seem like we were coming on bullshit. I chose to carry the 30 shot Glock 23, Nutso carried the Tech, T Stone had the Mac 10 and we decided that C Murder would sit in the car with the K. He would only pop out if things got too hectic for us.

"So, what I'ma tote?" Bone asked me while we were loading our clips.

"You not totin' shit nigga. You not even going," I replied not looking up from what I was doing.

"How Lil C and Binky get to go and I don't?" Bone whined jumping up acting like a big ass baby.

"Lil C not going either," I said looking up at him. "We need for y'all to stay here and hold the trap down just in case something go wrong. I told you. Y'all next up," I told Bone, but he waved me off.

"Suck a fat baby's dick," he mumbled. I didn't care how mad he was. He was my little brother and I planned on protecting him in every way that I could.

When we pulled up in the back of the building, in the C Section's parking lot, we saw a crowd of the guys standing in the field next to the tennis courts. There had to be close to 50 of the guys out there. We parked, hopped out and marched towards the crowd.

Big Risky stood with his arms folded across his chest listening to Wooski D talk. Big Risky was a cocky brown skinned man who stood about 5'9. He had a lot of rank and power radiated off of him. He was feared and respected throughout The Hundreds by every mob and hood who knew of him. His muscular arms told that he had did a little time. When he saw me approaching, he waved Reesie over to where he stood.

"Now, what the fuck is the problem?" He asked no one in particular. He wasn't speaking loudly but his deep voice commanded attention.

Reesie was the first to speak. "To be honest Unc, I don't know what this nigga problem is," he lied causing my jaw to drop. "The nigga shoot at me every time we run into each other. At first, I let him slide because he was one of my best friends but after he killed Lil E, I had to slide back," Reesie said lying with a straight face. Manipulation was something he was skilled at.

"Man, he lying!" I growled angrily.

"Calm down and tell him what's going on then," one of the older Moes named Ray Real told me.

"He begged for me to front him some weed so I tossed him a half a pound and told him to bring me back seven-fifty and after I approached him about my bread, him, and Lil 4 nem jumped me. Then, he robbed and killed my big cousin, Panda," I explained.

Big Risky rubbed his goatee before asking, "So what happened first?"

"He got down on me," I stated.

"Man, on the Foe, his cousin sold me some bogus work and when I tried to get my bread back, he got on some gangster shit so I left his ass right there," Reesie said and it looked like he was forcing himself not to smile.

"Y'all from the same building and y'all represent the same thing. Y'all supposed to be together, not against each other. We the brothers and the brothers don't move like that," Big Risky scolded us and all of the bros agreed with him. "So, from now on that shit y'all got going on is dead. Both of y'all leave that shit alone," he said firmly.

When Big Risky said that shit, I smacked my lips. "That nigga killed my blood and got down on me like I was some random ass nigga instead of his brother, one of his day ones. I'm not fuckin with dude bitch ass,'' I spat with venom in my tone.

"Niggas always on some fake tough shit," Lil 4 gruffed. "On the foe, that boy ain't gon be happy till we clap his bitch ass."

"Shut the fuck up!" Big Risky boomed. "Nephew, I said what I said and that shit final. It ain't nothing else to talk about. We got too much going on for y'all to be killing each other," he said looking at me before turning to the rest of the guys. "If any one of you lil niggas think y'all bigger than law then try me and see what the fuck I do," he said taking his time to lock eyes with everyone who was right there. Nobody responded and he walked off to talk to Henno, Baby Sco, Real and Thang.

Somehow, someway, Reesie ended up standing right next to my car. He had a devilish grin on his face. I knew him well enough to know that he was up to something.

"Look, since Big Foe say we gotta squash that shit how about you lil niggas flip foe and come work for me?" Reesie asked putting a hand on my shoulder.

"Don't touch me!" I said sharply smacking his hand away. "And ain't shit squashed you hoe ass nigga. On Stone, the first chance I get I'ma smoke yo' hoe ass," I promised.

Reesie looked unmoved by my threats. "That's probably the same shit Panda thought but I got him first. You should've saw how he was tryna run from them big ass nickel shells," he said with a chuckle.

"We had his goofy ass screaming like a lil bitch, on the Foe," Lil 4 chimed in and that was all it took for me to lose my cool. I threw a hard jab that connected with Lil 4's chin making him stumble backwards. I continued to swing trying to channel all my anger through my punches. I was beating Lil 4's ass but Reesie jumped in the fight and the tide quickly turned.

In seconds, the parking lot erupted into a big ass brawl. All of the older guys that were out there were trying to break the brawl up but to no avail. While I was fighting Cello, I heard somebody shout my name. I looked up to see Lil 4 running my way with his gun out. He opened fire towards me and I jumped behind somebody's Yukon Denali. A few more guns went off and then I heard the familiar sound of police sirens. I got up and saw that CPD patrol cars and the dicks were swarming the back of the building.

I took off and ran through the grass field we used to play football at before jumping a gate that led me to Maryland Street before darting across the street, hitting two cuts that put me on Corliss Street. I hit another cut that put me in my homie Wop's backyard. While in his backyard, I heard more guns going off, tires screeching and what sounded like a car collision. I beat on Wop's backdoor breathing hard and sweating profusely. I most definitely wasn't trying to go to jail. Just as a car was coming through the alley, Wop opened the door and I rushed inside.

I sat at Wop's crib until Nutso and T Stone pulled up to get me. He was one of the foes, but he was playing the middle due to him being locked in with both me and Reesie. T Stone was anxious to tell me how he had to get on C Murder's ass for not blowing the K when shit went up. He said he took the K from him and made him jump in the car with another one of the guys. While T Stone was going on a rant about C Murder and other hoe ass niggas, I got a call from Wooski D.

"Where the fuck you at, Moe?" he asked. It sounded as if he was crying.

"I'm at Wop crib."

"Who all over there?"

"Me, Wop, T Stone and Nut."

"Put the phone on speaker," Wooski D told me and when I did he spoke. "Man, Big Risky just got killed," he said before sniffling.

Those words were the last thing I wanted to hear. Big Risky was more than just one of the big guys. He was like a uncle to me. He was one of those guys who tried to lead us in the right direction. He got on our ass when he caught us ditching school. He knew we were in the field but he never did anything with us that a grown man wasn't supposed to be doing. He would always teach us gems that he felt we should know as young men. Big Risky was righteous and losing his was a big hit to the hood.

"What the fuck happened?" T Stone asked wiping a tear off his cheek. We were all crying.

"He tried to take the dicks on a high speed, but he crashed and when he tried to hop out and take 'em on a foot chase, the police shot him down," Wooski D explained.

The line got quiet. The only noises were of us crying.

"He told y'all to leave that shit alone," Wooski D said accusingly like it was our fault. The shot
he sent hit my heart like an arrow.

"Lil 4 started shooting," I said quickly.

"But you swung first," he shot back.

"But-"

"Ain't no buts!" Wooski D snarled. "All of you niggas bogus. Ain't no ifs ands or buts about it. I'm the one that's gon' have to tell Lil Risky and BT. Y'all lucky foe nem ain't out," Wooski D said and he was right. My brash actions ended up costing Big Risky his life. Guilt immediately started to eat at me and had me feeling like I had to throw up.

"This shit crazy man," Wooski D sobbed. "I'm 'bout to check on the rest of the guys. Y'all be safe, man."

"All well."

"Yes sir," Wooski D replied before disconnecting the call.

**

The next day Nutso and Lil C were riding down 103rd and Michigan rotating a fat Kush blunt while they listened to the latest Bump J mixtape.

"That mufuckin white Toyota been behind us for a lil minute now," Lil C said pulling his P89 Ruger off his hip and taking it off safety.

Nutso made a left on 105th Street and sped up a little. "Damn man," he mumbled when the Toyota did the same thing. He rode 105th all the way down until he made a left on Cottage Grove. When he made it to the light on 103rd and Cottage, he was about to make a right but an old Ford F-150 cut him off. The white Toyota screeched to a stop right next to Nut's car and a shooter opened fire out of the passengers window. Nutso stomped on the gas and rammed the Ford as bullets tore through his car's exterior.

"Bail out!" Nutso screamed to Lil C as he jumped out of the car and hauled ass. The masked man who was driving the Ford jumped out and sent shots at Nutso.

"Aarrgh!" He winced in pain as a bullet ripped through his spring Pelle jacket and into his arm. He continued to run until it felt like his lungs were on fire and he felt like he was safe. He hid in somebody's backyard on 103rd and Dauphin and called the paramedics.

Later that day, we had a candlelight vigil for Big Risky. There were no fights or confrontations. We all swallowed our pride and came together for a real legend. Reesie decided that in his memory we would now call the hood Risky Road. 104th and Maryland, our block, our building, was one of the riskiest blocks in The Hundreds so the name fit us perfectly. Not only that but the name foreshadowed our future and what we had ahead of us.

Chapter 11

True Love

I was laying in my bed contemplating my next move until my mom entered my room.

"Boy, what's wrong with you?" She asked me adjusting the collection of fitted hats that I had aligned on my dresser. I was the color of rich dark chocolate but my mother had flawless peanut butter-colored skin.

"I'm straight, ma," I replied dryly.

"I just got off the phone with Peaches. Why didn't you tell me Nut got shot?"

"I thought I did tell you. It wasn't nothing major. He good."

"I don't know what y'all out there doing in them streets but I know for sure that y'all involved in some bullshit. First you get shot, now Nut. I hope y'all haven't stolen somebodies money or drugs. I been noticing the new cars and clothes. I'm not blind or dumb. Just because I don't say nothing don't mean that I don't see it," My mom said snaking her neck like she was my age. She was a Registered Nurse and carried herself as a grown woman should but she was from the projects and sometimes it showed. All of her brothers were GDs from the Low End so she wasn't new to what I was doing.

"We ain't stole nothing, ma, you tweaking," I said getting a little irritated.

"Boy, I be seeing you and the rest of them purse snatchers all huddled up in this musty ass room having y'all little gang meetings," she replied scrunching up her pretty little face.

I had to laugh at that. "Them don't be gang meetings, ma. We just be coolin."

"How many of your friends have gotten killed lately?"

"I don't know like one or two," I lied quickly.

"Do you plan on being next?" She asked in a motherly manner.

"No, but at the end of the day I don't have no control over that."

"You sound dumber than you look," my mother quipped. "You can get yourself together and leave the streets alone. You already got a nice girlfriend," she paused to shoot me a worry filled expression before continuing. "I know that you dropped out of school. I got brothers that did the same shit you trying to do now look at them."

"Man, Uncle D was good until his homies told on him," I countered.

"So, you really think them little boys you be with wont give you up to save their own ass?" Her frustration showed in her face.

"Nope, my niggas solid. We don't even tolerate snitching," I stated proudly adding to her frustration.

"Boy, sometimes you show me just how much of a fool you really are. What the hell has any of your friends did to be considered solid?"

I thought in my head. If only if she knew that a few of my friends were sitting either in heaven or hell because of them trying to be solid.

"Them same friends gon' be the reason why you end up dead or in jail if you don't open your eyes and start seeing people for who their really are," she said preparing to leave my room.

"I hear you, ma."

"Whatever, Ugly. And if I smell smoke in my house again, I hope your friends solid enough to let you move in with them," she said stepping out of my room closing the door behind her.

"Shut the fuck up," I mumbled when I felt like she was out of earshot.

"'What the fuck you say?" my mom yelled.

"I'm on the phone ma!" I yelled lying.

The next day, I decided to take a well-deserved break from the trenches and spend some quality time with Ashley. I had bought her a Kia Supreme to get around in and I decided that it was best if we rode in her car because hers was more lowkey than mine.

"What's up baby?" I asked climbing into her passenger's seat and leaning over to give her a kiss on the lips.

"What?" I asked as I flamed up a Kush blunt.

She was shooting me a crazy look. "You know I don't like you smoking in my car," she complained.

"My bad, baby. I forgot," I lied after exhaling a lung full of smoke. "I left my phone in the house like I promised you I would. Now, I have nothing to distract me," I said trying to take her mind off the blunt I was smoking. We were on our way to Ruth Chriss Steakhouse so we were both dressed casually. She looked like a model in the black Alexander McQueen dress she was wearing. I noticed that she had on the necklace that I'd bought for her.

"You looking good as hell by the way, baby," I complimented her when we hopped out the car at the Steakhouse.

"Thank you," she said blushing like she did every time I complimented her beauty.

Once we got seated in the restaurant and ordered our food, Ashley broke the silence. "I guess you didn't even notice my new hairstyle," she said.

"I notice everything about you from your hair to the scent of your perfume to the color of your nail polish. I just told you how beautiful you are. What you tryna say ?You feel like I don't pay enough attention to you or something?" I asked while cutting a piece of my T Bone steak.

"I'm not saying that but I do feel like lately you have been giving your friends more time and attention than you've been giving me," she paused to take a sip from her glass of water then continued. "I know that y'all got a lot going on in the streets and I understand that but at the end of the day you're not fucking them—"

"And you not getting shot or dying for me!" I said sharply cutting her off.

"But I will if I had to," Ashley said softly but with certainty.

"But you don't have to and I would never put you in that position. When you're really in love with someone, you'll do anything to ensure that person's safety," I told her sincerely. "The bros are the bros. We signed up for this shit. However, it come but you're my woman. I do everything in my power to keep my love life and my street life separate," I said fearing the consequences of one spilling over into the other.

"I don't think you understand that you're my first love. My only love. What we have will never fade or pass away. I'm here for you in any and every way possible. I get so worried when you leave me to run the streets. I just feel like I could save you by keeping you in the house with me," Ashley said.

"Just hold me down baby and let me worry about the rest. It don't make no sense stressing over shit you can't control. I ain't going nowhere no time soon," I promised. I don't know how sure I sounded but I did know that she had a firm grip on my heart that I couldn't deny. The way she made me feel was hard to describe. She was the good to all my bad. The right to all my wrongs. She truly made me happy. I switched the subject up to a more positive note and we enjoyed the rest of our dinner, making each other smile and laugh the whole time. I know that they said that nobody was perfect but to me, Ashley was as close to perfect as a woman could get.

Chapter 12

Backdoor Wide Open

Smack's rank was rising within Reesie's crew. Some of them didn't trust him because he was a Stone and he was Bone's brother but after a couple successful shootings, they knew he was for real. He had ambitions on surpassing me and Reesie in the drug game. He didn't care if his baby brother was my best friend. He was on my ass every time he saw me. Smack was a different type of nigga. He didn't care about the hoes or the clout that came along with having money. All he wanted to do was make his money and get higher than everybody else. Everything else was a plus to him.

Reesie was the one who fronted him the pounds of Kush he needed to get on. Since we were always on D Block, Smack hustled in Goon Town. He had a cousin from Detroit who had a connect on the X pills. He shipped Smack five jars of pills to test his loyalty and it was safe to say that he failed that test. He was a party animal that smoked damn near a QP of weed a week and when he hosted kickbacks, he passed out X pills like they were candy.

After Smack had come up short on his last few loads, Reesie started shorting him on the weed. He was the type who was going to get his by any means possible.

If I clap Reesie after we clap Mo Money, then I can slide right in for that top spot. My only worries would be Cello, T Stone, Nutso or Lil 4 but shit, they could get it too. Smack thought to himself while sitting in his van in front of one of

Reesie's traps on 104th and Maryland. He had been waiting for Reesie to come out for about twenty minutes now and was becoming impatient.

"What's good law, man?" Reesie asked as he finally came out the trap and approached Smack's van zipping up his Louis Vuitton windbreaker. His dreads shook with every step he took.

"Shit," Smack replied dryly before lighting up a fat blunt of Kush. "I need five Ps," he said blowing smoke out his nose.

"How much you got for me?" Reesie asked leaning in the van's window.

"Fifteen-thousand-dollars."

When Smack said that, Reesie screwed his face up and said, "Aight, but where that lil eleven thousand that you already owe?"

Now it was Smack's turn to frown. "Damn bro, why you sweating me for that lil shit. On Stone, I told you I'ma get you together as soon as I'm straight."

"So, after you flip this five, I should be expecting twenty-eight five right?"

"Hell naw!" Smack replied quickly. "What the fuck did I just tell you?" He snapped trying to put his muscle down but he knew Reesie wasn't going for that shit. "Ima pay you yo' money when I get it."

"Who the fuck you think you talking to nigga?" Reesie asked looking from left to right like it was somebody else standing there. "You must've forgotten who the fuck I am nigga. Don't let that tough shit get you fucked up," Reesie barked using one hand to snatch open Smack's door and the other slid down to his waist. "Give me that bread and get yo' mind right before you lose it," he said with a threat.

Smack passed him a McDonald's bag full of money. He wanted to say something but he held his tongue.

"I'll have Shody Shod drop that shit off to you and I think you should leave them pills alone, Moe. That shit starting to fuck with yo' head," Reesie said with a chuckle while heading back into the trap.

Smack sat in his van heated. He couldn't believe that the nigga he was going against his own people for had just treated him like that. I got something for his bitch ass," Smack declared watching Reesie enter the trap. Not today, not tomorrow, maybe not even next week but soon he was going to put Reesie in his place until then he was going to plot and play his part.

***

After a small shopping spree with Ashley, I dropped her off at home and went to see how the crack we were selling on 105th and Edbrooke was doing. Bone was running that spot and it was generating some nice revenue. Bone was a natural hustler, and he knew how to make money and stack it. The thing that stuck out the most about him was his leadership abilities, he was young but well respected and carried himself as he was older than me.

"What y'all on?" I asked T Stone and Bone who were sitting on the porch of the trap with a few of the Moes rotating a few Kush blunts.

"Shit, trapping," Bone said slowly.

"What it's looking like out here?"

"This bitch boomin'," he replied with a smile. "I only been over here a couple hours and I done checked a couple bands," he said just as my phone started ringing.

"Hello?" I answered not recognizing the number.

"You have a collect call from Killa," an automated voice said.

I accepted the charges and Killa started talking. "What's the word lil bro?" He asked.

"What's up big bro? How you feeling?" I asked excitedly. He was locked up on drug and gun charges for a while now.

I heard it was looking ugly for him. It'd been a long time since we've spoken so I was happy to hear from him.

"I'm aight. These people tryna get me to cop out for eighteen years at eighty five percent. That shit dead doe. I can't do all that time."

"Hell naw, you can't," I agreed.

"I need to bond out and fight this shit from the streets but my money funny so I can't even do that."

"How much is yo' bond?"

"Fifty thousand to walk."

"Damn," I mumbled feeling sorry for him. Jail wasn't the place for a real nigga.

"I heard that yo' lil ass was out there running it up. I need for you to come through for me,"

"I'm doing good but not that damn good," I replied with a chuckle.

"So, what you got on it?" Killa asked.

I couldn't miss the disappointment in his tone.

"I can probably come up with twenty thousand for you."

"Twenty thousand!" Killa repeated damn near shrieking. "Bro, they tryna give me eighteen years and you can only come up with twenty grand? If the shoe was on the other foot you know how I would've came for you."

"I don't have it, bro!" I snapped. "Fifty bands ain't no small money. What the fuck do you want me to do, stick up a bank? I told you I got twenty stacks for you. I'ma holla at T Stone and Nut and see if we can scrape up another ten racks but you should be grateful for whatever I come with."

"Be grateful?" Killa asked like I had just said the most disrespectful shit he'd ever heard. I could only imagine the look on his face. "Nigga I'm the one that got you lit! You wasn't getting no money before I cuffed you and now since you done came up you feeling yo'self. Nigga fuck you then since you ain't tryna help," Killa said raising his voice sounding like he was ready to cry.

"Bro, I just told you that I was gon' try to come up with $30,000! How many other niggas can you call up for $30,000? On Stone, nigga don't ever come at me sideways like I'm on some fu shit. Get yo' goofy ass on!" I yelled back angrily.

The line was silent for a minute before Killa said, "You right lil bro. My bad for tweaking on you." His voice softened up a bit. "Good lookin' doe. I'm 'bout to make some more calls and see if I can round up some more bread. I'll have my peoples call you later so they can come scoop up that bread," he said and hung up before I could reply.

Later that night, I was in one of my traps with C Murder. He told me that he had a cousin who was trying to buy two bricks of coke. All we had left from our last robbery was five bricks and I was thirsty to get that shit off. The drug money was great but I liked making that fast and easy robbery money.

"What's that for?" C Murder asked me as I counted out the $30,000 for Killa's people to pick up from me.

"This for Killa's bond. I told him I had 30 bands for him. You came through with this serve just in time," I told him with a smile. He had talked me into looking out for his cousin and giving him the bricks for $28,000 apiece.

"Aye, do the stick you got in yo' Glock fit in mine?" C Murder asked while looking out the living room's window. "I don't know why it wouldn't doe?"

"Because yours is a Glock 19 and mine a Glock 26."

"They both nines doe, but here." I passed him my gun. "Check and see."

While C Murder was playing with our guns, his phone rung. He answered and said a few words before opening the front door for his cousin.

"What's up folks?" he asked shaking up with his cousin who was a brown skinned, tall, lanky guy with a low cut.

"What's up folks? I got some shit to do. Where that shit at?" C Murder's cousin asked impatiently. I don't know why he was so impatient and he was holding no money. The tall dark skinned dread head he had with him gave me a bad vibe by the way he was standing and shifting from side to side.

I was stuffing all of my money into a Louie backpack. I was lowkey blew that C Murder let his peoples in before I could put my money up.

"Aye, bro, go in the backroom and look in that Toys 'R' Us bag. Them bricks in them X-Box 360 boxes," I told C Murder while making a mental note to change my spot as soon as everyone left. C Murder re-entered the living room holding the bag with all of the X-Box boxes inside. "Fuck is you doing? I thought they only wanted two?" I asked him with a frown on my face.

"Naw, we want all that shit," His cousin said before him and his homie upped their guns.

I reached for my Glock but then I remembered that I had given it to C Murder.

"G, what the fuck yo' peoples on?" I asked. My voice was an octave higher than it normally was.

"You heard what he said. They want all that shit," C Murder said showing his true colors. I searched his face looking for some sign indicating that he was pranking me but I couldn't find the joke.

"That's what you on bro?" I asked trying to swallow the lump that was forming in my throat. "Why you getting down on me?" I asked sadly.

C Murder pulled out the 30 shot Glock that I'd just given him and smacked me across the face with it. "Where the rest of that money at?" he growled.

"That's all the money I got here," I lied after kicking the Louie bag towards him.

"Stop playin' with me Moe," he replied. "Tell me where that shit at or we gon' leave you in this bitch." His threat sounded more like a promise to me.

"It's in the bathroom in the back of the toilet," I said defeatedly. I would've lied but my hiding spot was weak as hell and I didn't want to find out if he was making a threat or a promise about killing me. Inside, I was kicking myself for going out this sweet. I should've been seen that C Murder was a snake ass nigga.

"Tie his ass up," C Murder's cousin said to his homie but C Murder stopped him.

"Naw just go get the car ready and blow the horn when y'all ready for me to come out," he told them. They grabbed all the money and drugs and ran out of the trap.

I sat on the couch staring daggers at C Murder. "On Stone, you bogus as hell bro. I never thought you would pull a hoe ass stunt like this," I said through clinched jaws.

C Murder chuckled. "Fuck you, nigga. You lucky I don't smoke yo' hoe ass. I wish T Stone was here. I would've smoked him fasho," he said and that's when it hit me. He was doing this because of how T Stone treated him after he didn't shoot in the back of the building. His cousin started honking the horn and C Murder flew out of the trap. For a few minutes, I sat there mad and stunned. I was back to square one basically. No money except for the money that I had on the streets. Other than that, I was back fucked up. It hit different because I was back in a fucked up position behind trusting someone who I thought was a friend.

***

The next few weeks passed by extremely fast. Ever since C Murder had backdoored me, T Stone and Nutso had been on a manhunt for him. We all wanted him dead.

Me and T Stone were riding around looking for somebody to shoot. I had a lot of built up frustration that I needed to relieve myself of and nothing eased my mind more than sliding. As we rode past the Gas station on 103rd Street, we saw Lil 4 and Cello amongst a crowd of the bros.

"I'm about to blow they ass down," I told T Stone chambering a round into my Glock. When we came back around the block, he slowed the car down while I hung out the window shooting.

"Shit! There go twelve!" T Stone shouted as I sent shots at the fleeing crowd.

I'm not going back to jail, I thought to myself before making one of the dumbest decisions I ever made. I sent a flurry of bullets at the blue and white CPD car that was pursuing us.

"Stomp this bitch, moe! You driving like a bitch!" I yelled feeling a jolt of nervousness. T Stone went through the alley on 105th and Edbrooke and bailed out of the car. I did the same thing. "Meet me at Nut crib!" I screamed to him as I ran in the opposite direction as he did.

I ran straight up 105th Street until the Blue and Whites got on me. I hit the alley leading to State Street before hitting two gangways and hopping a big, wooden fence to a house on 105th and Perry. I banged on the house's backdoor.

"Who the fuck is it?" A young boy yelled through the wooden door.

"Open the door for me, Baby Charles. This Dre," I yelled frantically and out of breath.

"Nigga what you want? FeFe sleep!" Baby Charles said cracking open the door a little bit.

"I got some money for you," I told him pushing my way inside and closing the door behind myself. I could hear the police cars riding through the alley. I felt like I had dodged a big bullet. I reached in my pocket, pulled out a crumbled up dub and handed it to Baby Charles.

"FeFe!" he screamed running off.

A few minutes later, FeFe came downstairs in a small T-shirt and a pair of boy shorts. Her small but nice ass jiggled with every step she took towards me. Her long hair was pulled back into a ponytail. "What are you doing here, Money?" she asked, putting her hands on her slim hips. She didn't look very happy to see me.

"The jakes was on my ass. I need to stay here for a minute until shit cool down."

"No," FeFe said smacking her lips. "You not about to have the police running in my mama's house."

"Man, be cool," I scoffed brushing past her, heading for her bedroom. Once in her bedroom, I plopped down on her bed and tried to catch my breath. That police chase had me tired as hell. "Yo' lil big headed ass starting to get dark," I told FeFe looking at her toned brown skin. She was one of my exes. She was beautiful in the face with a slim model's body. She was a bad bitch but her looks weren't enough to make up for her craziness.

"Boy, I know you not talking about nobody being dark because you the darkest nigga I know," FeFe said with a laugh, taking a seat next to me.

"Do you miss me?" I asked pulling her back so that her head was laying on my chest.

"Yes."

"No, you don't."

She smacked her lips. "Why would you ask me if I missed you if you was gon' tell me I'm lying when I answered?" she asked

"I just wanted to see if you was gon' lie to me."

"Boy, you not my man no more. I don't have to lie to you," she snapped.

"Well show me how much you miss me,"

"How am I supposed to do that?" she asked, playing dumb. She knew exactly what I wanted.

"Give me some of that good ass top that I been missing out on," I said trying to contain my smile.

"Boy, no," she said turning to look at me. "You got a bitch and I'm sure she give you all the top you need."

"Now you know don't nobody suck me better than you do," I replied honestly. "Now, stop playing," I urged her pushing her head towards my already hard dick.

Fefe unbuckled my belt, unbuttoned and unzipped my jeans and pulled my dick out. She took her time and slid my whole dick down her throat. "You happy?" she asked after pulling my dick out of her mouth.

"Hell yeah, keep going," I told her with a broad smile. I closed my eyes while she took me to heaven with her mouth. It took everything in me not to moan. FeFe was the best dick sucker I ever encountered. After twenty minutes I was in a trance, drowning in pleasure until she abruptly stopped sucking. I opened my eyes to see that she was undressing.

"Fuck is you doing?" asked watching her get naked.

"You think I'm just about to suck your dick? I want to feel you inside of me," she said trying to climb on top of me.

"If I wanted to fuck, I would've asked you for some pussy, don't you think?" I retorted.

"Well, you can leave," FeFe snapped angrily.

I weighed my options for a second. I could either give her some dick or I could leave and possibly go to jail. "Fuck it, give me a condom." I gave in to her demands.

"What do you need a condom for? It's not like we never had unprotected sex."

"I don't know who you been fuckin lately."

"Bye. Get out."

"Okay. Okay, come on," I said with a chuckle. I had her pressed for real. I climbed on top of her and put both of her long legs over my shoulders before sliding my dick inside of her. FeFe still had some good pussy and her shit was wetter than I remembered it being.

"Go faster," she moaned. I had almost forgot that she loved rough sex. She enjoyed getting her pussy beat up. I sped up and started fucking the shit out of her. It must've been good because I saw real tears slip from the corners of her eyes. I turned her over and watched my wet, creamy dick slam in and out of her pussy. I held onto her hip with one hand and grabbed her ponytail with the other, while beating her pussy up trying my best to make her tap out. Her sex was good but I just wasn't feeling it at the moment.

"I'm about to cum," I lied after thirty minutes of me pounding her out. I was sweating bullets. "Swallow it," I told her laying on my back. FeFe went right to work, sucking my dick, making my toes curl in my Retros. She sucked my dick while I finger-fucked her. Her legs started to tremble and then she came on my fingers. I was busting my nut within minutes. She slurped and drank it all up. I swear her head was so good that I vowed to always come back to her.

"That's the FeFe that I love right there," I told her as I got up from the bed and went to the bathroom to wash myself off.

"Hello?" I heard FeFe say as I was washing my dick off. "Bitch yo' man over here enjoying this good pussy that you obviously don't have," I heard her snap.

I quickly bolted out of the bathroom and into FeFe's room. "What the fuck is you doing?" I asked when I saw her with my phone to her ear. Before she could respond, I snatched my phone and muffed the fuck outta her. I looked at my phone and saw that Ashley was still on the line. "Hello?" I said putting my phone to my ear.

"I'm over here stressing, worried about you and you at a whole 'nother bitch house. You crazy, Dre," Ashley said. I could hear the anger and sadness in her tone.

"Before you jump to conclusions, just hear me out. The police was chasin me and I had to run in FeFe's house or else I would've gotten locked up. I was just in the bathroom taking a shit when she picked up the phone. Do you think I would actually let a random bitch answer the phone when you calling?"

"Why wasn't your phone in your pocket?"

"It was on the charger," I lied quickly.

"I don't believe you," Ashley replied sadly. She was now crying.

"Dre, I never once lied to you. I never cheated on you. I never did anything to hurt you and this the type of shit you doing when you supposed to be outside with your friends. You know what Dre?" she asked sniffling. "Just leave me the fuck alone. Don't call me. Don't text me. Don't come near me. I told you in the beginning that loyalty is everything to me and you showed me that you're disloyal. I don't want anything to do with you," she said and hung up in my face.

"Fuck!" I shouted while trying to call her back. "You a dumb goofy ass bitch on Black Stone. That's why I don't fuck with yo' goofy ass now!" I told FeFe as I prepared to leave. I was so mad that I didn't give a fuck about the police anymore. I dialed Nutso's number.

"Yoooo," he answered on the first ring.

"Where you at, cuz?"

"I'm on the block. Where you at? We thought yo' goofy ass got booked."

"Hell naw, I got low on twelve and ran to Fefe crib. Come pick me up."

"Bet," Nutso said and hung up.

I left out of FeFe's crib and sat on her neighbor's front porch until Nutso pulled up.

***

T Stone, Nutso and one of the Moes were in a stolen car in front of C Murders mother's house on 113th and Eggleston. They had been camped out in front of the house for almost two hours patiently waiting for C Murder to pull up.

"Y'all ain't never smoked none of that loud that Reesie nem got? I ain't gon lie that shit some gas!" Moe said from the backseat.

"Fuck that nigga," Nutso spat staring out of his window.

"All I'm saying is that the nigga got some good ass weed. I was at Red Lobster with him and he was saying how we can be getting some real paper together."

"Nigga, we getting enough money by ourselves so like I said: *fuck that nigga!* And why the fuck were y'all at Red Lobster together," Nutso asked with a mug. He was fingering the .45 he had sitting on his lap.

"We weren't together," Moe said making air quotation marks with his fingers, "I was with my bitch and he came in with some bitch and we had a few words. Nothing major doe. Like you said fuck that nigga."

"It sound like you should be fuckin with that nigga," T Stone said sarcastically.

"Hell yeah, maybe I should be," Moe joked, making himself laugh.

"What?" Nutso growled, turning around, jamming his gun in Moe's neck.

"Bro, you tweaking! I was just joking." Moe was scared shitless.

"Naw, nigga *you* tweaking. I don't joke like that," Nutso told him as a white Malibu with dark tint pulled up. Nutso and T Stone immediately jumped out the car.

"C Murder, what's the word, ku?" T Stone asked aiming his Mac at him.

"Shit nigga, put them guns up. What the fuck wrong with y'all?" C Murder asked looking like he'd seen a ghost. His eyes were big and his skin was pale.

"Nigga, you know what the fuck going on. Where them bricks and that bread at?" Nutso asked.

"Man, my cousin took all that shit. He didn't give me shit. I know where he live doe. I'ma kill his hoe ass," C Murder lied throwing on a fake ass mug like he was truly mad.

"Who the fuck you think you playing with?" T Stone asked frowning.

Instead of responding, C Murder took off running towards his mother's front door.

"Shoot!" Nutso told Moe. Moe shot recklessly until a bullet hit C Murder in his ankle, knocking him off his feet.

"Nut, don't do me like this, gang. We like family, bro, you know that," C Murder pleaded.

"Fuck outta here," Nutso said before pumping four shots into his face.

"Aye law," T Stone called out to Moe from behind him.

"Wha—" Moe couldn't even get the word out before T Stone put two bullets in his forehead.

"Tell C Murder I said fuck him!" T Stone smiled as he pumped three more shots in Moe's chest before running off to the car.

Chapter 13

Precious

"Damn Foe, you don't even gotta do this," I told Reesie, who was standing over me with a AK pointed at my face.

"It's fucked up you going out like this, Moe," Reesie said with a chuckle. He had me. I couldn't run or nothing. "You still my nigga doe," he was saying. At that moment, I figured that since I was about to die anyway I might as well try my luck. I reached for the choppa he was holding.

Boom. Boom. Reesie started dumping his clip in my face.

"Arghhh !" I woke up sweating bullets. My phone was ringing loudly.

"What's up?" I answered erratically.

"What's the demo big bro? You well?" Bone asked.

"Yeah," I replied running a hand over my face. The nightmare I had just had really had me shook up. "I was just having a crazy ass dream. What's the demo, doe?"

"You must've forgot that we gotta go meet that Mexican mufucka," Bone replied reminding me that we had to go meet up with this Mexican cat named Lopez. Lopez had bricks for days. We met him through some Latin Kings that were buying weight from Nutso. Word on the street was that Lopez was one of the older Kings and he had sent his nephews to us to cop some work just to scope out the quality of work we had. When he found out that not only were we small fries in the drug game but that his work was a better quality than ours, he extended his hand to do business with us. The only money we had left was the $65,000 that we scraped up and put together.

Once I picked up Bone, we went to Lopez house in Oak Brook, Illinois. His security searched us, took our guns, and led us to Lopez's huge living room.

"Mo Money, it's nice to finally meet you in person," Lopez said giving me a firm handshake. He was a short Mexican with long hair, beady eyes, and a thick mustache." And who is this young man?" he asked, looking at Bone.

"This my lil brother Bone," I told him. "I brought $65,000 to get things started, you feel me? You already know we capable of moving that shit so I'm thinking you should give us the work for twenty a brick—" I was saying until Lopez held up a hand indicating for me to be quiet.

"Hold on, primo," he said. "For twenty-thousand-a-brick you could only afford three bricks," he said with wrinkles in his forehead.

"That's true," I agreed looking stupid. "But I was thinking that I could give you this whole sixty-five racks, My *last* sixty-five racks, for three bricks and you give me three more bricks on consignment."

Lopez stared at me for almost a full minute before speaking. "How do I know that I can trust you?"

"You don't, and you won't be able to find out unless you give me a chance."

Lopez stuck his hand out for a shake. I smirked and grabbed his hand. He tightened his grip and pulled me in close to him. "Listen, and you listen close," he said in a low, ominous tone. "If you fuck up my money or try to run off with my shit, I will find you and kill you personally and while I'm looking for you, I'll make sure everybody from Risky Road and D Block die slow deaths. Trust me," he said and let me go. I handed him a Wendy's bag full of money and we arranged a location where I could pick the bricks up at.

"Thanks for the opportunity, amigo," I quipped shaking his hand again one last time before leaving.

With so much going on in the hood it seemed like the winter came quick. After Lopez started fucking with us, we took off and started seeing more money than we'd ever seen. All of us had given up robbing, except for T Stone and Binky. It seemed like Reesie was always one step ahead of us because he was doing very well for himself. He was in his bag and still active in the field. Even though he was making money, he was still robbing and getting over on whoever he could get over on. Nobody was safe from him and niggas were starting to carry him as a chief.

Ashley had been avoiding me for the last few months. She wouldn't answer my calls or respond to any of my texts. I had gotten so desperate that I had even reached out to her mother for help but Ashley wasn't tryna hear it. I really had hurt her and she was making me pay for it. I was heartbroken. I tried to hide it but I was going through it. I felt incomplete without my other half.

***

Nutso was riding in a smoke grey Dodge Challenger that he had recently rented. He had been serving all morning and decided to slide downtown to treat himself to a quick shopping spree.

"Somebody tell these hoes I'm single for the nighttt," he sang along with Lil Wayne as he parked his car and hopped out. A small group of women admired him as he stepped out of his car in a pair of jet black True Religion jeans, a True Religion Skully and even though it was cold outside he left his Pelle in the car to show off the True Religion Crewneck he had on. "Lil thick ass," he said smiling as he walked past a thick, dark skinned woman and into the Burberry store.

"Hay P-Nut," he heard someone sing as he looked through the many pairs of Burberry shoes. He looked around in curiosity trying to see who was calling him by his childhood nickname. His eyes stopped on Tati, a short, light skinned, young woman with round brown eyes. They went to school together but never spoke much.

"That ain't my name, shorty," he said heading her way.

"Boy, yes the fuck it is," she replied rolling her eyes. "What are you doing in here?" she asked. Her eyes rolled over Nutso checking him out.

"Shit, tryna spend a lil money," he replied nonchalantly. He was dying to up his bankroll and show her that he was getting it. "What you on?" he asked.

"In here with my cousin. What you 'bout to buy me?" Tati asked getting to the point. She was his friend on Myspace so she already knew that he was getting money. He gave her a once over. She had a nice, petite body and wore her hair cut on one side like the singer Cassie. That's who she favored too. He had to admit that she was bad.

"You can get whatever you want," he replied cooly as the young lady who he assumed was Tati's cousin walked up. "You want something too?" He flexed.

"No, thank you."

"You sure, shorty?"

"My name is Precious not *shorty* and like I said, *no thank you*," Tati's cousin snapped.

Tati and Precious accompanied Nutso on his shopping spree. Once he spent close to four racks, he asked. "Y'all tryna kick it with me today? I got a cousin for you Precious."

"Yes," Tati said.

"I don't want your cousin," said Precious

I was in the trap bagging up when my phone rang. "Yooo," I answered.

"Where you at Moe?" Nutso asked me.

"I'm in the trap on the side block. What's the demo?"

"Shit, I'm with my baby Tati and her cousin Precious tryna see how you coming," Nutso lied with a big smile while looking at Precious through the rearview mirror. She was shooting him an evil look.

"Pull up on me," I told him and hung up. When he called me to come out the trap, the first thing I noticed was his car. "Where the fuck yo' Porsche at?" I asked as he lifted his seat to let me climb into the backseat.

"Smack hoe ass Swiss-cheesed my shit, so I had to grab this to get around until my shit get out the shop. You like it?" Nutso asked smirking.

"On Stone I do. You a flashy lil bitch," I joked. "Take me to the liquor store," I told him before turning to look at Precious. From the moment I locked eyes with her, I knew I had. to fuck. Even though I was still pressed over Ashley, I was going to push her to the back of my mind. Precious was the perfect shade of brown, like mocha. She had long, wavy hair that stopped in the middle of her back with the prettiest, slanted, almond shaped eyes. Precious was exactly as her name suggested. "What's up," I said nodding at her. She simply nodded back and turned to look out of her window.

"I like yo' shoes boy," Tati said looking over her seat.

"Thanks, and my name Mo Money," I said looking down at my red patent leather Pradas. "Why yo' cousin acting so anti?" I asked.

"I don't know. Ask her," Tati replied with a shrug before turning around to mess with the radio until Nut smacked her hand away.

"You got some pretty ass eyes, Precious," I told her with a small smile.

"Thank you," she mumbled still not bothering to look my way.

"I wish you would look at me. I know I'm not that damn ugly," I joked.

Precious smiled and finally made eye contact with me.

"It gotta be my hair, right?" I asked running a hand over my now shoulder length braids. They were nappy and rough-looking because I hadn't gotten them touched in weeks due to me stressing. We pulled up to Hilltop Liquors on 103rd and Michigan and had a hype go in and buy us a fifth of Remy. "Where you from?" I asked Precious after we got the bottle and pulled off.

"Pocket Town but I been living in The Hundreds for a lil while."

"How you been living in The Hundreds and I don't know you?"

"Boy, who do you think you are? You must be a little rapper or something," Precious said with a giggle.

"Shorty, loosen up with yo' mean ass," Nutso said as we pulled up to his mother's house.

When we got inside, we poured cups of Remy and knocked back shots while rotating Kush blunts. After we made a little small talk and damn near finished the bottle, Nutso and Tati disappeared into his room.

"So, you just gon' sit there all quiet and shit?" I asked Precious after a few minutes of me sitting there watching her.

"I *could*," she replied flatly.

I was used to women throwing themselves at me but she wasn't doing that and it made me want her even more.

"That's crazy how you treating me so bogus." I shook my head.

"How am I treating you bogus?"

"You ain't fuckin with me. Treating me like I'm some type of goofy."

"I never said that," Precious smirked. "But for all I know you could be a goofy," she added.

I stood up and looked down at myself. I had on a Red Prada polo, a pair of black jeans and a pair of low top red Prada shoes. "Stop playing with me," I said pulling out a thick wad of money and thumbing through it.

"Boy, I know a lot of lames that got money and know how to dress," Precious said unimpressed. I stepped closer to where she was sitting on the couch. Once close enough, I knelt down and pushed her back before lifting her shirt to kiss on her flat stomach.

"What are you doing?" she asked as I moved my kisses down to her panty line.

"Just enjoy the ride," I told her while unbuttoning her jeans and pulling them down to reveal her Love Pink panties. The Remy had me feeling freakier than I usually was because I was about to eat this lady's pussy and we just met. The only pussy I was eating was Ashley's but Precious had this effect on me that I couldn't explain at the moment. I spread her legs and began to kiss the insides of her thighs. I could feel the heat coming from her pussy. I pulled her panties to the side to see one of the prettiest pussies that I'd ever seen. She was clean shaved not a hair in sight and her clit peeked out perfectly. I kissed her southern set of lips and felt her legs slightly tremble. She moaned and put one of her legs over my shoulder as I went to work with my tongue.

"Ooohhh," Precious moaned running a hand over my nappy braids. I rapidly flicked my tongue over her clit before sucking and nibbling on it. I shoved two fingers inside of her wet pussy and my dick jumped with excitement when I felt how tight her pussy was. It was like a vice-grip was holding my fingers. I could feel her pussy throbbing as I fingered her. Precious' pussy tasted so good. I didn't even mind when she came on my lips. I got up, pulled my pants down to my knees and sat on the couch.

"Come here," I commanded anxious to feel her insides. I pulled my rock hard dick out of the slit of my boxers, and she came and straddled me. She was so sexy to me that the sight of her made my dick even harder. "Damn," I whispered when she slid down on my dick. Her pussy was so good that I didn't know the words to use to describe it. We started kissing while she bounced up and down on me taking all that I had to give. The faces she made in between our kisses were amazing. I knew she was having an orgasm when she slowed down. Her body was shaking with pleasure. She slowed her pace down and we kissed passionately while she rotated her hips. I grabbed her waist and held her still while I thrusted my dick in and out of her. She threw her head back and moaned loudly. Her juices were dripping out her of pussy, soaking my nuts.

"I'm 'bout to buss," I told her, expecting for her to get up but she didn't. Instead, she wrapped her arms around my neck, looked me deep in my eyes and started bouncing like she was trying to make me nut even faster. I grabbed two handfuls of her small ass and matched her energy. That pussy was too good for me to want to pull out anyway.

"Ahhhh," she moaned sounding like she was crying. I pulled her all the way down on my dick and busted a gigantic nut inside of her. She kissed me and tried to stick her tongue down my throat. "You probably still a goofy," she joked breathing heavily as she got up and began to fix her clothes. I couldn't help but to smile to myself because I knew that she was mines now and she probably was exactly what I needed to take my mind off of Ashley.

***

Killa walked out of Cook County Jail smiling hard. He had did damn near two years and was finally able to bond out. Reesie, Lil 4, and Cello were sitting in Cello's white 2009 Chevy Tahoe. "So, y'all the ones who really getting money, huh?" Killa asked climbing in the backseat next to Lil 4.

"That lil fifty racks you needed for yo' bond wasn't shit," Reesie stated before taking a hit off the thick Kush blunt he was holding.

"Okay, so what's up?" Killa asked. Reesie told him that if he bonded him out he would only want one thing in return.

"I want you to clap Mo Money hoe ass," Reesie told him looking at him through the rearview mirror.

"Huh?"

"That nigga be hiding from us but I know that you'll be able to get next to him. I want you to wack his dumb ass," Reesie explained.

"We gon' pay yo' lawyer and put you in play so you can run yo' bag up and all you gotta do is stand on that business," Lil 4 said.

"I got you," Killa said looking through the truck's tinted window. "That bitch ass nigga was acting funny when I called and asked for him to bond me out, so fuck him," Killa said with ice in his tone.

"Say less then," Reesie said turning up the MMG Rome that was playing. He had a plan and everything was starting to fall in motion for him. Pretty soon, he was really gon' be the last one standing, the King of The Hundreds.

***

Hi, you've reached Ashley. Sorry I couldn't answer the phone right now but leave a name and a number and I'll get back— Ashley's voicemail said for the fourth time in a row. It'd been almost three full months since she cut me off and she still wasn't answering my calls. To keep myself busy I had been fucking every eater I ran across. I had also been kicking it with Precious heavy. She was my unofficial girlfriend. I had caught feelings for her but I wasn't trying to make our relationship official because I was still holding on to hopes of Ashley coming back to me.

It was New Years Eve 2009. I had tried calling Ashley a million times. I only wanted to hear her voice and that would've been enough for me but she was standing on not fucking with me so I decided to bring in the new year with Precious.

"Hey bae," Precious said seductively answering my call on the second ring.

"What you doing, baby?" I asked.

"Nothing, I was just about to call you. We need to talk," I could.hear the sense of urgency in her voice.

"About what?"

"Something very important but I want to wait until we're face to face,"

"All well. Get sexy for me. I'm 'bout to come pick you up so we could go out."

"Okay, just call me when you're pulling up," Precious said before disconnecting the call.

A knock at my front door stopped me from heading to the shower. I opened the door to see T Stone standing there. His already low eyes were even lower and his long hair was all frizzy.

"What's the demo, law?" I asked shaking up with him before letting him inside.

"Shit," he replied taking a seat at the living room's table. He pulled out a pack of blunts, a seven of Kush and started breaking a blunt down. "I just caught that lil nigga that always be with Smack and popped the shit out of his goofy ass," T Stone told me laughing.

"And I just saw Reesie in a new Porsche truck with some bad ass thot that with him. I tried to kill both of their ass," he laughed patting the gun that rested on his waist. His eyes suddenly got big.

"Speaking of thots, I saw yo' lil bitch Ashley at IHOP with some lame ass nigga. I wanted to approach they ass but I was with my OG nem so I let them slide. Plus, I remembered that you got that Pocahontas-looking bitch now so you good," he said.

His words hit me like a punch in the gut. Here I was stressed and depressed over Ashley and she had a whole 'nother nigga. My heart was shattered but I couldn't let it show.

"Man, fuck all them hoes," I said feeling shitty. "I'm not tripping over Ashley. I got a different bitch for every day of the month," I lied. I was lowkey going crazy on the inside.

I was seeing red. I wanted to find out who this new nigga was and go shoot his face off. I wasn't ready to accept the fact that I'd lost the love of my life to another man. I was so thrown off by that shit that I didn't even go pick up Precious to take her out. I went to the liquor store, grabbed two bottles of Remy, and brought in the new year drunk and alone.

The next afternoon, I was with Arab and T Stone. We were in a crackhead's car that we had rented for three rocks. We were riding through London Towns on 101st and Cottage Grove. We knew that Lil 4 lived in London Town and Reesie had a crack house in the back of the row houses that was making a lot of money. It was time to hit a lick and hurt his pockets.

Shody Shod was overseeing the crackhouse. He had never shot at me and I still had a lot of love for him so I didn't want to hurt him. I had Arab call him and set up a deal for nine ounces. We smoked a Kush blunt and talked shit before he called Shody Shod and told him to come outside. I was in the back seat laying down with my .40 aimed at the window. T Stone sat in the front passenger's seat with his hat pulled low so Shody Shod couldn't see his face from a distance.

"Hop out," Shody Shod was saying as he approached the car. When he was close enough, he saw that it was two guns aimed at his face.

"Don't do it foe," I said sensing that he was about to try to run.

"Man, I don't got shit to do with what y'all got going on. I ain't never shot at none of y'all. I'm just tryna get this money on the Foe," he said pleading his case. He was most definitely thinking that he was about to die.

"How much work y'all got in there?" T Stone asked.

"Just a few more zips," Shody Shod said a little too fast. I knew my homie well enough to know that he was lying.

"Now if we go in that bitch and find more than what you say it is then the next time we see you it's gon' be on somebody's shirt," Arab threatened. He was the only person in the car that Shody Shod didn't know so he didn't take his threat lightly.

"Okay. Okay, it's like two bricks and a few pounds of Kush in that bitch," Shody Shod confessed.

"And how much bread?" I asked.

"Like twenty-eight bands."

"Aight call for somebody to bag all that shit up and bring it out. If a mufucka move funny, I'ma clap yo' ass," I said and Shody Shod complied. Moments later, one of the lil foes came out carrying a black Glad bag.

"Tell him to drop that shit right there in the grass and go back inside," I ordered. Shody Shod did as told and T Stone jumped out and retrieved the bag.

"Shody this shit wasn't personal, solid but tell Reesie I said fuck the Foes and he a hoe," I said as Arab pulled off laughing.

***

I was sleeping comfortably in my bed when I felt a presence standing over me. I reached for the 30 shot Glock that I kept under my pillow as I pretended to still be sleeping. When the person standing over me reached out and touched me, I pulled the gun from under the pillow and aimed it at the person's face.

"Boy, what the fuck!" Precious shouted flinching hard.

"My bad shorty," I said lowering my weapon. "Why you sneaking up on me anyways? That's how people get hurt."

"Boy, I didn't sneak up on you. If you wasn't snoring so loud, you would've heard me," Precious quipped. "But look," she said rubbing her belly which was poking out further than it usually did.

"Yo lil ass gaining weight. That's all them crab legs you be eating," I joked.

"No, stupid. I'm pregnant,"

"By who?" I asked with a smirk.

"By you, goofy. You the only nigga that I've been having sex with," she said sitting on the bed next to me.

I got up, grabbed my jeans off the floor, reached in one of my pockets and pulled out a wad of bills. "How much you gon' need for that abortion?" I asked nonchalantly while peeling off a few hundred dollar bills. I fucked with Precious but I wasn't ready to have a child with her or anyone else. I had too much shit going on to be trying to bring a child into the world.

"I'm not getting no fucking abortion!" Precious snapped, getting loud. "You got me all the way fucked up!" She jumped in my face. She had veins coming out of her neck.

"Shorty, I got too much shit going on right now. It's niggas tryna kill me. I'm not tryna get killed or locked up and leave you out here raising a baby on yo' own," I explained. "Just think about that part. An abortion may be what's best for us," I added after a few seconds of silence.

Precious took a deep breath. Her face was balled up into a mug and I could almost see the steam radiating off of her. "You know what? I'm just about to leave because you blowing me right now," she said before getting up and storming out of my room.

"Damn man," I said shaking my head, throwing the wad of money I was holding against my wall. Having a baby on the way added to my plate which was already full enough as it was.

Chapter 14

Tears

Nutso and a gang of the Moes sat on D Block smoking and joking with Killa. This was their first time seeing him since he'd been home. Nobody even knew that he was out up until about an hour ago when he rode through Indiana looking for Mo Money.

"Damn where the fuck Money black ass at?" Killa asked for the third time while breaking down a Swisher.

"His goofy ass should be on his way through this bitch if he ain't somewhere chasin that lil bitch, Ashley. She got my nigga brain," T Stone said with a chuckle.

A white Toyota rode up the block going a little too fast for Nutso's liking.

"On that car," he said alerting one of the lil moes that was out there on security.

"That probably ain't nobody," Killa said. "Lil Nut, I see you done upgraded from wearing them fake ass corner store chains."

Nutso glanced down at the chain he was wearing. It was the same one that I had robbed SBE Randy for. "Hell yeah, I came a long way," he said proudly.

"Aye Killa I saw you the other day with Malcolm. Foe, I wanted to flag y'all down but I didn't want Malcolm to see me," One of the Stones named Mike Moe said just trying to kick it.

"What the fuck is you talking about?" Killa asked screwing his face up.

"I was riding past Cello grandma house and y'all was standing—"

"That wasn't me. On the G, you tweaking boy," Killa snapped frowning extra hard like he was ready to slap Mike Moe for his mistake.

"On Stone Moe, stop tweaking. You almost had me thinking that big bro was on some other shit tryna play both sides. You know we ain't playing that over here," Bone said, flicking his lighter to light the blunt that hung from his lips.

"I gotta piss," Nutso said walking to the alley while watching oncoming traffic at the same time. From the alley, he saw the same white Toyota coming up the block again. This time the car had its windows rolled down. Nutso heard the shots going off before he saw the guns coming out the windows. As he fixed himself up, he watched Killa and Mike Moe take off into the opposite alley trying to avoid getting shot. He pulled out his Tech, ran out the alley and started blowing at the Toyota as it sped off the block. He heard a few more shots and jetted to the corner to see the car turning on Michigan. He ran to the alley that he saw Mike Moe and Killa run through and immediately broke down when he seen Mike Moe laying in a pool of his own blood with two bullet holes in the back of his neck and head.

"Damn Moe, not you," my homie Von D said running past Nut to where Mike Moe was laying.

"On Stone, I'ma kill every one of them bitch ass niggas," Nutso vowed as tears flowed down his face. He crouched over Mike Moe's lifeless body, kissed his fingertips, and touched Mike Moe's heart before pulling his phone out to call 9-1-1. Mike Moe was one of the guys that chased hoes and sold his weed. He wasn't fucking with nobody and it hurt to see him go.

I was in a deep slumber before my phone started ringing loudly. I knew it was Nutso by the Gucci Mane ringtone I had set for him.

"Yooo," I answered sleepily.

"Man, Mike Moe just got killed on the block," he told me.

"Damn, who was it?" I asked. The bad news had awakened me completely.

"I don't know but it was the same white Toyota that shot me. It had to be the Foes."

"Damn," was all I could say.

"That shit really got me fucked up because that was my shorty. I shouldn't have had Moe out there in the first place."

"Who all was out there?"

"Shit all the bros. We was out there fuckin with Killa—"

"When he get out?" I asked surprised. I couldn't believe he was out and hadn't reached out to me.

"I don't know, but I do know that Reesie nem was behind Mike Moe getting killed. I don't wanna trap. I don't wanna kick it. I don't wanna do shit until we get our lick back," Nutso said before starting to cry. I could hear him sniffling and I felt his pain.

"I feel you, cuz. Get at his OG and let her know we gon' pay for the funeral," I told him.

"All well," Nutso said and hung up.

***

I pulled up to Mike Moe's funeral with a million different thoughts racing through my mind. I was a wreck mentally. I took a swig from the bottle of Remy that I had been drinking on and prepared to enter the funeral. I stepped out of my car dressed in a black Burberry button up, a pair of jet black jeans and a pair of black Timbs. I wore a pair of Gucci shades to hide my swollen, red eyes. I had been crying all morning.

"You straight lil bro?" A voice asked from behind me.

I looked back to see that it was Killa who was speaking to me. This was my first time seeing him since he'd been home. He hadn't even called my phone. I just figured he was salty that I wasn't able to come through with the bond money I had promised him.

"Hell naw, I'm not straight. I'm going through it bro but it's good to see you back down," I said honestly giving him a brotherly hug.

"We all going through it for lil bro but we gon' catch Reesie, Lil 4 and whoever else with that shit."

"Why you say Reesie and Lil 4? You heard they names come up in that shit or something?" I asked because as far as we knew nobody knew exactly who killed Mike Moe. All we had were our assumptions.

"Ain't them the only mufuckas y'all into it with?"

"Hell naw. We into it with UPT, Dirty Perry, 1O-4L and The Snakes, too. It could've been anyone of them hoods that did that shit. Just because them niggas been put up don't mean they forgot," I said. We were so focused on the war we had going on with each other that we forgot about the rest of our opps.

"You right but ain't nobody been sliding like Foe nem. I was just putting two and two together," Killa replied with an awkward smile.

"Let me go holla at bro OG real quick and make sure she straight. I'ma holla at you in a minute G," I told Killa before quickly walking off.

I didn't like the vibe I was getting from him. His energy was off. Something wasn't right about him I just couldn't pinpoint what it was. Maybe I just didn't like the fact that he was able to smile at a time when it was absolutely nothing to be smiling about. Maybe I was just irritated at the moment. Regardless of the fact, I had to get away from his weird ass.

"How you doing, Ms. Hall? That dress looks beautiful on you," I complimented Mike Moe's mother while giving her a hug and a peck on the cheek.

"I'm okay, baby. Just trying to hang in there. I'm trying to be strong but it's hard," she sighed before continuing. "Thank you so much for helping out with the funeral. It meant a lot to the family and to myself. I'm grateful that Michael had friends like you and Nut."

"No problem, Ms. Hall. I know that he would've did the same for me if the shoe was on the other foot. He was one of my closest friends."

Ms. Hall started crying. She gave me another tight hug before saying, "You're a good kid, Dre. Do something with yourself while you still have a chance. It's not too late for you to get out of these streets. If you don't walk away now, the streets will consume you. Once you die, you can't come back, start over, and see if you could get it right. Life isn't a game." She looked at me and gave me a weak smile. She knew deep down that I was already neck deep in the streets and me being consumed was all a part of God's will. She had to say what she said just to be able to say that she tried to warn me.

I sat in the second pew of the church. The funeral was packed. I looked around and saw Nutso, Von D ,Binky, Bone, T Stone, and a few of the Stones from D Block and From Risky Road. Smack was even in the back of the church with a mug on his tear stained face. I didn't speak to anybody. I greeted everyone with silent head nods. As I looked over at Mike Moe's grieving family, I saw Ashley. I had forgotten that her and Mike Moe were second cousins. I got up and made my way to be by her side. On my way to her, I noticed that everybody in the funeral faces were wet with tears except for Killa, who was sitting not too far from Smack. For some reason, that irritated me even more.

"Please leave me alone, Dre," Ashley told me as soon as I took a seat next to her.

"Damn, so you can't hear me out for a minute?"

"No!" Ashley snapped. "Do you see where my little cousin at because he hangs with you? Everything around you is toxic. I don't want to be around you," she said with tears dripping from the corners of her eyes.

"I been stressed out, missing you like a mufucka. I feel like I can't function without you. I move better when you're by my side. I never felt like this for no other woman. I need you back," I said honestly. I was feeling my emotions getting the best of me.

Ashley stared deeply into my eyes and at that moment it seemed like I could feel all the pain that she was feeling. She stared at me like she was searching for my soul through my eyes. Her big, brown eyes burned with sadness and hurt.

"It's too much going on right now, Baby Dre," she said finally. "We're about to bury my cousin so just call me later and we'll talk but I can't do it right now, I can't even focus," she said.

I couldn't do shit but respect her wishes so I didn't respond. I just got up and left the funeral. I couldn't be in the same room as her knowing she didn't wanna speak to me when I had so much to say. I sat in my car gulping the bottle of Remy while listening to R. Kelly's 'I Wish' Remix. My pain started to transition into anger and that anger was in my ear telling me to do all type of crazy shit. I pulled my .40 off my waist, sat it on my lap and sped off with murderous intentions.

***

Reesie, Lil 4, Cello and Reesie's younger brother, D Thang sat in one of the Foe's crib on 103rd and Corliss playing NBA 2K10 while a few of the bros chopped and bagged up rocks in the kitchen of the home.

"We should go clap Mike Moe's funeral up. That nigga Smack called me and told me that all them hoe niggas in that bitch," Cello suggested while playing with a SKS assault rifle.

"Hell naw Foe, you tweaking," Reesie said pausing the game. "You must've forgot that the nigga Smack was a Stone, too, and he from D Block at that. He might be on some backdoor shit."

"He can get it too," D Thang said.

He was 15-years-old and determined to be just as grimey and cutthroat as Reesie was. They were almost identical in appearance. They were the same skin tone, the same height, about the same weight and D Thang even had shoulder length dreads that were only a tad bit shorter than his brother's. Reesie was his idol, and he was anxious to prove to him that he was just like him. He had even been on a few hits.

"Naw, Smack my homie, and it's kids and old people at that funeral. Plus, Mike Moe wasn't on the same time as them other niggas. He just got caught up in the mix. Killa said he only clapped him because he was saying that he seen him with you," Reesie said nodding towards Cello.

"You right, Foe, but I left my phone in yo' car. Let me see the keys," D Thang told his brother.

"Here," Reesie tossed him his car keys. "And grab that Racks Rude mixtape out the radio for me," he called out to D Thang as he left out the crib.

***

I was riding up Corliss when I spotted Reesie's Porsche truck. I silently thanked God as I got closer and I saw that he was leaning inside the truck, apparently looking for something.

Just the bitch ass nigga I was looking for. I looked over at Mike Moe's obituary, which was laying on my passenger's seat before I rolled my window down. Reesie was on the passenger's side of the truck so when I eased up and stuck my .40 out of the window. I was so close it was no way that I could've missed him. I squeezed the trigger and his body jerked violently as bullets slammed into his back as well as the back of his head and neck. I screeched off when Lil 4 ran out of the house and started blowing a Choppa at me.

***

"Stay woke, lil bro. Keep breathing," Reesie cried holding his brother. D Thang convulsed and twitched trying hard to fight to keep breathing but it was a fight that he couldn't win. D Thang was on his way to Paradise.

***

"Yeah, it was Reesie. I'm positive. I was right behind him," I told Killa over the phone. He was on the other side of the phone huddled up with Reesie and a bunch of the Foes.

"Fuck him. That's what he had coming," Killa said. "Ima find out when the funeral is so we can take care of the rest of them niggas."

"Naw," I said before sighing, "that shit was personal between me and Reesie. I'm 'bout to run my bag up and fall back, you feel me?" I asked sadly.

I thought I would be happy after killing Reesie but I wasn't. I was hurting even more than I already was. We had our differences but deep down he was still one of my best friends. It was crazy how now I wished I could turn back the hands of time and just say fuck that lil money he owed me. I had finally realized that it wasn't worth all this.

"Yeah, I feel you and if that's what you want to do then do it. I'ma hit you right back doe," Killa said before hanging up. I thought Reesie was dead but he wasn't. He was alive and ready to kill me and everyone close to me. He wanted us to pay for what I did to D Thang.

Chapter 15

Locked In

Everything was going good with us and Lopez until a few of the older Moes got locked up while picking up nine bricks of coke. Now, we owed Lopez $132,000 because six of those bricks were being given to us on consignment. All I had to my name was about $28,000 and three bricks of Crack.

My phone rang early one morning, It was Lopez.

"How is everything going? I heard about some of your men getting arrested with my work. What happened with that?" he asked calmly.

"The State Troopers were trying to pull them over for a routine traffic stop and bro nem took them on a high speed but they ended up getting caught."

"So, do you have the money to cover the six bricks of mine that you lost?"

"Damn, amigo, they just got booked yesterday!" I gruffed. "Let me make a few moves and then I'll have yo' money."

"How much time do you need to make *your moves*?"

"I don't know. Maybe a few months," I said not trying to hide my irritation.

"That won't do," Lopez replied flatly. "I cannot wait a few months for my money. I'll give you a month. I can't risk you getting killed or locked up in the between time."

"I feel you but at least give me a month and a half," I said.

After a moment of silence Lopez finally spoke. "Okay, Mo Money, but only because we've been doing great business together but if I don't get my money then you can expect for you and your whole team to get killed in the worst ways," he said grimly and hung up in my face.

I knew for a fact that Lopez meant every word he said. What type of plug played about his money or drugs? I knew I had to do whatever I had to do to get that Mexican mufucka's money or be ready to fight a war that I knew I couldn't win.

***

I was at a prenatal doctor's appointment with Precious when I got a call from a familiar number. I almost thought that my phone was playing tricks on me.

"Yooo," I answered cooly.

"Hey, Baby Dre," a soft, angelic voice said. It was only one person in the world who called me by that name. It was a special name that she'd made up for me.

"Ashley?" I asked.

"The one and only." She giggled. "I can't believe that you forgot my voice. That's crazy."

"Naw, I could never forget yo' voice. I'm just surprised that you called me. What's up with you, doe?"

"Nothing much. I'm on my lunch break and I was thinking about you so I decided to stop being stubborn and give you a call," she said and I started laughing loudly.

"What's so funny?" she asked.

"That new nigga you fucking with must be broke as fuck!" I said and erupted in more laughter. "You never had to work when I was yo' man," I added cockily.

"What new nigga is you talking about, crazy boy?"

"The nigga you was with at IHOP."

"Let me find out you had yo' friend stalking me," Ashley said after a moment of brainstorming.

"Naw, Moe just knew that I was going through it over you and he was calling himself looking out for me but he don't even know that he broke my heart to pieces when he told me that shit."

"How?"

"Because the thought of you with another man was too much for me to handle. That shit killed me," I admitted. Usually, I would've taken that to the grave but I always felt comfortable being open with Ashley. She never judged me or looked at me different after seeing certain sides of myself that I hide from the public.

"Aww that's so sweet," she said playfully.

"I'm saying doe. Can I pull up on you later and holla at you face to face?" I asked when I saw Precious coming out of the doctor's office.

"Yeah, I get off at six. Just call me," Ashley told me before I disconnected the call.

***

Nutso, Lil C and Killa were riding around in Killa's new Infiniti truck listening to *'With Me'* by C Money, a local rapper from 114th and State. He had a buzz in The Hundreds and was sure to take off sooner or later. They had been riding around smoking and serving for almost an hour now.

"This a rental?" Nutso asked Killa.

"Naw, I leased this bitch. It's decent doe?" I asked with a smile. He was running his bag back up fucking with Reesie nem but he wasn't as well off as he used to be. It was strange to him seeing how far his shorties had come.

"On Stone, I could have sworn that I saw Reesie the other day in the back of the building," Lil C said from the backseat flaming up a Kush blunt.

"Hell naw, it couldn't have been him. They had a private funeral for him the other day," Killa replied.

"Man, I haven't heard about no funerals. I ain't seen his face on no shirts. I haven't even seen nobody post *'Rest in*

Peace' on Facebook," Lil C said but Nutso spoke before Killa could.

"Pull up on that thick ass bitch right there," he said pointing at a thick, caramel colored woman who was walking up 75th and Cottage Grove.

"What's up?" he asked leaning out of his window.

"What's up?" the woman asked with a slight attitude. When her eyes landed on his diamond screw in earrings and then the chain he was wearing, her whole attitude changed.

"Shit, I'm tryna see what you on."

"I'm looking for some gas."

"We got it. Hop in," Nutso said with a smile while popping the locks. The woman looked vaguely familiar but he couldn't place where he knew her from. "We at the spot," he told Killa before pulling out a pack of Swishers and a seven of Kush.

Thirty minutes later, they were in one of Nutso's traps halfway through a fifth of Patron that had two X pills crushed up in it. Nutso was getting his dick sucked by the eater while Lil C hit her from the back.

"This some good ass pussy," Lil C told no one in particular as he pounded shorty out. He couldn't help but to watch his dick slam in and out of her pretty, fat pussy.

"Killa come get you some of this top boy," Nutso told Killa who was sitting on the other side of the room smoking a Kush blunt while nodding his head to the Lil Durk song that was playing.

"Man, I'm not touching that lil ass girl," Killa mumbled.

Nutso was on his second nut and almost came again when the woman took all of him in her mouth damn near swallowing his whole dick.

"Damn shorty, slow down," he said with a grin as he gripped her head and took control. Lil C had his thumb in her ass while he hit her from the back. She had came multiple times. He did too but the liquor and pills had everybody energized. Lil C pulled out and shot his load all over the

CITY OF SMOKE | MOLOTTI

eater's back. She continued to suck Nut's dick like she didn't care. He let a low moan escape from his mouth as he bussed in the woman's mouth.

Me, Bone and T Stone walked in just as the woman started to suck Lil C's dick. Me and the bitch locked eyes and it looked like she had just seen her worst nightmare.

"This snake ass bitch!" I growled charging over to the woman and hitting her with a few powerful punches to the head. The woman yelped and Bone pulled me off of her.

"Fuck is wrong with you, Moe?" He asked me trying to keep me in his grasp.

"That's the bitch Mieysha that set me up and got Herron killed," I said and Bone turned around and hit Mieysha with three heavy handed punches to her face.

"I didn't set you up. Boy, you tweaking," Mieysha cried, and Bone hit her with two more punches.

"Aight put that ass in the air for me then," I told her.

"No," she shook her head. "Just let me go home," she said. She was so scared that she was shaking.

"Naw, you say that you didn't set me up so I'm wrong for accusing you. Let's keep the party going. I want some," I said licking my lips. Mieysha looked at me for a few seconds trying to read me before she got down on her hands and knees. "Stay just like that," I told her walking to the closet and grabbing our AKs.

"What you doing?" Mieysha asked looking back over her shoulder. She saw the K and tried to get up, but I kicked her as hard as I could.

"Stop moving, bitch!" I huffed. She got back down and screamed one of the loudest screams I ever heard when I shoved the barrel of the AK up her ass. "How you like that bitch?" I asked her over her howls.

"G, what the fuck is you doing?" Killa asked grabbing my shoulder.

"Bitch ass nigga don't touch me!" I said shoving him hard with one hand. "If you wanna save this hoe, you can get it with her. Goofy ass nigga," I threatened.

"What?" Killa asked pulling out his .45.

Click Clack!

"Don't do that, bro," T Stone said coldly, aiming his Glock at Killa's head.

"You right," Killa replied adjusting his attitude as he looked around the room. He knew everybody there would side with me.

I went back to what I was doing. I was shoving the K so far up Mieysha's ass that she had involuntarily shitted on herself and was dripping blood.

"Keep throwing that ass back until you make it cum," I told her never taking my eyes of her. I fucked her with the K for five more minutes and then I pulled the trigger with the barrel still in her ass.

T Stone finished her off with two shots to the face.

"Cuz, that was just some sick, nasty ass shit," Nutso said with a frown.

"Call somebody to come clean this shit up," I said stepping over the dead body and leaving out.

Later that night, I was at Ashley's house. We were sitting on her queen sized bed catching up on missed times.

"So, what's been going on with you?" she asked laying her head on my lap looking into my eyes.

"Same shit." I shrugged. "I owe the plug a hundred thirty something dollars or me and all the guys gon' be dead men walking," I replied brushing a loc of hair out of her face.

"And after you pay him, then what?" she asked.

"Then, hopefully after I make another hundred thousand, you stop playing with me and I could leave this shit alone. We could start us a family."

"Why do you feel like you need to make another hundred thousand? Why can't you try to make a honest living?"

"Cause I ain't no honest mufucka," I said with a chuckle. "I can't leave the streets alone when the streets is all I know. What else I'ma do? I never really took the time to think about the future. I'm not even sure if I'ma make it to see the future," I said truthfully.

"Don't think like that dummy," Ashley said playfully punching me in my chest. "The lifestyle you're living doesn't last forever. You're always supposed to have an alternative."

I chuckled and said, "You in this bitch sounding like my OG."

"Look, how about you just pay the plug and then we can run away and settle down together," she said seriously.

"I just can't up and walk away like that. It's niggas that's depending on me. I just need some time to get everything situated and I promise that shit gon' get greater for us," I said before kissing her on the lips. After the kiss she got up and put her Trey Songz CD in her radio. She seductively switched her hips as she sashayed back to the bed.

"Look at you tryna model and shit," I joked as she approached me.

"Lay back," Ashley demanded as 'Upstairs' played. She kissed me from my chest down to my stomach before unzipping my jeans and pulling out my rock hard dick. She held my dick with both hands and licked around the head. Her mouth was warm as she slid only half of my dick inside.

"You don't even deserve this," she told me holding my dick.

"Yes, I do," I replied, and she put me back inside of her mouth while using her tongue to please me. I was ready to bust already. That's how excited I was.

Ashley took me deep inside her throat and started to gag. She stared up at me looking into my eyes while she sucked my dick.

"I'm 'bout to bust," I whispered after a few minutes. She sucked faster and sloppier until I exploded in her mouth. I immediately pulled my dick from her mouth, laid on the bed and pulled her down on top of my face. She rode my face like it was her dream car and I drunk all the juices she had to offer. After she came, I flipped her over and continued to suck and nibble on her clit as I entered two fingers inside her pussy. She was just as tight as I remembered her being. 'Neighbors Know My Name' came on while I was tongue fucking her, making her moan my name. I knew she was having an orgasm once her legs started quivering and her moans turned to cries. I kept licking. I even took a few licks around her ass hole until she told me she was ready to fuck.

I climbed on top of Ashley holding my dick. I slowly rubbed my head up and down her opening before slowly sliding inside of her soaking wet pussy. I kissed her passionately while taking my time gently stroking her body. The sounds she made drowned out the music we had playing.

"Ummm, it hurt," she moaned and that only made me stroke faster. By the time I flipped her over to hit it from the back, we were both sticky with sweat and other sex juices. I was going strong killing her insides. After about 45 minutes of making love, I knew my show was coming to an end so I started picking up the pace of my strokes.

"Slow down," she whispered out of breath. I did as told and made love to her until I busted inside of her. I fell over on the bed next to her breathing hard.

"Damn, I missed that good shit," I smiled rubbing her pussy. We laughed and kicked it until she fell asleep in my arms.

The next day, me and the gang were all at Bone's crib smoking.

"I think I'm about to fall back and go back to school," I said out of the blue to no one in particular while blowing smoke out of my nostrils.

"On Stone Moe, what type of goofball shit is you over there thinking about?" T Stone snorted screwing his face up.

"I'm thinking about getting my mufuckin shit together so me and Ashley can be straight for the long run."

"Moe, you 18-years-old checking a fuckin bag and you tryna go back to school just to impress that skinny ass bitch? What about the baby you got on the way? Ain't yo' other lil bitch pregnant? How the fuck you gon' feed all those mouths while you going to school?"

"I'ma figure all that shit out along the way," I said with a shrug." Lately, I been thinking about the future. I'm tryna be able to live comfortably without worrying about shit. We all know it's only two ways out these streets. I'm tryna leave on my own terms before I have to take one of those roads."

"Nigga, you already chose yo' route! You chose to be a gangster, so don't hoe up now," T Stone shot back angrily. His face was turning red. "You think Lil 4 or Cello ain't gon' step up and take over for Reesie? This shit ain't gon never be over," he gruffed.

"Man, law let that nigga do whatever he wanna do," Nutso said flatly. "We can't force him to stay in the field with us. Some niggas get active. Some niggas die. Some niggas get rich and some niggas run when that pressure come. So, if Moe wanna run, fuck it let him run."

"You saying run, like I'm running from the streets like I'm some hoe ass nigga or something," I said to Nutso with my face balled up.

"Cuz, I'm just callin' it how I see it," he shot back at me.

"Fuck outta here," I snapped getting up and leaving out of the house. Those niggas had took everything I said and misinterpreted it and made it seem like I was ducking my shit. They had me heated. One thing I never did was duck anything except for jail. They had me fucked all the way up questioning my gangsta. I called Killa as soon as I got in my car.

"Where you at?" I asked when he answered.

"I'm put up. What's the word?" he asked.

"I'm tryna pull up on you," I told him and he gave me his whereabouts. I pulled up on him about thirty minutes later.

"What's the word lil bro?" Killa asked climbing in the passenger seat and shaking up with me.

"Shit, I got a few bricks left and I need to get these bitches off ASAP."

"Why what's wrong? That shit must be garbage?" he said with a chuckle.

"Naw, I'm just tryna pay my connect the lil bread I owe him and then get out the game while it's still a chance," I said, flaming up a Newport.

"Get out the game?" Killa asked shooting me a crazy look. "Why you tryna quit so early? You still ain't even touched yo' prime yet. You gotta get outta Chicago and see the world before you give this shit up. Have some fun with yo' money. That's what you supposed to be focused on," he stated.

"You right, but all the friends I lost. I got their blood on MY hands. That shit be keeping me awake at night. I be feeling like I'm next, on stone and that shit lowkey drivin' me crazy. I'm 'bout to have a baby. I can't keep living like this," I said stopping at a red light on 75th and Stony Island. A white Toyota pulled up behind me just as Killa started speaking.

"I'm not gon' be the one to lie to you and say that this shit last forever. You could fall off tomorrow, but I can say that just because you might feel like you done with the streets don't mean the streets gon' be done with you. On the G, it's still gon' be niggas hating on you on some jealous shit. Still gon' be niggas that want you dead and you still gon' have problems," he said.

I looked in my rearview mirror just in time to see a masked up dread head coming out of the passenger side window of the white Toyota. I stomped on the gas just as the masked man waved his Tech from side to side. Bullets pinged off my car, shattering my back windshield. "Shoot back!" I yelled to Killa ducking down trying to avoid crashing into another car.

"I don't got my pipe," Killa shouted back

"Grab my shit off the floor!" I yelled trying to maneuver through traffic. He reached over and felt around for a while before coming up with my Glock. He stuck his arm out the window and shot four times.

"Damn," Killa muttered. "I dropped the pipe."

I hurried up and whipped into the McDonald's parking lot on 65th and Stony Island. "Bro, how the fuck did you drop the pipe?" I asked Killa while watching the white Toyota keep straight up Stony. I locked eyes with the gunman and his gaze gave me an eerie feeling, like I was staring into the eyes of a ghost.

"I don't know how I dropped that bitch. Yo' goofy ass hit a pothole or something," Killa replied, looking stupid as hell.

I looked at him with nothing but disgust in my face before saying, "On Stone, you just pissed me the fuck off with that goofy ass shit. Yo' weird, scary ass. You could have just got us killed." I shook my head. "Matter fact, where you going? I'm about to drop yo' goofy ass off," I said angrily.

Killa shot me a small smirk like he wanted to say something smart. "Just drop me off on 100th Street. I'll be straight right there," he said dryly.

After dropping Killa off, I went to Precious' house. My mind was everywhere and I just wanted to relax.

"Baby, what's wrong? Talk to me," Precious said lying next to me all in my face. I had already told her I was bothered but she insisted on bothering me even more.

"I didn't come over here to talk. If you want to talk, call one of yo' friends or something," I said not hiding my irritation. I regretted not going home.

"Well lets have sex. You haven't gave me none in a minute," she said reaching down and rubbing my dick.

"Naw shorty, I don't even feel like fucking," I said gently pushing her off of me and getting up. "I got a lotta shit on my mind and I can't even think straight right now. I'm 'bout to jump in traffic and hit some blocks," I told her, rushing out before she had the chance to protest.

The next few hours all I did was ride around the city while smoking Kush blunts back to back. I was so overwhelmed with emotions and frustrated that I felt like my head was about to explode. I had my mind set on bettering myself but my brothers made me feel like I was doing something wrong. I didn't understand. I ended up calling Bone and telling him to meet me and the D Block trap so we could talk.

"What's the demo, law?" Bone asked me as I entered the D Block trap.

"You think you ready to step up?" I took a seat at the table we had in the living room.

"What you mean?" he asked taking a seat across from me.

"After I pay Lopez, all I'ma need is one last run to stack me up some paper and then I'ma fall back. You can have all this shit. I'm giving you my seat at the table and all I need from you is for you to cut me in on some of the profit just so I can provide for my family. How that sound?" I asked.

"How Nut nem feel about that?"

"I didn't ask them. I know they gon' do them and be straight. I'm tryna make sure you straight."

"If that's what you wanna do, then I'm with it. I'm ready," Bone replied.

I didn't know if I was making the best choice for my lil brother. A part of me felt bad for pushing him deeper into the same lifestyle that I was trying to get away from but he was determined to be a part of what we had going. I made myself feel better by saying that I was doing the right thing by putting him in position where he could be a boss instead of just a worker, just like Killa did me.

***

Smack and Cello rode through the hood in Smack's new Jeep looking for someone to kill. They needed to get back for D Thang's death so they were on a mission. They rode all through 107th until they rode past T Stone.

"There go T Stone hoe ass right there!" Cello said anxiously pointing towards where T Stone was standing serving a hype. "Hit the block. I'm bout to smoke his hoe ass," Cello told Smack, chambering a bullet into his .9.

When they came back around, T Stone was nowhere to be found. Smack stopped his Jeep in the middle of the block.

"Where the fuck he just go?" he asked Cello out of nowhere. T Stone popped up from a gangway shooting a Millennium .45. After his eighth shot, he turned around and took off running.

"Go wack that bitch!" Smack told Cello who hopped out and chased T Stone down only for Bone to pop out a cut blowing at him. Cello ducked down and turned to run back to Smack's Jeep. As he made his way to the Jeep, a Blue and White hit the block with its lights on and Smack sped off. Cello ran towards the jeep hoping Smack stopped and let him in but he didn't. As he drove away, Smack could see the officers hawking Cello down.

***

Reesie, Smack, Lil 4, Killa and a bunch of the foes were sitting in the back of the building plotting their next move.

"I'm ready to end this shit," Reesie said before turning to Killa. "Tell them niggas you got a lick or a big serve and get them all in the spot at once and we gon' kill all they dumb asses," he said before lighting up a blunt.

"Man, them niggas ain't on shit! It ain't even fun no more. I say we just squash that shit and focus on running our bag up," One of the Moes that sided with Reesie said making everyone look at him funny.

"What?" Lil 4 asked twisting his face into a scowl.

"Fuck them niggas. We giving them too much energy. We got the building. They don't even come around no more," the guy replied.

"Man, fuck what he talking 'bout," Smack said waving Moe off." They killed D Thang so we ain't squashing shit, on Stone!" He added.

"Look, lil bro," Reesie said to Moe. "Go get up with Mo Money nem and tell them that I said everything good and I wanna squash that shit. Make sure you let them know that I'm alive and I just been tucked but I'm tired and I'm done with all that goofy shit."

"Aight, I'm 'bout to go do that right now," Moe said happily. He was excited to be able to hustle all day without worrying about getting killed. He turned around to leave but before he could make it to the door, Reesie put three bullets into the back of his head.

"Anybody else wanna try to squash some shit?" He asked looking around the room. "Get foe nem together and take 'em to slide, "He told Lil 4 before leaving the trap.

Nutso and T Stone were on Harrison and Sacramento, out west, waiting to serve two bricks of crack to some Traveler Vice Lords that they had met in the club. The Lords had told T Stone that they had pounds of Kush for sell and that they were looking to buy a couple bricks. He planned on selling them the bricks and buying a few pounds after he checked out the weed.

"Man, we should have made these niggas come to us," Nutso gruffed climbing out of the car. Out West was way out of his comfort zone.

"We good. You got yo' pipe?" T Stone asked.

"Nope," Nutso replied. "You got yours?"

"Hell yeah, I don't know why you came all the way out here without yo' pipe. We don't even know these niggas," T Stone said patting his waistline where his .40 rested.

"You the one that made it seem like dude nem was good."

"That don't mean I trust them," T Stone replied as two guys approached his car. "What's up bro?" He asked a tall, lanky, brown skinned guy with long dreads. He was accompanied by a shorter, darker guy who sported a mohawk. The guy with the Mohawk looked kinda nervous like he thought Nutso or T Stone would up at any moment and try to rob him.

"It's hot as hell out here. Lord, grab that shit and follow us," The dread head said. They led them into a court way building. Once they entered the building, the dread head said, "Let me see them bricks."

Nutso flashed him a small smile that said, "Yea right." before saying. "Where is that bread at?"

Mohawk man returned the smile before telling him, "Go in apartment 1-C."

"Aight, come on," Nutso said not budging. He was starting to get a funny feeling about the whole situation. Before anybody could say anything else, two men holding AK-47s ran into the hallway with red bandanas tied around their faces. One of the men had his AK pointed at T Stone's face before he got the chance to reach for his gun.

"Give that shit up 'fore we smoke one of you Southside ass niggas," the guy who held T Stone at gunpoint gruffed.

"On Stone," Nutso said shaking his head in disbelief. He knew something wasn't right. "You niggas broke as hell! I thought y'all was getting money out here," he said as they searched him.

"Aye T make sure you kill him first since he don't know how to shut the fuck up," the dread head said.

"Y'all think we was dumb enough to come out here alone?" T Stone asked. "In a few minutes, if we don't walk up outta this bitch, Moe nem gon' be on they way in. Y'all got the bricks. I advise y'all to take that shit and run with it. It ain't shit. We ain't fucked up about that lil shit. Y'all can have them two bricks. Just let us go and we gon' chalk that shit up as a loss," he said trying to talk the men out of killing them.

Nutso stood there fuming with his jaws clinched. He was mugging everybody in the room, including T Stone.

"Get the fuck on," the dread head said nodding towards the door. "If y'all even look crazy, we gon' put on of y'all ass down," he threatened.

Once they got inside the car Nutso exploded. "MAN YO' GOOFY ASS JUST GOT US POKED BY THAT ROSCOE DASH LOOKIN ASS NIGGA!" he roared. "I knew we shouldn't have came out here man. Damn, "he said mugging T Stone. "Cuz bout to be mad as hell."

"On Stone, stop talkin' to me like I didn't just get robbed right along with yo' goofy ass," T Stone replied angrily. He knew that Nutso was right about how mad I was going to be.

"This shit crazy as hell," Nutso mumbled knowing that they had some explaining to do once they made it to the hood.

"HOW THE FUCK Y'ALL GET POKED!" I screamed in Nutso's face after they met me in one of the guy's crib on D Block and explained to me what had transpired. "Why the fuck you bitch ass niggas ain't let me know what y'all was about to do? You niggas lame as hell," I said getting louder and louder as my anger continued to rise.

"Nigga that wasn't just yo' shit," T Stone stated. "We all put in blood, sweat and tears to get that shit, and I'm not yo' mufuckin son, nigga. So, watch how you talkin' to me," H
he checked me.

"Who you talking to, Moe?" I stepped in his face.

"You!" he said giving me a two handed shove that made me stumble a couple feet.

'Crack'

I hit him in the eye with a lightening quick jab and followed up with three more punches that landed on his face and head. He ducked the fourth and hit me with a powerful three punch combination of his own before scooping me up and slamming me on my back. We traded blows, going blow for blow, rolling around on the living room's floor. Bone snaked T Stone causing him to roll off of me. I quickly got to my feet and started to punch him in the head. Bone joined me and we went to work punching and kicking him until Nutso broke it up.

"We supposed to be the Moes and y'all gon' roll me like that?" T Stone asked climbing to his feet with blood leaking from his mouth. "Don't trip I got something for y'all," he said before rushing out the crib.

"I should beat yo' ass too!" I threatened Nutso. I was mad as hell. Because of them we had just lost two bricks, setting us back from being able to pay Lopez. I don't know how serious they took it but I knew the clock was ticking and we had to get that money together or end up dead.

The next day, I decided to stay in and plot on how I was gonna come up while I chilled with Ashley. I was happy to have her back in my life. I felt more complete. She was the only peace I had these days. She was my motivation. She drove me to figure everything out.

"You hungry, bae?" she asked me snapping me out of the daze I was in.

"Yeah, go make us some tacos." I lightly smacked her on the ass.

"Boy, you love you some tacos, don't you?" She walked out of the room just as the doorbell rang.

"Hell yeah, almost as much as I love me some Ashley and answer that door for me. That's probably Nut nem," I said loudly before falling back into my thoughts. I anticipated Nut bursting into my room but as the minutes passed, I brushed it off as somebody ringing the wrong bell or something.

"D'Andre, you got company!" Ashley yelled. She had a sharp edge to her tone that I caught. I was a little thrown off because she never called me by my real name.

"Who is it?" I asked a little paranoid, thinking maybe it was the police.

"Come down here and see!"

I cautiously walked down the steps. I wasn't expecting to see a pregnant Precious to be sitting on my living room couch but there she was.

"What the fuck is you doing poppin' up on me without calling?" I snapped angrily.

"I just wanted to come over and let you know that we was having a girl. You haven't been responding to my text or calling me back so I decided to come over," Precious said trying to hand me a couple ultrasounds.

"We not havin' shit," I said, shaking my head. "*You* having a girl and you could've called and told me that over the phone," I said harshly. I knew that her being here would start some shit between me and Ashley because I hadn't told her about Precious or the baby she was carrying.

"And when were you going to inform me on this baby you got on the way?" Ashley asked frowning. I thought she was going to wait until Precious left to confront me but she was ready to address it now.

"I was but a lot of shit going on and it slipped my mind—"

Ashley held a finger up indicating for me to shut up before asking, "How could you having a child on the way slip your mind?"

"I was gon' tell you as soon as the time was right,"

"When was the time going to be right? When she went into labor?" She asked with a look of disgust on her face. She was hurt and couldn't hide it. "You know what, Dre. Just save it. You ain't shit and I don't even know why I wasted so much of my time with a nothing ass nigga like you. Enjoy your family," she said before storming out of the front door.

I was beyond angry and due to Precious being the cause of my angst I lashed out on her.

"See!" I yelled. "Yo' dumb, stupid ass comin' over here uninvited and shit!" I growled.

She opened her mouth to say something but I continued my verbal assault before she could speak.

"That's what I get for fuckin dumb bitches like you with no condom. Fuck you. Yo' stupid ass should've gotten an abortion," I screamed, not even thinking about what I was saying and the effect that my words would have on her not just emotionally but mentally too. The power of the tongue was immense. Precious just stood there staring at me with a shocked but hurt expression on her pretty face. I could tell by the mist in her eyes that my words cut her deep. She got up and shot me a look that almost instantly made me regret every word I had just said to her before she walked out. If she cried, she didn't give me the satisfaction of seeing her drop a tear .

Bone and a crowd of the lil Moes were standing on 106th and Indiana serving crack, talking shit and rotating Kush blunts. "Pretty soon the whole hood gon' be ours," Bone said speaking to no one in particular. "On Stone, whoever not standing on business can't even hang with us. Everybody already know how me, you, and Von coming," he said to Binky, who was a dark skinned kid with a low cut. He was one of the Black Stones from D Block and even at the young age of 15, he had two bodies under his belt and was thirsty to catch more. He was already considered a problem by their opps.

"On that van!" Von D said clutching as a Ford 1500 van hit the corner and screeched to a halt right in front of where they were posted. The driver of the Van was a 14 year old 4 Corner Hustler from Risky Road named Bands.

"What's up?" Bands asked with a mug.

"What you want to be up?" Bone asked returning the mug. "You riding around like that big ass van bulletproof or something," he added.

"On the Foe, all that tough shit a make a mufucka find out if you bulletproof," Mylo yelled from the passenger's seat of the van.

"Mylo, who the fuck you talking too?" Bone asked reaching for his .45. As he pulled out his gun, the van's backdoor opened to reveal Sauce pointing a AR-15 at Bone and his crowd.

"Put that lil ass gun up," Sauce told Bone with a chuckle.

"Blow that bitch!" Binky provoked him. He was itching to get it on. "Y'all lucky Big Foe ain't give us the greenlight on you hoe ass niggas. Next time we slide through this bitch it's gon' be a scary situation," Mylo said dropping the five with his hands before Bands pulled off.

"Damn, they got yo' boy Bands with that shit now?" Bone said to Binky, who was very close to Bands.

"You should've known Reesie was gon' cuff him. He be tryna play crazy," Von D said.

"Well, I'm glad they just fronted their hand. Now, we can go hit them before they hit us," Bone told his crowd. He knew that with him, Binky, Von D and MCK Reese leading the way, his generation of Stones could make some noise and shake the hood up a bit. In his feeble mind, he thought that this would be the perfect time to test his men out and weed out the savages from the fakes. Little did he know that most of them were only boys trying to play a man's game and they weren't ready for what the streets had to offer.

Chapter 16

Fast Money

I was in traffic with Arab about to hit a big lick. We were smoking a Kush blunt going over our plan.

"Turn that shit up," I told Arab referring to the newest Lil Durk song that was playing on the radio. I nodded my head while taking heavy pulls off the blunt, listening to Lil Durk rap about being a hitta by himself. I only had a few weeks left to get Lopez's money, so I was back getting my hands dirty by hitting licks. "This nigga decent as hell on the rap side," I said complimenting the Chicago native.

"Hell yea, but my nigga Bump J still the best out the city," Arab replied.

"On Stone, Bump raw as hell too but give it some time and he gon be up there with him and Keef," I said before taking another pull and passing the blunt to Arab. We were about to rob a nigga named D Baller from 46th and Woodlawn, who was sitting on a few bricks of coke and I needed that shit badly.

An hour later, we were at D Baller's backdoor. We had picked up Nut just to have an extra set of eyes and an extra gun if needed.

"1-2-3," I counted out before kicking in the backdoor with my SKS aimed, ready to blow. The kitchen's light was off and from where I was standing, I could see the empty living room and the stairs that led to the basement. I heard multiple footsteps above my head. I looked at both Nutso and Arab and pointed upstairs. As we crept up the stairs, the light to the second floor's hallway flicked off. I slowed down when I made it to the top of the stairs, reached around the corner and ran my hand along the wall until I found the light switch and flicked it back on. The pungent aroma of Kush and Newports attacked my nostrils.

It was two bedrooms and a bathroom on the second story. The door to the room furthest down the hall was cracked open with the light off. My intuition told me that there was an ambush waiting for us behind that door. I put my finger to my lips indicating for Nut and Arab to keep quiet as possible while we contemplated our next move. I motioned my hand toward the door that was closest to us which was completely closed. It had a hand painted sign on the door that read A'myra.

I pushed the door open hard and swung my rifle inside with my finger curled around the trigger. A young girl who couldn't be any older than ten years old jumped out of her bed startled.

"Daddy!" she screamed when she saw the three of us masked up with guns drawn.

"Shhh," I told her trying to calm her down. "We not gon' hurt you, just get up."

"Don't touch my daughter," a smooth voice said from behind Arab. He had a chrome Desert Eagle pointed at Arab's head.

'Click Clack'

Nutso chambered a bullet into his tech. "Look man," he said to D Baller aiming his Tech at his daughter. "We not tryna hurt yo' lil girl, you know. We know what you got so give that shit up so we can leave. Don't be a tough guy because it's not gon' end well for y'all," he said.

D Baller stared at him with a ugly mug on his face. "Yella," he shouted. "Bring all that work up here!"

"And drop that gun," I told D Baller.

"Why, so y'all can kill all of us?" He asked defiantly.

"I advise you to do what the fuck he asking you to do because you starting to blow me," Arab said clearly agitated.

A brown skinned guy with shoulder length dreads who I assumed was Yella entered the room and dropped ten bricks of coke on the floor right next to the gun D Baller had just dropped.

"Drop yo' gun bro," D Baller told him calmly.

"Hell naw. On Chief, you got me fucked up!" Yella shouted with veins coming out of his neck and forehead.

"I'm tired of playing with you goofy ass niggas," Nutso growled grabbing A'Myra by her arm and putting the Tech to her head.

"Do what the fuck they say and drop the gun!" D Baller yelled stepping in Yella's face. He was almost in tears. He was that mad. Yella reluctantly dropped his gun and as soon as it hit the floor, D Baller hit him in his mouth. He was furious that he was acting so stubborn while his daughter's life was in jeopardy.

"Whoa! Whoa! Whoa! Don't make no more sudden moves. I almost started popping mufuckas," Arab warned before snatching the sheet off A'Myra's bed and using it to wrap the bricks in.

"Now this how things 'bout to go. If we search the house and find anymore drugs or money, then we killing everybody. If you know it's in here, stop playing and give that shit up so we can slide," I said.

"Fuck!" D Baller gruffed leaving the room. He returned moments later, holding a duffle bag holding some money and four more bricks.

"It's always a slick ass nigga tryna do some raw shit," I said hitting Yella in the face with the butt of the SKS. "Okay so now yo' daughter gon' walk us to the car and if you do something stupid then you gon' be the reason she die," I said meaning every word. If I didn't get this money, I would be dead so I couldn't have feelings at the moment.

"Deno, stand down!" D Baller screamed as we backed out of the room. I had his daughter clutched tightly. I didn't want to hurt her but if they forced my hand, then so be it. When we made it to our rental, I told the little girl to run back to the house as fast as she could. As we sped off, I thought about how close we could've come to dying. If the little girl wasn't there, things could have taken a terrible turn for the worst. We came up on $150,000 and 14 bricks of coke. We split the money up evenly. Me and Nutso kept 9 bricks and let Arab keep 5 since it was his lick. I was excited because we had enough drugs to flip and be able to pay Lopez. It felt like a huge weight had been lifted from my shoulders.

By the next night, we had put the word out that we had some good coke for sell. We had hard or soft, however you wanted it. We didn't actually know if it was good or not but we said it was. If a nigga had a problem with the quality after he paid us for it then that was on him. We set it up so Bone and Lil C both had their own separate blocks where they could sell bags and small pieces on. Me and Nutso would handle the big deals. The only problem was that none of us knew how to cook soft coke into crack. We found a local hype who agreed to cook up for us for a small fee. His name was Buck. Back in the day he was getting big money in Chicago Heights with a group of 4 Corner Hustlers who called their clique S.T.O. Somehow, he started experimenting with his own product and fell over onto the dark side. He was a cool, funny ass hype who had a lot of wisdom. He knew a lot because he had seen and been through a lot.

"On the Foe, my whip game so nasty y'all gon' have hypes coming from Alaska to buy this shit, ya hear me?" Buck said to us. It was me, Nutso, Bone and Lil C sitting in his kitchen paying attention to his every move. "You can ask anybody about Foe Buck. I'm one of the best. This wrist is legendary on the Foe," he complimented himself with a big smile.

"Just shut the fuck up and whip nigga!" Nutso growled flaming up a Kush blunt while bobbing his head to Gucci Mane's 'Making Love To The Money'.

It took Buck longer than it should have because he kept stopping to talk shit but in no time, he turned three bricks of Coke into four and a half bricks of crack. "Try a piece out," I told him when he was all done.

"You ain't gotta tell me twice," he said whipping out his pipe with a big Kool-Aid smile. He smoked a fair sized rock right in our face. I could tell by his body language that he was instantly high as a cloud. His eyes glossed and he had a goofy ass smirk on his face as he stared into nothing.

"That shit stank," Lil C complained covering his nose.

"Is that shit good?" Bone asked Buck who was just standing there staring at nothing.

"Does a bear shit in the woods and wipe his ass with a fluffy white rabbit?" He asked showing his stained teeth. Me and Nutso erupted into a fit of laughter. You could always count on a hype to say some slick, funny shit.

"Good lookin' Big Foe. You can keep an eight ball. I need for you to put the word out there that we got some glass," I told him.

"Thanks, lil brothers. Anytime y'all need me just call me. Anytime!" he repeated, looking extra ugly.

"Aight, we will but until then go get yo' old, ugly ass in the shower. You stank!" Nutso joked as we prepared to leave.

In less than two weeks, we ran through two bricks, probably because I sold them wholesale for $30,000. I had enough money to pay Lopez and get him off my back but money was coming so quick that I didn't wanna leave the game anymore. I wanted to pay Lopez what I owed him and then grab a whole nother load. I hadn't heard from Ashley or Precious lately, so I was fucking every bitch that looked my way.

I had no worries. I was living my best life. The blocks that Bone and Lil C ran were making at least $3500 a day. Me and Nutso only saw a small percentage of that. I felt like we were back on top.

The first week of May, we all took a trip to Lopez house to pay him his money and re-new our business agreement.

"Hello, primo, once again you didn't let me down I see," Lopez said as his nephew Chito counted out the $132,000 that I had for him. "Bone, my friend," Lopez nodded at Bone. "And who are these other men you've invited into my home once again without letting me know beforehand," he asked referring to Nutso and Lil C.

"That's my cousin Nutso and my homie Lil C. They're also my business partners. We're all equals in this shit so I wanted you to meet them because it might not always be me who comes to do business with you. Speaking of business, I got a new proposition for you," I told him rubbing my hands together.

"I'm all ears."

"We want you to give us 15 bricks on consignment. We gon' operate in different areas as a whole and we'll bring you $300,000. That's $20,000 a brick," I said already knowing the play I had in motion.

Lopez chuckled and stared at the four of us for a second. "Can you little guys handle that type of deal?" He asked.

"Hell yeah, on Stone. All you gotta do is try us," Nutso said speaking for the first time.

"How long will it take for you to have my money?"

"Not long. We'll pay you before we feed ourselves but if we sell all fifteen bricks for at least $30,000 apiece. We'll make $450,000. We agreed to bring you $300,000 but how about we give you the whole $450,000 and you give us 10 bricks and we don't owe you nothing. We'll just continue to cop from you for $20,000 a brick after that?" I asked him.

"That's kind of a hard decision for me to make. I don't see how it would be benefiting me," Lopez said with doubt, covering his face.

"Well, we'll bring you back $500,000," I said and waited for Lopez to give me an answer. When he took too long to respond, I added. "Well, just take that lil bread we owed you and we'll find somebody else to do business with. Good lookin' for everything you've done for us. I appreciate it," I turned to the guys. "We gone y'all," I said preparing to walk out the door.

"Wait a second, Mo Money," Lopez said stopping me. "I like how you carry yourself. If you could stay alive and stay out of jail, you could have a very bright future in the drug game. You got a magnetic personality, and you make people want to deal with you. I see potential in you and your team so I'm going to trust you this time. You have three months, not a day later to have my money. I will have fifteen bricks delivered to you tomorrow morning," he said.

"Gracias, amigo," I replied making Chito burst out laughing. He liked when I said lowkey racist shit because he knew I was just a funny ass nigga, and I meant no disrespect. Everybody spoke their goodbyes and we left feeling like we were the Supreme team.

Chapter 17

Mo Money, Mo Problems

Reesie and a couple of the guys were riding in his black BMW 530 listening to Gucci Mane's 'Gucci 2x' while plotting on killing their opps.

"Tonight, I want you to take lil Foe nem to slide through D Block. I don't care who y'all catch. Just make sure y'all fuck somebody up," Reesie told Sauce, who was sitting in the backseat smoking a Kush blunt. "Smack, I need you to have Killa get up with Moe nem and see where the fuck they heads at and I need for you to see what the fuck Cello booked for," he instructed.

"Aight, I'ma see what's up," Smack said with no real intentions of doing what was asked of him.

"Aye, Foe Buddy you can drop me off in the hood so I can have Lil 4 and Bands slide with me," Sauce told Reesie before handing him the smoldering blunt.

"Make sure y'all clap one of them hoe ass niggas. I'm getting tired of this back and forth, tit for tat ass shit," Reesie replied turning up the volume on his radio.

***

T Stone sat in his 09 GMC Envoy." These niggas out here lacking, on Stone," he said to himself as he rode past Bone and a few of the Moes. When he reached the corner of 107th and Indiana, he saw a black BMW with too many heads in it sitting at the stop sign on 108th Street. He thought his mind was playing tricks on him cause the driver of the BMW looked just like Reesie. The even crazier part was that the passenger looked like Killa. The sight threw him all the way off because he could've sworn that the driver was Reesie not somebody who looked like him but him living and riding through the hood. He couldn't believe it.

I was hopping out of my car to drop some work off to Bone when T Stone pulled up and hopped out of his truck.

"Bro, I just saw Reesie and Killa riding down 108th in a black BMW. I know I wasn't just tweaking, on Stone," he said frantically.

"You lying bro. I smoked Reesie fasho and Killa said he went to the funeral. You tweakin with all that lying shit. You gotta slow down with them pills you been taking," I told him with a straight face.

"Nigga, on Mike Moe grave, I just seen them niggas together," T Stone said seriously. He was certain that he saw who he thought he saw and that was the only reason why he murched it.

"Stop lying on bro grave you goofy ass nigga!" Bone gruffed angrily.

Before T Stone could reply, shots went off. Damn, I said to myself as I jumped in front of the big oak tree that sat in front of Bone's house. I watched T Stone run to his truck, jump in and speed off. Bone grabbed the .40 that he had stashed on the tire of a parked car and fired shots at T Stone's truck as he fled the scene.

"On Stone, that bitch ass nigga just tried to get us killed! If I catch his ass in the hood again, I'm fuckin him up," I stated angrily while dusting off my jeans. In my head, I was thinking that T Stone tried to throw Killa under the bus to cover up his own backdoor intentions.

"Say less Moe, we on his ass," Bone replied eager to put in some work. He didn't care who caught his wrath as long as somebody was getting it.

After a few weeks, business was doing great. We had flipped seven bricks at $32,000 apiece. On a good day, Bone or Lil C would check a little over $5000 off one of their blocks just off selling bags, sixteenths, eight balls and ounces. We were all eating good and having fun with our money. We were young, lit and stepping on shit so nobody could tell us a damn thing. We got into a few more unnecessary wars but we didn't give a fuck. The whole world could get it. I still hadn't heard from Ashley or Precious. I didn't even know how the baby inside of her was doing. A part of me felt bad but most of the time I was too high or drunk to give a fuck. I also felt like they were the ones who abandoned me so I wasn't wrong at all in my mind.

Bone had just bought himself a white on white 06 Range Rover. He was stacking his money way better than me and Nutso was. We bought everything that we thought looked good and we partied hard every day. We were young niggas who came from nothing and now that we had a little bit of something, we didn't know how to act. Who could blame us doe? The only thing I'd heard about T Stone recently was that he had been behind a few people getting shot and robbed. I hadn't heard from him or seen him since the shootout on D Block and I found that a little bit strange.

Reesie was still moving in the shadows. His money was growing as well as his influence. The guys who was on his side looked at him like some sort of God. He was really on his Chief shit. He wasn't fucking with Killa and Smack like that because he felt like they weren't getting shit done. He moved Sauce to the frontline and was only fucking with him, Lil 4, and Bands hard while Cello was away. The police had ran in one of his spots and found 22 pounds of Kush. He wasn't hurt about it though because he was moving pounds like they were dime bags. He was hellbent on taking me out. It was almost like he had an obsession with killing me. He felt like The Hundreds weren't big enough for the both of us.

He wanted all the money, hoes, and respect for himself. It was almost time for him to make his move and show his face.

**

September 2010

Me and Nutso were riding in my 2011 Chevy Camaro that I had just leased. I was in love with how the Red paint sparkled in the sunlight while we drove through the trenches. "Let's go get up with some eaters," Nutso suggested while rolling a blunt.

"What eaters? You be fuckin with them stuck up ass hoes. I'm not on that," I replied focusing on the road.

"The Nuk Ladies want me to slide on them up the hill," he replied flaming up his blunt.

The Nuk ladies were a group of young women who we went to school with. They called themselves 'Nuk Ladies' after their brother, Nuk who had gotten killed. We pulled up on 110th Street between State and Perry to see that it was a fiesta going on out there. The block was packed with people. When we hopped out, all eyes were on us. I had on a black, green, and red Gucci t shirt, a pair of black jeans, a black Gucci cap that I had cocked to the left over my hair that was pulled into a puffy ponytail and a pair of black Timbs. Nutso was dressed in a Prada outfit with a pair of matching Prada sneakers and a black and gold Pittsburgh Steelers snapback over his mohawk.

"Heyyy, Nut," a caramel skinned woman with a nice body sang as she ran up and gave him a hug.

"What's up, Mami? Y'all shit bussin' today. Fuck y'all got going on? "Nutso asked while still holding her in his arms.

"Today is my brother, Nuk birthday. We do this every year for him," Mami replied before turning her attention to me. "What's up, Moe? You actin funny now?" she asked.

"You know it ain't never like that, sis. What you on?" I asked giving her a hug. We were the same age and had started high school together. We had been very tight since our freshman year.

"I'm tryna get some money like y'all."

"It's gon' take a long time for a mufucka to catch up with us. It's worth a try doe," I said arrogantly.

"Boy stop!" Another female said from behind me. I turned around to see that it was Mami's best friend, Cinnamon.

"Damn, Cinnamon I ain't seen yo' lil fine ass in a minute," I said glancing at her thick thighs. "On Stone, you lookin too good," I complimented her. She was wearing a wife beater and a pair of denim shorts that barely covered her ass.

"Thank you," she said with a smile that showed her gap. She resembled Keyshia Cole. They had the same skin color. Cinnamon's gap was a little wider and she was thicker than Keyshia Cole was.

"What you doing up here?" she asked. Me and Nut were from Down the Hill and we were into it with a lot of hoods that were Up the Hill so we usually didn't mingle on that side.

"Shit, we was just sliding through. We seen that y'all shit was bussing so we decided to pop out—"

"Plus, Mami invited us," Nutso said cutting me off.

As I looked around, just trying to be aware and observant of my surroundings, I saw the most heartbreaking sight. Ashley was sitting on some ugly ass nigga's lap, laughing, and smiling like she was talking to a celebrity. I immediately got heated and jealous at the same time. Instead of approaching them like I wanted to, I played it differently.

"Damn Cinnamon, I can't get no hug? You mean as hell. You 'bout to make me leave from up here," I said extending my arms until she fell in and gave me a tight hug." Stop acting like you ain't want to hug me," I whispered in her ear, purposely brushing my lips against her earlobes.

"Boy, shut up," she replied with a smile.

"What? I can't be yo' nigga? On Stone, yo' lil boyfriend must be out here," I said with a smile of my own.

"Get off my bestie Moe," Mami joked while rolling a Kush blunt.

"I'm hungry as hell. What's up with that food they got over there?" Nutso asked pointing at a couple of tables and grills that were going while he rubbed his stomach.

"Go over there and buy yourself a plate," Cinnamon told him.

The grills were close to where Ashley was, so I saw that as my opportunity to get close to her. "I got you, Nut. Walk with me, Cinnamon baby," I said with a smirk. I wrapped my arm around her shoulder as we casually strolled to where the food was.

"So, what's the deal? You gon' see what's to a nigga or what?"

"Didn't you try to talk to Cherry?" She asked referring to Mami's younger sister who I did want a piece of.

"Hell naw, that's just my homie," I lied.

"Whatever. I'ma see what's to you but the minute I feel like you playing with me, I'm cutting yo' ass right off."

Once we made it to where they were making plates at, I caught Ashley watching me all over Cinnamon. She had a shocked, dumb ass expression on her face. She was pretty as hell but Cinnamon was slightly badder with a raw ass body to match her looks. She made most women feel insecure or intimidated.

"What's up Ashley?" I asked while eyeballing the nigga whose lap she was sitting on.

"Hey, Dre. What you doing up here?" she asked.

"Shit, cooling with Cinnamon," I replied spitefully before reaching into my pants pocket and pulling out a thick wad of money. "Here, grab Nut something to eat and get you and

Mami something too," I said to Cinnamon passing her a hundred dollar bill. I had smaller bills. I was just tryna flex.

"You hungry, Ashley?" I asked with a smirk pointing another hundred dollar bill her way.

"No, I'm okay, "Ashley replied.

"Aight then be safe out here. Let me know if you need me," I said before turning my attention towards Cinnamon who was talking to a group of women.

"Aye, where you from fam?" a male's voice gruffed from the side of me.

I turned to see that it was the guy whose lap Ashley was sitting on. He was now standing up damn near in my face.

"I'm from Risky Road where the money at," I replied curling my upper lip a bit. I hated to be called *fam* so that was strike one for the character. I already was mad that he had my bitch on his lap. I was hoping to find a way to smoke his ass without making it seem like it was over a bitch. I was glad he was confronting me.

"Dolla, sit down!" Cinnamon said already seeing the confrontation before it got the chance to unfold.

"Naw, this goofy ass nigga waving money in my bitch face. He tryna flex on the wrong block. This ain't that," Dolla spat sizing me up. He was a few inches taller than me and a shade or two lighter with bad acne all over his ugly face.

"On Stone, you betta watch yo' mufuckin mouth boy," I warned twisting my face up. Both Cinnamon and Ashley quickly got between us.

"Dre, you doing too much! Just get from up here," Ashley said tryna make it seem like I was the one in the wrong. That only made me angrier.

"What's up, cuz?" Nutso asked with his hood over his head and his hands stuffed in his Prada Hoodie pockets.

"This bitch ass, broke ass nigga actin crazy like I'm not Mo muthafuckin Money. He better check my background before he get fucked over," I gruffed as a crowd of people gathered around us trying to see what was going on.

"Shorty y'all better get the fuck from up here!" A big, fat light skinned guy yelled.

"They with me and Dolla started all of this so y'all should be telling him to leave," Cinnamon said defending me. By now, we were surrounded by all of their friends and family members. We were outnumbered but we weren't worried at all. Everybody in The Hundreds knew it was consequences behind something happening to one of us.

"What's up, bitch ass nigga?" Dolla asked, stepping up with a few of his guys behind him. He was extra tough now that he had a crowd.

"What, you think y'all bout to jump us?" I asked looking at how everyone was mugging me and Nut. They didn't know that they would be fighting a whole bunch of bullets.

"Mane Mane, don't let them jump my boyfriend," Cinnamon said to Mami's older brother. He was a brown skinned, cut up guy with a big head. He was one of the top guys off their block.

"Sis, say that you started this shit, Dolla so fight him one on one if y'all got a problem," Mane Mane said.

At first I was hesitant because I thought that they would jump us but I knew that Mane Mane knew that I was one of the Moes so I trusted that he would make sure it was a one on one fight.

"We can do that," I said before taking off my hat and shirt. I was determined to beat Dolla's ugly ass in front of Ashley.

"You better beat his ass foe!" A tall dark skinned dread head told Dolla as he came out his shirt.

"What's up?" I asked squaring up with him. He threw a wild hook that missed. "Aw yeah, On Stone, I'm 'bout to beat yo' ass," I said before he caught me with a stiff jab. He threw another wild hook that I ducked and countered with a lightening fast two punch combo. We circled around each other until I faked a left and landed a powerful right haymaker. Dolla stumbled and dropped from the impact of the punch.

"Don't touch him while he on the ground," another dread head warned before I could stomp his hoe ass out.

When Dolla got up, he rushed me and threw a flurry of crazy, unorthodox punches. A few of the punches connected before I hit him with a uppercut that caused blood to squirt from his nose. Once he grabbed his face, I went to work punishing his head with hard blows until he scooped me up and slammed me on my head.

"Damn!" I heard Mami say.

Dolla started stomping me out until Nutso snaked him from behind dropping him.

"That's what I'm talkin' about!" one of his homies said as a few of the younger men out of the crowd started to move in on us. By the time I got to my feet, Ashley, Cinnamon and Mami were still pushing and pulling people away from us.

"What's up now?" Nutso asked after he was finally able to pull out his Glock 26. "Who wanna fight now?" He asked waving the gun around. "I should smoke one of you hoe ass niggas!" He snarled pointing the gun from person to person. Somebody had hit him in his ear hard as hell. He wished he knew who it was so he could smoke him.

"Please don't shoot, Nut," Mami pleaded with him.

"Come on, cuz," he said to me, and we took off to my car. Just before we made it to the car, Sauce popped out of a cut shooting at us. Somebody must've let him know that we were up there. Nutso returned fire and everybody who was out there scrambled to get out of the line of fire.

"Call Mami phone," I told Nut once we were in the car. He called her and put the phone on speaker. "Aye Mami give Cinnamon my number and tell her I said grab my shirt and hat," I said before hanging up.

"I'm clappin' Sauce hoe ass for shooting at us," Nutso said. He was steaming. I was mad too but more about Ashley and Dolla than about the shooting. I was pressed and I couldn't even hide it.

**

T Stone sat in a stolen grey Acura waiting for me and Nutso to hop out of my car. He had a sawed off double barrel shotgun on his lap. He wasn't for sure if he wanted to rob us or shoot us but he was positive that he wanted to do something to us. As we climbed out the car, he jumped out of his and was right up on us aiming his weapon.

"What's the demo? Y'all still tryna fight?" he asked glaring at me with death in his eyes.

"T, what the fuck you on, law? You tripping. This not how you supposed to be coming at the Moes," Nutso said.

"You niggas flipped on me," T Stone spat angrily. "Y'all moving bricks while I'm out here robbing mufuckas still. The guys wouldn't let they man starve while they eating good so miss me with that we the moes shit," he said raising his voice.

"Man, you set us up and had somebody blow us down the other day," I said mugging him.

"Nigga, on Black P Stone, I would never set y'all up. I love you niggas like brothers. Blood couldn't make us no closer. When everybody turned on you, I was by yo' side ten toes. I never let you down. When we was broke, fucked up and at our lowest, I was right there starving with y'all. You ain't never have to question my loyalty so why y'all so against me now?" T Stone asked sounding truly hurt.

"Man, is you 'bout to shoot or put the gun up and talk to us like men? Cause I can—" I was cut off by T Stone letting off a shot. I instantly hit the floor and Nutso followed suit. T Stone let off another shot before saying, "Get up, we gone!"

I got up and saw two bodies stretched out. One of the guys was still clutching his chest, struggling to breathe. I recognized him as one of the older Foes. He was a money

CITY OF SMOKE | MOLOTTI

getting ass nigga but he had just gotten caught trying to creep. Fuck him.

By the first week of December, I had just fully paid Lopez off and now we were running through our own bricks. Me and Nutso had planned to throw a Christmas party at Adrianna's, a club in Harvey, Illinois. We really had a few weeks to get things situated before Christmas came.

While we were planning our party, Reesie was planning his reappearance. Once word got out about our party, he knew that the party was where he would show his face at. Lately, Bone's crew and Sauce's crew had been sending shots back and forth.

Me and Bone were riding through the south and east sides of the city putting up flyers for our party. We wanted everybody to show up and show us love. Our names were ringing loudly throughout the city, so we knew that a lot of people were going to show up just to see how we were coming.

As we rode up 93rd and Halsted, I saw a familiar face walking down the street.

"Kahidijah, what's the word? You just forgot about me huh?" I asked pulling up beside one of my exes.

"Boy, you phony as hell. You started acting funny ever since you started fucking with that skinny bitch," she replied walking up on my car.

"I'm 'bout to drop bro off. Hop in and ride with me," I said popping the locks.

She quickly jumped in the backseat. Once I dropped Bone off, I shot to the liquor store and bought a fifth of Remy. "So, what you been on shorty," I asked before taking a sip from my cup.

"Nothing just working and going to school .I always hear about you and Nutso. Y'all came a long way. I'm so proud of you," she replied before taking a big gulp from her cup.

"Yeah, I bet you wish that you didn't break bad on me while I was doing that time," I said letting my eyes roll over her thighs. She had gotten a lot thicker since the last time I'd seen her.

"I sure do and I miss that dick too," she replied seductively, reaching over to rub my dick through my jeans.

"How much?" I asked feeling my dick start to harden.

"Enough to put this pussy on you right here in this car," she said reaching over to let my seat back. We were parked on 106th and Indiana and it was nighttime so I didn't see a problem with me getting my rocks off real quick. Even though I was in a redzone for shootings.

"That sound good but what I really need is some of that good ass top," I said putting my hands behind my head. Kahidijah didn't respond even respond. She went right to work, sucking my dick like she got taught by the porn star Lethal Lips.

After about thirty minutes of nonstop sucking, she was swallowing my nut. Jeremih's 'Waiter' played while she continued to suck. I had my eyes closed enjoying the head a little too much when something told me to open my eyes and check my surroundings. I looked in my mirror and saw two young boys who couldn't be older than 16 approaching my car dressed in all black. I recognized Bands instantly.

"Shit!" I said to myself as I hurriedly put my car in drive and screeched off. As I sped off, Bands and whoever he was with filled my car up with shots.

"Shut the fuck up, bitch!" I yelled at Kahidijah who was screaming dramatically. "You got hit?" I asked her.

"No," she whimpered.

"Well, be the fuck quiet then," I snapped speeding down 107th Street. Once I reached the red light on 107th and King Drive, I unlocked my car doors. "Hop out," I told her.

"Why? Where am I going?" She asked after taking a sip from her cup.

"I don't know where you going but you ain't goin' with me. It was nice seeing you doe?" I said before passing her a fifty-dollar bill and pulling off.

***

I was laid up with one of my lady friends named LaLa when I got a call from Precious. "What's up?" I answered.

"I'm going into labor at Little Company of Mary's Hospital," she said hurriedly. She sounded out of breath and in pain.

"Okay," I said dryly. "I'm kinda tied up right now. I'm not gon' be able to make it up there. Call me when she come out or something."

"Bitch, stop playing with me and bring your dirty ass up here to see our daughter be born!" Precious yelled angrily.

I laughed before saying, "Congratulations baby," and hanging up in her face.

I guess it was the drugs that had me tweaking but at the moment, I didn't realize how goofy and childish I was being.

"Bae, who was that?" LaLa asked laying her head on my chest.

"Mind yo' mufuckin' business and what did I tell you about calling me bae?" I snapped before tuning her out to continue watching the movie Juice.

The next morning, I was sitting in front of Ashley's house in a dark blue Dodge Charger that I had rented until my car got repaired. After about an hour of idle sitting, she finally walked out of the house wearing pink North Face coat, a matching pink North Face skullcap and a pair of pink Ugg boots. "Damn it's been a couple months since the last time I got a call from you," I said hopping out my car, surprising her.

"Boy please! Fuck you. What are you doing over here? Shouldn't you be at Cinnamon house?" she asked sarcastically while continuing to walk down the block.

"Slow down," I said jogging a little to catch up with her. "I just wanted to personally invite you to the Christmas party I'm having at Adrianna's. It would be nice for you to get out and have some fun," I said trying to read her facial expression. So far, I wasn't liking what I was reading.

"I been having enough fun lately and anyway why should I come be around you, Dre? Go invite your BM," she replied jealously.

"Fuck shorty, I only had her because I couldn't have you. You the one I want, the one I'm in love with but just like you doing now, you always get scared and put that tall ass wall up. I climb all the way to the top just for you to push me down and make the wall taller," I replied with a chuckle. "But here," I reached in my pocket, pulled out a wad of money and passed it to her, "buy you something sexy to wear if you gon' show up. If not, then it was nice seeing you," I said blowing her a kiss and walking off to my car with my head down.

Nutso was posted on D Block with a few of the moes, just hanging out. "Which one of y'all got your pole out here?" he asked the crowd.

"I got it," Bone said standing amongst the crowd of young men.

"Let's go slide on them hoe niggas real quick," Nutso told him. As they walked off to get in his, car, a blue and white CPD cruiser turned the corner at full speed.

"Twelve!" MCK Reese yelled as he took off running as fast as he could. Nine times out of ten, he had his gun and some drugs on him. A few of the moes ran too so the police wouldn't just chase Bone. Nutso felt like because he wasn't dirty. He didn't have to run.

"Hands in the air!" A young black cop screamed at Nutso with his gun drawn.

"Aight, man, be cool," Nut gruffed raising his hands as the officer grabbed him and shoved him onto the hood of his patrol car and started to search him.

"What's this?" The officer asked holding a dub rock of crack.

"Shit, I don't know. I don't sell no mufuckin' crack," Nutso snapped to the dirty officer. He did sell crack but not anything as small as a dub rock.

"If you don't sell crack, then why did you have this rock in your pocket? Are you a smoker?"

"That shit wasn't in my pocket. You never even dug yo' hand in my pocket," Nutso replied.

"Okay, smart-ass. Move around. If I catch you back out here, you're going to jail," the officer replied pushing him away from the car.

Nutso smacked his lips. "You ol' Uncle Tom-ass nigga!" Nutso shouted to the officer. "Instead of trying to uplift, help, protect and serve a young, black man, you tryna plant drugs on me and make me a statistic. You ain't got no kind of respect for your badge. You should be out here solving a murder or preventing one but instead, you rather waste time harassing an innocent man. With all due respect sir, you can suck my dick!" he said giving the officer a much needed reality check. For a moment, the officer stood there looking dumb. He thought about locking Nut up but decided against it. He just got into his squad car and rode away.

Chapter 18

Christmas Bash

My nigga Bucky wasn't too much in the hood now-a-days. Once shit got serious between me and Reesie and he couldn't pick sides, he decided to dedicate all of his time to the rap game. He put in endless hours in the studio, dropping mixtape after mixtape until he signed a deal with an independent record label. He was preparing to drop his debut album 'Risked it All' .He had a strong buzz off his latest mixtape. I decided to call him to see if he could spare some time to perform at my party.

"Hello?" Bucky answered slowly. I could tell when my boy was high and I knew he was leaning hard.

"Damn law, who selling that shit that got you sounding like that?" I asked laughing.

"What's the demo, Moe?" He asked with a chuckle

"Shit, I'm tryna get like you. Put me on a song or something."

"Whenever you ready bro. I got some new shit I need somebody to drop a verse on anyway."

"I'm having a party at Adrianna's on Christmas and I need for you to come through and perform some of that new shit."

"Man, Moe, the last time I performed with the guys like nine mufuckas got popped and that was on Christmas."

"On Stone, law that was some fluke shit. We not on none of that this year. We just tryna have a good time," I said convincingly.

"Look, I got two new songs that we can shoot videos to during the party. How that sound?"

"That sound like a plan to me broski. That bitch gon' be lit fasho, But be safe, fat ass and I love you my nigga. I'll be in touch with you," I said before disconnecting the call. Now that I had Bucky online to perform, I knew the party would be epic.

***

Me and Nutso sat on 64th and King Drive waiting for Five to come out of his building. We had two bricks of coke in a black bookbag for him. He finally approached our car wearing a black hoodie under a black leather Pelle coat, a pair of black Timbs and a black skully over his long dreads. He had a Nike backpack over one of his shoulders.

"Damn pussy, you got us waiting on this hot ass block," I complained. Parkway Gardens AKA O-Block was a red zone in the city. The BDs and GDs were in a bloody war.

"Shut yo' crybaby ass up," Five joked waving me off before turning to Nut. "Wassup skud?" he asked him.

"Shit, tryna run this bag up, you good?"

"Hell yea," Five replied before reaching in his pocket and pulling out a thick wad of hundred dollar bills. It took him about ten minutes to count and recount $50,000.

"Hold the fuck up man if the money in yo' pocket then what the fuck you got in the bookbag? Why the fuck do you always have on a fuckin' bookbag every time I see you?" I asked him.

Five laughed before digging into his bookbag and pulling out a Colt .45 with a lemon squeeze on it and a thirty shot Glock 19."I was about to drop this off to one of the guys," he said lifting the Glock. "But I be keeping an extra pole and extra clips in my shit. You never know when it might go down. I bet y'all in this bitch naked as hell," he said.

"Come on now, Five. I thought you was smarter than that," Nutso said pulling out his Glock 27 at the same time as I upped my Glock 17.

"Okay cool," Five said with a chuckle. "Where that work at doe? I gotta whip that shit up before I shoot O.T.," he said and Nutso tossed him the bookbag with the bricks in it.

"I'ma be ready for y'all in about another week and a half," Five said opening the car door to get out.

"I'm having a Christmas party at Adrianna's and King Bucky performing and shooting a video in that bitch so make sure you show up."

"Man, the last Christmas party I showed up to I lost a homie," Five said. It seemed like the Christmas party of 2008 haunted everybody.

"Ain't shit going on this year bro. I promise you," I replied.

"Aight skud, I'll be there," Five said closing the door ,looking to his left and his right before walking off.

***

Nutso waited in a stolen Honda watching Sauce and his boys. He had a .40 on his lap while he smoked a Kush blunt. He opened the door and climbed out. "Y'all got some weed out here?" he asked the crowd of men that were closest to him. He wanted to get up on Sauce but he would recognize him immediately.

"Yeah, what you tryna get?" A short, dark skinned kid asked.

"Check it out," Nutso told him sliding his hands in his hoodie pockets under his coat. The kid approached him telling him the different deals that he had. When he got close enough, Nutso pulled out his gun and put three slugs in the kid's chest before unloading his clip at the rest of the crowd who were scattering away. He watched another guy fall and was satisfied with his work as he ran to his car and peeled off as somebody started shooting at him. It was too late though.

Killa sat in the backseat of Bone's Range Rover with a smug look on his face. I was in the passenger's seat. We were riding around smoking and talking about the Christmas party. Killa had a compact Millennium .45 in his inside coat pocket, secretly debating if he should kill both of us while he had the chance.

"Aye law, I just took a big L and I'm tryna get back on my feet. You think you could front me a brick?" Killa asked me.

"Yeah, but I'ma need $34,000 back."

"Damn, you gon tax me like that?" he asked raising his voice a little.

"Hell yeah. I'm taxing everybody. Plus, you the one that need it. I'm doing you a favor," I replied flatly.

"Damn lil bro, you starting to let that shit get to yo' head."

"Yeah, whatever nigga," I snorted. "$34,000 take it or leave it," I shot back causing Bone to erupt in laughter. One thing Bone was great at was instigating. He knew how to put the cables on any and everybody.

"You back there sounding broke as hell crying over thirty five racks. What you need a Gapper?" Bone asked before grabbing a knot of money out of his cup holder and tossing it on Killa's lap.

"Aye Bone, on the G, stop playing with me before I fuck you up. You a shorty to me," Killa said seriously.

"On Stone, you must be some new type of fool if you think you gon' fuck me up," Bone retorted looking at Killa through the rearview with his face screwed up.

"On the G, you better stay in a lil boy's place before you end up in a grown man's casket," Killa replied threateningly. He would never tolerate disrespect from a shorty that he watched grow up.

Bone didn't take threats lightly but by the time he turned around pointing his Glock at Killa, he was staring down the barrel of Killa's .45.

"Is y'all gon' shoot or have a mufuckin staring contest?" I asked looking from Bone to Killa. "Y'all both grown ass men so if y'all want to kill each other, then go head. I got enough funeral money for both of y'all," I stated.

"Drop me off on 105th and State," Killa said lowering his weapon.

"I should smoke yo' hoe ass for uppin' that pipe on me," Bone said still pointing his gun at Killa's chest.

"That shit over with lil bro," I told him.

Killa sat there steaming. The only thing he could think about while we dropped him off was how my time on earth would soon be over with. He vowed to send Bone with me if he had the chance.

The next day, me and Cinnamon were downtown on Michigan Avenue shopping for something to wear to my party. The party was in less than a week and neither one of us had an outfit. My first stop was the Burberry store. She found a few items but I didn't see anything that I wanted so we went to the Louis Vuitton store. As I grabbed a black and white Louie bubble coat, a familiar voice spoke from behind me.

"I know that's not Mo Money looking like new money," the voice said.

I looked back to see that it was L.O.'s skinny ass standing there with a grin on his face.

"Shit if I'm looking like new money, what you lookin like?" I asked admiring his white Prada shoes.

"You know how I do it," he replied looking down at himself. "Aye, do you remember the nigga Keem? He one of the Moes from 72nd and Merrill. He was next door to us in the hole when we was locked up together."

"Yeah, I remember him. What about him?"

"That's who I'm in this bitch with. I been out west hustling dope in K-Town with him," L.O. said leading me to the front of the store where Keem was standing.

"Keem, you remember Mo Money? He was my celly when I was fighting that pipe case." he said.

"Yes sah, what's the demo Law?" Keem asked me as we shook up.

"Shit, getting this money. I see you niggas out here on the same shit," I said before pulling out a wad of hundred dollar bills. "Go grab whatever you want and take it to the register while I rotate with them," I told Cinnamon passing her the money and the coat I had grabbed before turning back to L.O. and Keem.

"I'm having a party at Adrianna's on Christmas and my homie King Bucky performing. If y'all ain't busy, slide through and fuck with us. It's gone be fulla thots, free drinks, and the best gas," I told them.

"On Stone, I'll be there," L.O. promised before we all exchanged numbers and went our separate ways.

After I finished shopping, I decided to slide through 61st and Kimbark to let Lil Mike and 50 know about my party. When I pulled up, it looked like they were having a block party. This block was packed with women and men of all ages even though it was freezing cold outside.

"What's going on out here, law?" I asked my younger cousin Killa Key as I hopped out my car, leaving it running.

"Nigga, you know it's Panda Day. We all out here for Big cuz," he replied. In Chicago, whenever someone died, their birthday and the day they died on became their day. People celebrated that person in whatever way made them feel the best. Some partied, some mourned and some put in work.

"Where Lil Mike at?" I asked Killa Key after we shook up. "They in Big Johnny hallway shooting dice."

I headed for the court way building. As soon as I stepped in the hallway, the smell of Kush, liquor and Newports flooded my nose. Before I could make it to the basement where the dice game was being held, I was stopped by a tall, brown skinned guy with a long face and long dreads.

"Look at Lil Dre!" he said with a broad smile. "You grew the fuck up! You was just a little rugrat running around with a snotty nose and a fat ass pair of fake ones on," he said making everyone who was right there laugh at me.

"Damn, One Eighty when yo' old Busta Rhymes lookin ass get out?" I asked shaking up with him. He was my big homie, one of the Generals for the Stones. He was always catching a case and doing stretches of time.

"I been home for like a month now. I thought you wasn't gone show up for Panda Day. I was gon' fuck yo' lil crusty lip, Dave Chappelle lookin ass up," he joked. When we were together, we would crack jokes on each other all day.

"Mo Money, what's the demo law?" Lil Mike asked reaching out for a handshake. "What's the word, law? Where 50 fat ass?"

"In the basement getting his dumb ass hit on the dice."

I walked up on the dice game with a few fifty dollar bills in my hand. "What y'all shooting?" I asked no one in particular.

"Fifties and hundreds. The lil kid dice game in the corner," a brown-skinned guy with a smooth voice and a low wavy cut told me. He was my older cousin, Gio.

"Well, I got you faded for a hundred and you don't hit a hundred, big mouth," I told him before pulling out all the money I had on me and dropping two hundred dollar bills on the floor.

"Bet," Gio said before rolling the dice and catching a ten.

"You don't ten-four. A hundred and straight Ten a hundred," I said dropping four fifties on the floor.

Gio bet and then re-rolled his point. I was salty and it showed. Everybody knew I hated losing on the dice.

"Who got me?" he asked after scooping up his money.

"Shoot two hundred, hit two hundred, sweet ass nigga," I said dropping my money.

"On Stone, y'all done got this nigga started," 50 said with a sigh.

They all knew that I was an avid gambler and once I got started I wouldn't stop until I was broke or I won everything.

Gio rolled a six and we bet a six-eight and a straight six for two hundred apiece. He shot a few times before crapping out.

"I shoot two hundred and hit two hundred to anybody who want it?" I said dropping the money for the bet.

Thirty minutes later, I had stripped down to my wifebeater and I was down on one knee winning a lot of money. After so long, Cinnamon had come into the hallway. I had forgotten that I had left her in the car. Out of nowhere, I felt something get jammed into my ribs.

"You know what time it. Empty them pockets," Someone disguising his voice gruffed.

"You can have this lil money. It ain't shit," I said arrogantly. My arrogance was hiding my anger. Cranktown was a Black Stone hood and majority of the Moes from Cranktown were related to me. A lot of them considered me one of their own, considering that I was always around when I wasn't in The Hundreds. I couldn't believe somebody had the nerve to rob me.

"Yo' scary ass," the voice said with less edge. I turned around to see that it was Arab playing with me.

"Stop playin' so much," I gruffed while everyone laughed.

"Nigga, fuck you. I'm tryna figure out why the fuck you in the hood and you ain't hit my line. I could have had a stain lined up for us," he replied pulling his skullcap over his face. He actually looked like a damn fool due to his long, puffy ponytail poking out the back of his cap.

"I'm straight right now but on Christmas I'm having a party at Adrianna's and my homie King Bucky gon' be there so y'all make sure y'all come out and fuck with me," I told him and everybody else.

"You know I'm in that bitch," One Eighty said, doing a little dance.

"Let me holla at you real quick Moe," I told him.

"What's the demo, lil bro?" He asked once we were outside standing in front of the court way.

"Here bro. Welcome home," I told him passing him all the money I'd won in the dice game.

"Gratitude beloved," he said giving me a brotherly hug.

"It ain't shit bro. I'm just glad to see you home."

"Did you stand on that business for Panda yet?"

"Naw, not yet but the nigga who did that shit gon' die. On Stone, I ain't letting up until then," I told him before walking to my car, hopping in, and pulling off.

"You a pretty ass lil girl," I said holding my newborn daughter, Paradise, in my arms. She was beautiful. She shared my dark brown skin tone. She had my eyebrows and the most beautiful brown eyes I'd ever seen. The moment I laid eyes on her, I fell in love. I had been playing with her for over an hour. I was so amazed by how much she looked like me.

"You my lil twin, ain't you?" I asked her in a baby's voice.

Holding Paradise in my arms, I instantly regretted not being there when she came out. I should've been the first person she saw. I felt remorse for how I was carrying Precious too.

"Go in my pants pocket and grab a few racks out of that money that's in there," I told Precious pointing at a pair of True Religion jeans that were crumbled up on my floor. "Spend all that shit on Paradise. Make sure you get her everything she need," I told her as she counted out the money.

"You sexy just like yo' daddy. Let's hope you be smart like yo' daddy and not dumb like Mommy," I said to Paradise loud enough for Precious to hear me. I was intentionally trying to irritate her. It seemed like ever since she got pregnant, our relationship deteriorated. I suddenly wanted some of her attention. She was my child's mother so she was special to me.

"I love you, baby," I whispered to Paradise before planting kisses all over her face.

***

While I was in the house playing daddy, Nutso sat in the passenger's seat of a beat up pickup truck that Buck was driving.

"Let me taste some of that kill you smoking on," Buck asked reaching out for the blunt Nutso was smoking.

"Naw, just keep telling me what you saw," Nutso replied dumping ashes on the floor.

"I saw Reesie in the car with Smack. On the Four Corner Hustler, I know for sure it was him because I walked up on the car," Buck replied holding up four fingers. They were sitting on 111th and Vernon. Buck had told him he knew where Sauce and his crowd hung out at on cold days like this one. Binky, Bone and MCK Reese were in a stolen Nissan parked behind Buck's car.

"You need me?" Buck asked quickly upping his .38 Special. He pulled it out so quick Nut didn't even see his hand move.

"Naw man," Nutso chuckled. "Here go something for you to get right with," he said handing him a eight ball of crack. "Now, I need for you to throw a rock through that window and run,"

"Good looking, nephew, just bring my car back in one piece," Buck told him getting out of the truck. Nutso chambered a bullet in his Tech as he watched Buck find a rock or a chunk of ice and sent it crashing through the front window of a big red house before taking off running .He couldn't help but laugh when Buck slipped and fell face first in the snow. A few seconds later, a few young niggas were coming out of the house. Nutso hopped out the truck at the same time as Binky and MCK Reese. He squeezed his trigger as Binky shot the SKS that he was cradling. They let off every round they had while watching the guys fall and try to scramble away from the shots. Once all the shots stopped and bodies dropped, all you heard were tires screeching from Nutso and Bone burning rubber trying to get away from the scene.

***

Reesie was steaming when he heard the news. "Fuck is wrong with you hoe ass niggas? Y'all acting like straight bitches, steady letting them hoe ass niggas put pressure on y'all. On the Foe, I'm bout to show you niggas how to slide," he told Sauce and a few of the foes before grabbing his Glock 30 and storming out of the house.

I was standing on D Block talking to a bitch who I had recently fucked but forgotten her name. I was really there dropping off some work to Von D because Bone was somewhere with Nut. Bone had all of the bros his age serving with him. They were mostly shorties from the hood just trying to be a part of something. I didn't judge them because not too long ago I was in the same boat.

I noticed a black Porsche truck with tinted windows creeping up the block. I tried but I couldn't see how many heads were in the truck. "Which one of y'all got pipe out here?" I asked no one in particular. "Y'all got cars creeping through this bitch and ain't nobody saying shit. What the fuck going on?" I asked mad that they weren't on how they should've been.

"I'm on point, big bro," a kid wearing a ski mask said clutching by his waist. A few seconds later, the Porsche truck was hitting the block again.

"On that mufuckin truck!" I said loudly once the truck was damn near in the middle of the block. The truck stopped and I started to walk off as the windows dropped and shots started ringing from every window. I upped my Glock and returned fire while taking cover behind a parked Mazda. "Shoot back!" I yelled to the shorty wearing the ski mask as I watched him run away with his gun in his hand. Once the shots stopped and the Porsche truck peeled off, I got up from where I was to see that four people had gotten shot, including the woman who I was just talking to.

"Aye lil bro check it out!" I yelled at the kid who was supposed to be protecting the block. I think his name was Rod.

"What's the word, Moe?" Rod asked slowly approaching me.

"Why the fuck didn't you blow back?"

"Shidd." he shrugged then said, "They had four guns. I only got one, shit just didn't add up to me."

The stupid ass look on his face blew me. I looked around the block. I knew that soon police and paramedics would be everywhere.

"Let me see yo' pipe," I told Rod and he passed me the Ruger he had on his waist. "This bitch work?" I asked examining the gun.

He nodded, and I shot him in the thigh.

"Next time, use it you hoe ass nigga," I gruffed before running off to my car. I watched Rod fall out in tears as I screeched away. I decided to keep his gun since he wasn't going to use it anyway.

The day of our Christmas party came quick. I watched Cinnamon stand in the mirror looking amazing in a Lime green Chanel sweater, a pair of dark blue jeans, and a pair of white and lime green Chanel shoes. I was dressed in a black and Lime green Dior Crewneck sweater, a pair of black True Religion jeans, a Dior beanie, and a pair of black Timbs.

"Are you ready yet?" Cinnamon asked.

"Yeah, you can go start the car up," I told her before grabbing my Glock and throwing a white Obama head pill in my mouth. Ever since Arab introduced me to Ecstasy, I had been hooked.

"Tonight, is my night," I sang as I filled every pocket I had with wads of hundred dollar bills before leaving out for the party.

When we arrived at the club, I could see that it was already jammed packed inside. I skipped the line and walked straight in to see Nutso and Bone surrounded by a crowd of women.

"Yo' goofy ass always late for some shit," Nutso told me as we half hugged.

"Let me find out you goofy ass niggas tryna be twins," I laughed when I peeped that both of them had freshly cut mohawks.

"Naw, this just my son son," Nutso joked grabbing Bone's head.

"I see you niggas was tryna get it in without me," a voice said at the same time as I felt a arm wrap around my shoulder.

"T Stone, what's the demo bro?" Nutso asked T Stone who was dressed in a Dolce and Gabbana outfit and a pair of wheat Timbs. His long hair was freshly twisted hanging down past his shoulders. "On Stone, I'm hurt that the brothers, MY brothers." he stressed, "Didn't invite me to the party. It's cool doe. I know what it is," he said walking off. He took a couple steps before turning back around. "Aw yeah, I got a plug on the pipes too. Hit me up if y'all need a crate or something," he added with a sly grin.

"That nigga ain't got no mufuckin' plug on no pipes. He fronting his shit," I spat watching him walk off. I was still in my feelings about that fight we had.

"I don't know. He probably do doe. If so, I hope he don't sell none to the wrong mufuckas," Bone said.

By 1AM, the party was in full effect. Everybody was high, drunk, and enjoying themselves. King Bucky arrived, and we were in our section, rotating Kush Blunts and popping bottles while we waited until it was time for him to perform. When the DJ played 'Jeremih's '5' Senses' all the women in the club went crazy. I was mingling around the dance floor trading what's ups with different people until I bumped into Ashley.

"What's up, shorty?" I asked extending my arms for a hug. I tried to hide it, but I was over excited to see her.

"Hey," she said softly, flashing a smile and giving me a tight hug.

"Damn, I miss yo' scent," I said giving her a kiss on the neck. The perfume she had on was intoxicating. It was her favorite Chanel perfume.

"I miss you, too, Baby Dre."

"Huh?" I asked faking like I couldn't hear her. "It's too loud in here. Let's go outside and talk."

"Talk about what, Dre? I came here to get out the house and have some fun. I don't feel like dealing with feelings or going through any bullshit tonight," she said.

"Just give me a few minutes," I told her, grabbing her hand and leading her to the front exit.

"And where the fuck are y'all going?" I heard Cinnamon scream over the music just as we made it to the front door.

"We going out front. I need to holla at her about some shit," I said quickly letting go of Ashley's hand.

"What you need to holla at her about that say in here?"

"Don't start tweaking baby. Trust me, I'll be right back," I said smoothly.

"Don't play with me, boy. I'll beat your ass in this club."

"That's not for us baby. Go grab a drink and shake some ass and I'll be right back," I said with a smile. I held eye contact with her until she rolled her eyes and walked off.

Once we were outside, I looked at Ashley up and down admiring how good she looked in Alexander McQueen dress she had on.

"What creep?" she asked with a smile.

"It seem like you happy as hell without me."

"Boy, didn't I just tell you that I didn't want to do this tonight?"

"I just wanna know if you happier without me because if you is, then I'ma have to accept that but if not, I need to know what I could do to make this shit right."

After a few seconds of thinking, Ashley spoke up. "The question should be are you happy without me?" She asked looking down at her pumps.

"Hell naw," I replied quickly. I didn't even have to think about that. "I think about you all the time and to be honest, the only reason I'm out here fuckin with these hoes is because you not around. What do you expect for me to do, beat my dick?" I asked jokingly.

"No stupid," she replied with a giggle. "I just don't know, Baby Dre. I honestly don't know if I'm happier with or without you. It's just so much confusion, pain and worry that comes with being with you. I don't know what I want to do because I don't want to be without you either," she said, and I could see the conflict on her face.

"So, you don't know?" I asked raising an eyebrow.

"No, I don't, Dre."

"All well," I said sadly. "Whenever you figure it out, get at me and let me know," I said before kissing her on the lips and walking off back into the club. So many thoughts and emotions were running through my mind all at the same time. Part of me was hurt but the rest of me was angry. I felt like I was too young and living too fast to be this pressed over a woman.

When I walked back into the club, I saw Bucky's camera man, ChipSet setting up his equipment so I knew that it was time for me to put my emotions aside and throw my game face on for the video shoot. I hopped on the stage and grabbed the mic.

"Where the fuck gang nem at?" I asked and the club went crazy. "All my niggas get the fuck up here," I said and everybody from the hood and the people that I invited personally flooded the stage. "Merry muthafucking Christmas. Get you a Stone, we do it better!" I yelled as 'Show Out' by Roscoe Dash came on and we all started flashing and throwing money.

As the song was going off, King Bucky was walking onto stage wearing so many iced out chains that I didn't know which one to admire first. The crowd went crazy as his song 'Took The Risk' came on and he started performing.

The X pill I was off of had me super charged and I was having the time of my life. When King Bucky's song 'Chain Glow' came on, Nutso pulled out a couple diamond chains of his own and put them on. He was standing next to Bucky while he rapped in front of the camera. All of us were sweating, dropping, or throwing up gang signs or throwing money. We all felt like celebrities, at least I did. I felt an arm go around my shoulder and thought it was T Stone again until I saw him on stage by Breezy doing his shit. I noticed that Nutso's face dropped and the color from his skin drained.

When I looked to my right, I almost thought I saw a ghost. Reesie was standing right next to me with his arm draped around my shoulder. I backed up a few steps, unintentionally bumping into Ray Real, who was doing his thing in front of the camera.

"I ain't on shit, you good," Reesie mouthed to me as he pulled his money out of his pockets and started thumbing through bills.

I looked around to see Sauce, Shody Shod, Beezy, Smack, Lil 4, and everybody else who fucked with Reesie, on stage with us. You could tell who was important because they all wore matching gold Rolexes. Once the performance was over, me and Reesie stood face to face.

"Back from the dead, huh?" I asked with a mug.

"It look like the back of the building in this bitch. All these members in here, I had to show up. Plus, I wanted to see yo' face when you found out that I'm still here, still on yo' ass," Reesie said smiling, showing his gap. I could smell the Kush on his breath and the Patron seeping out his pores. He could see the surprise hidden in my expression. "You took my lil brother, I'ma take everything from you. On the foe," he vowed looking me dead in my eyes.

At first, I was confused by his last statement but then I quickly put two and two together and figured it out. It was D Thang who I had shot up the day of Mike Moe's funeral. That's why we never heard about Reesie dying or having a funeral.

"I didn't know that was D Thang. I thought he was you. I would've actually let him slide but it is what it is. I'm glad yo' scary ass done hiding."

"I haven't been hiding. On the foe, I been real close," Reesie said with a chuckle while making a gun with his fingers. "Y'all better stop all that lacking y'all be doing," he said moving his dreads out his face and over his shoulders.

"I promised fat ass that I wouldn't be on no bullshit tonight, so you get a pass."

"Well, I didn't promise him shit. So, I just might shoot this bitch up but then again, I wanna fuck Ashley before I smoke you," Reesie shot back with a laugh. "Keep yo' eyes open, hoe nigga," he said dropping the five at me and fading into the crowded club.

"You want me to smoke his ass?" Five asked.

"Naw, I got him," I said. Even though we were uneasy, we continued to party for the rest of the night. All of us were uncomfortable knowing that Reesie and his crowd were in the same building as us but fortunately the night ended with nobody getting shot or killed.

The next day, the loud ringing of my phone woke me up. It was Killa calling. "What's up folks?" I answered through a dry, scratchy throat.

"On the G, why the nigga Lil 4 rob me last night after the party," Killa said speaking a mile a minute.

"How you let him get up on you?" I asked gazing over at Cinnamon who was out cold, slobbing on my pillow.

"You know that nigga sneaky as hell. He was waiting for me by my whip. The nigga took my chain, and that money I owed you for that brick you gave me," Killa replied.

Hearing that caused me to fully wake up. "So, you let that nigga take my bread? You a straight fuck up bro. I see how yo' goofy ass got caught with all that work. You don't know how to move at all on Black Stone!'' I snapped.

Killa tried to speak but I kept going in. "I don't care how you gotta do it but get my mufucking bread bro or else we gon' have a mufuckin problem," I said before hanging up in his face.

"Let a nigga get some of that pussy," I told Cinnamon while feeling on her trying to wake her up.

"Boy stop," she said aggressively. She killed me by acting like fucking her was such a privilege.

"Let a nigga get some of that pussy," I repeated more demanding this time.

"No, stop acting so thirsty," she mumbled sleepily.

"You ain't never tryna let a nigga fuck. You can take yo' ass home," I said under my breath.

"What?" She asked turning around to face me. She was looking mean as hell.

"Girl, I ain't say shit. Take yo' ass back to sleep," I said laying back down.

Chapter 19

Snakes In The Grass

Bone, Binky, Lil C, and a few of the lil Moes were out early serving fiends, left and right.

"We got all the thots on our dick. All these lame ass niggas wanna be gang. We ain't never going back to being broke and even if we did, we just gon' turn our savage up like Money and Nut nem did and rob everybody," Lil D claimed smoking a Kush blunt, leaning on a gate. They were posted on D Block. Lil D was a frail, yellow kid who followed after Bone and Binky. He wanted his name to hold as much weight as theirs did.

"First off, we not gon' fall off. It's impossible," Binky said snatching the blunt from his fingers. "Secondly, we not Nut nem. Go grab some more blunts from the store. I need a break from yo' mouth for a few minutes," he added after taking a pull from the blunt.

"On Stone, I already met the plug. Pretty soon, we gon' be able to branch off and do our own shit, you feel me?" Bone said to Binky as they watched Lil D and his cousin turn the corner.

"You think the plug gon' give you the same prices he giving bro nem? "Binky asked but before Bone could respond, they heard what sounded like thirty shots go off. They both upped their pipes and took off towards 107th Street where the shots had come from. They made it to 107th Street to see Lil D lying face down with two bullet holes in his back and one in the back of his head.

"Damn bro," Bone mumbled trying to fight back tears. He looked down the street to see Lil D's cousin who was also stretched out.

"Call up Nut and tell him to bring that big boy over here," he told Binky wiping tears from his cheeks.

As soon as the heat from the police cooled off, Bone, Binky and Nutso were riding in a stolen Mazda with tinted windows. Binky had a Mac 90 laying across his lap.

"On Stone, we gotta clap one of them hoe ass niggas. I don't give a fuck who it is," Nutso said as they rode through London Town where they knew Sauce was staying at. They spotted a crowd of young niggas walking with Sauce leading the pack. "Spin back around," Nutso told Bone who was driving.

As they rode back up on the crowd, Binky hung out the window cradling a Mac 90. He started shooting rapidly trying to hit everyone in the crowd. He smiled when he seen Sauce drop and heard him scream.

"I hit Sauce bitch ass!" Binky said excitedly as Bone cruised off like nothing happened.

***

Later that night, I received a unexpected call from Ashley.

"Hey boy," she said when I answered.

"What's up, love?" I replied smoothly.

"What you doing? I hope you not laid up with one of your hoes."

"Naw, today is my *me* day. I been in the crib, coolin, playing the game. What you on, doe?"

"Nothing, bored," she replied with a sigh.

"I should have known that. It seem like the only time you call me is when you bored."

"That's a lie. I call whenever I feel like talking to a friend."

"A friend?" I asked screwing my face up as if she could see me.

"Boy, you know what I meant by that. Just because we not together, don't mean that I don't be wanting to hear from you. I still care about what you're doing, who you're with, where you be at and how you're feeling."

"Fasho," I said and then it got awkwardly silent for a moment.

"Hello?" Ashley said.

"Yeah, so you still don't know if you happier without me?" I asked.

Ashley took a deep breath before responding, "No, I'm still not sure about that yet. Maybe if you would stop pressuring me to be happy without you, I wouldn't be. It almost seem like you want me to say yes so you can be free and be a hoe. I feel like you're pushing me away from you," she said ·

''Naw, it ain't like that at all. The last thing I'm tryna do is push you away. I want you right here with me. I been questioning our bond lately and it should've never gotten to this. I'm in love with you and it's not easy cause you sooo...''

"So, what?"

"So quick to run away when shit start getting hard."

Ashley smacked her lips. "Whatever Dre, how is your daughter doing?" She asked sarcastically.

"Don't start with that shit."

"I'm just asking. Maybe, I want to meet it."

"*It* has a name and it's Paradise," I replied slightly offended.

"Damn, I see you're the world's greatest dad now," she replied with even more sarcasm.

"Call me back when you not on yo' goofy shit," I said, and Ashley hung up in my face.

She couldn't hide the fact that she was jealous that I had a baby with another woman. I knew that was a scar that wouldn't heal anytime soon. I felt like I couldn't win for losing with her. I had real profound feelings for her, but I guess our best days were behind us. At least, that's what it was starting to look like and that was really fucking with me mentally.

The next few weeks dragged by; business was good but nothing special was going on besides a lot of back and forth shootings and a few of Bone's homies getting locked up. We weren't tripping because we had bond money for everybody.

My birthday was at the end of January, and it came quick. Me, Nutso, Bone and Breezy were riding in a jet black Maserati that I had rented just for my birthday.

"This shit be having me in my glory, on Stone," Bone slurred holding a red Transformer head pill in his hand before throwing it in his mouth and washing it down with a shot of Remy.

"Yo' baby ass don't be rolling for real," Nutso quipped knocking down a shot of Remy.

"Turn the radio down. This Buck hype ass calling me," Bone said in his usual slow slur.

"Hello?" he answered. "You sure?" he said after a few moments of him listening. "Where you at? I'm 'bout to pull up," he said and after a few seconds he hung up the phone. "Pull up on 111th and Edbrooke," he told me.

Buck was already waiting outside for us on 111th and Edbrooke when we pulled up.

"What's the word ?" Bone asked him after he climbed in the backseat smushing breezy in the middle.

"Y'all know my nephews be hanging out with Smack. They was all at my crib smoking and playing the game and I overheard them talking about they know where yo' bitch or yo' BM live and they gon do' something to get you back for what you did to somebody," Buck said.

"Who?" I asked already knowing he was talking about me because I was the only one in the car who had a child.

"You," he said nodding towards me. "But that ain't all. They was saying something about somebody named Killa."

"What was they saying about him?"

"I can't remember all I know is that they kept saying his name. I'd advise y'all to stay away from him," Buck said screwing his face up looking ugly as hell.

"I don't like his bitch ass anyway," Bone spat.

"As I think about it, I remember them saying something about somebody bonding him out and some more shit but don't get me to lying and making shit up."

I pulled out a fifty dollar bill and handed it to Buck.

"Slide through the block tomorrow and Bone gon' give you a ball on GP," I told him before popping the locks so he could hop out.

"So, what you think they on with yo' BM ?" Nutso asked me as I drove off.

"I don't know, cuz. I was thinking the same shit. I don't even know how them niggas knew about my BM," I replied.

"You think that nigga Killa on some backdoor shit?"

"We gon' see. That nigga sholl be actin weird as hell lately."

"I hope he is on some snake shit so I can be the one to nail his dumb ass," Bone said.

Shit was getting deeper by the day with the war we had going on. Reesie was a grimey ass nigga and you never knew what he was up to or how he might strike. I didn't put anything past him. Hearing that them niggas were plotting on my family had me heated. They were ready to cross the line so I had to touch them niggas before they touched me or one of mine.

The next day, Killa called my phone early in the morning. I was laid up with a bitch that Lil C introduced me to.

"What's up?" I answered groggily.

"Bro, I got a sweet ass stain for you," Killa claimed sounding excited.

"Talk to me," I said wiping the crust from my eyes.

"My cousin put me in tune with some clowns that's tryna pay $40,000 a brick for some good work."

"Where they at?" I asked ready to jump up and get dressed.

"They flying in from Utah. They'll be here Friday,"

"How many they tryna grab?"

"Ten."

"Murch it."

"On the G, "Killa replied with a chuckle.

"Aight well, whenever they land just have them pull up on us. I'ma have the ten ready."

"Them out of town niggas scared of us Chicago niggas just off the reputation we got. We gon' have to make them feel comfortable."

"Whatever, nigga, but I been meaning to ask you what's up with yo' case?"

"Shit, really my lawyer still waiting on discovery."

"You never even told me how you ended up coming up with that bond money."

"My OG had to put up her house as collateral. I promised her that I was gon' stay out the way. What made you ask that doe?"

"I was just wondering, gang."

"Fasho. This my lil bitch calling me. I'ma hit you back in a minute," Killa said quickly hanging up on me. My intuition was telling me that something was up with him. I didn't believe he was on no snake shit but for some reason I felt like he was living by the motto.

Why do ten when you can tell on a friend?

I was starting to think that he was trying to get me jammed up.

Chapter 20

Choices

Later that night, I was parked outside of Ashley's house while arguing with her over the phone.

"Dude, I'm telling you that you don't need to bring shit. I'll buy you some mufucking clothes to wear!" I yelled in frustration. After thinking about the info that Buck had given us, he wasn't sure if Smack said my bitch or my BM so I was putting Ashley up in a hotel just in case they tried something stupid.

"Ugh, I'm on my way out," she said hanging up on me. A few seconds later, she was storming out of the house and stomping to my car with her face balled up. "I just can't comprehend how you continue to find some way to ruin my life! Why the fuck would anybody want to do anything to me? I'm not your bitch no more," She screamed after climbing into my passenger's seat.

"Would you please shut the fuck up with all that screaming?" I asked calmly.

For the rest of the ride, Ashley sat quietly, staring out the window. She didn't even look at me. I already had Nutso and Bone at the Cambria Hotel with Precious and Paradise. I was going to have them staying there until I found them somewhere else to live.

Once we stepped inside the room, all hell broke loose. "Seriously, Dre!" Ashley asked angrily.

"You really gon' bring me to the same room you got this hoe in?" she asked as soon as she seen Precious.

Precious didn't respond she just gave Ashley a deadly stare.

"Chill the fuck out," I told Ashley.

"Naw you got the wrong bitch. I'm not her or any one of them other bitches you deal with. You might as well drop me off back at home."

"Yeah, that bitch need to go because she doing too much in front of our daughter," Precious stated.

"Bitch, fuck you!" Ashley spat taking a step towards Precious. It was kind of funny because she was tall and skinny and Precious was short and skinny, and neither was truly aggressive so I kind of wanted to see them fight.

"Man, both of y'all shut the fuck up," I snapped fighting back the smile that threatened to spread across my face. "I can't even fuckin think with y'all going back and forth like lil ass girls. Now, if y'all wanna go home and get smoked then get the fuck on. I don't even care no more. I tried playing Captain Save-a- Hoe but y'all making this shit too difficult," I said pulling out a blunt and breaking it down. "Matter fact, Nut go pay for another two rooms," I said and cuz got right on it.

"On Stone, y'all need to be on Maury," Bone laughed eating a box of Lemon Heads.

"Fuck you fat ass," Precious said mugging him.

"I know you wanna fuck me but big bro might not like that," Bone countered cracking himself up.

"Bitch never."

"That's what they all say before Daddy long dick get to 'em," he said once again cracking himself up. I wanted to laugh too but Precious looked too mad and I didn't want to make her any madder.

"Rooms 101 and 201," Nutso said entering the room throwing me two key cards.

"Bye, go make yourself comfortable," I told Ashley tossing her a key card. She left the room without a word.

"Give us the other room. We gon let y'all spend some family time together," Nutso said. I tossed him the other key and him and Bone left the room.

"I'm about to get in the shower. Paradise been woke all day. She just fell asleep so don't bother her," Precious told me before pulling her shirt over her head. She didn't have on a bra and her small, perky breasts were calling my name. I waited about five minutes before going in the bathroom to see her washing up under the shower water with her eyes closed.

"Get out," she said flatly without even opening her eyes. If she did, she would've seen that I was already naked and on my way inside the shower with her.

"Stop acting like that," I told her in a hushed tone as I climbed in the shower. I stood behind her and reached around and started rubbing her clit.

"You always try to treat me so bad but just expect for me to be so in love with you," she said turning around to face me. She wrapped her arms around my neck and stared in my eyes as I massaged her pussy.

"It ain't like that, P. I really do love you and you mean a lot to me but it's just so much going on in my life right now that I can't show you the love that you want me to show you. I know you don't understand that right now but hopefully one day you will. One day me and you gon' be happy as hell together," I promised before kissing her passionately, shoving my tongue deep inside her mouth. I picked up one of her legs, wrapped it around my waist and entered my hard dick inside her wet pussy. I loved how she always was soaking wet for me. I rammed my dick in and out of her hard and fast while she cursed, scratched my back, and planted kisses all over my face and neck. Twenty minutes later, I was exploding inside of her.

"Now, let me wash you up," I told her while pouring Dove body wash on her bath sponge. We took turns washing each other up from head to toe. For a moment, it felt like we were connected by more than just our daughter. We felt right, like she was the one I was supposed to be with. I felt loved and looking into her beautiful eyes, I knew deep down I really loved her more than I thought I did. I didn't want our moment to end.

"I'm about to go check on everybody else before we call it a night," I told her after we dried off and got dressed.

"That's all I am to you huh, a good fuck?" Precious asked, hurt by the fact that I was leaving.

"Naw, you my daughter's mother," I told her before leaving out of the room before the conversation went any further and I said something that would get both of us hurt.

When I entered Ashley's room, she was sitting Indian style on the bed, in her bra and panties, with her laptop on her lap.

"It look like you was waiting for me to slide in," I said plopping down on the bed, pushing her back so that she was laying on her back and I was laying between her legs.

"Nope, I was actually waiting for Dolla to text me and let me know he was downstairs," she said with a evil grin.

"Yeah, aight. Dolla ass a be dead before the elevator close," I said not hiding the fact that her comment struck a nerve. "Damn. So, I can't get a taste?" I asked kissing my way down her stomach. She pushed my head down to where her panties were, to eat her pussy. I licked her pussy like a man on a mission.

After she came twice, I climbed on top of her. "Give me a kiss?" I said and we kissed a few times before I pulled out my throbbing dick.

"What are you doing?" She asked in between kisses as I rubbed the head of my dick up and down her wet opening.

"Fuck you think I'm doing?"

"Naw not tonight, Daddy, you better go fuck ya baby momma," she said flashing another evil smile before pushing me off of her and grabbing her laptop.

When I entered the room Moe nem was in, it looked like there was a fire going on due to how foggy it was with Kush smoke. "Fuck you looking like a lil bitch for? Fix yo' mufuckin face," Nutso told me making Bone laugh.

"On Stone, these hoes blowing me. Let me hit that gas," I said before snatching the smoldering blunt he was holding.

"That's because you a cuffin' ass nigga, Yo' lame ass fall in love with every bitch you bump," Nutso teased me making Bone laugh even harder. Bone knew that his laughing was pushing my buttons. I hated when he laughed at me.

"On Stone, you lying," I replied. "Something ain't right about the sale Killa supposed to be setting up. I got a feeling that that nigga on some police shit," I said before taking a deep pull from the blunt I was holding.

"Hell yeah, cause if they overpaying for the work, then nine times outta ten they the feds. If they under paying, they the feds and if they coming correct then it just might be a stick up and Killa taught us that himself," Nutso said with a chuckle.

"On Stone!" I said joining in on the laughter. "I know it's something fishy going on and if it is, I'm going out shooting. I'ma try to smoke all they ass before I let them walk me out in cuffs. They gon' try to slam a mufucka either way it go," I said feeling high as hell off the potent Kush.

"I was thinking the same thing because but I was thinking we should have some more of the bros go with us just in case," Nutso replied reaching for the blunt with his long fingers. I intentionally passed the blunt to Bone just to irritate him.

"Naw, just get at T Stone and let him know that we need him and tell him to bring some of them pipes too."

"Hell naw, fuck his snake ass!" Bone growled.

"He won't snake us. I know that for a fact. He been down since day one."

"Reesie was, too," Bone shot back.

"Yup, you right so if T Stone tweak, we gone smoke his ass too," I told them and for the rest of the night we smoked and plotted.

Thursday came and I wasn't even feeling like myself. I spent most of the day thinking about what I'd been through over the course of the last five years and everything that got me to where I was now. Shit didn't add up to me. I had a bigger bag than most 19 year olds in the city but I wasn't even enjoying that shit. I hadn't even been out the city. I spent more time frowning than smiling.

Every day I was facing a different struggle that came along with living in the city. It was a million niggas that hated Risky Road so not only did I have to be on point for them but I had to watch out for my own homies, the niggas who should've been on the same side as me. I really wished that things could've played out differently. I wish I would've let Reesie have that half a pound instead of me letting my pride get in the way and letting that small shit tear the hood apart. Looking back on it now, I could honestly say that that shit wasn't worth it at all. I wanted to go back to the days when it was all of us against whoever, but it seemed like those days were another lifetime ago.

A million different thoughts ran through my mind while I played with Paradise. I wasn't sure if tonight would be the last night I got the chance to hold her so my plan was to cherish this little time that I had left with her.

"You such a pretty, pretty baby," I told her rubbing our noses together. "Ugh, come on Pooka. Stop slobbin' on my face dude!" I laughed calling her a nickname that I'd heard her mother call her plenty of times. "Ughhh man!" I laughed even harder as I held her in the air above my head while she giggled and continued to slob all over my face and neck.

"That is your twin, boy. She looks just like you," Ashley said walking up to where I was sitting on the bed. I hadn't even heard her enter my room.

"Say thank you," I told Paradise facing her towards Ashley.

"Can I hold her?"

"Only if you promise not to throw her," I joked.

"Shut up," Ashley giggled, grabbing Paradise out of my hands. "Look at you, you a heavy little baby," she said rocking her in her arms. "I'm glad she not as black as you," she joked.

"You just a hater. Give me my princess back," I replied taking Paradise from her just as Precious entered the room.

"I know she wasn't just holding my daughter," she said mean mugging me.

"First off, she not yo' daughter. She is *our* daughter and secondly, shut the fuck up sometimes. You be worried about the wrong shit," I snapped.

"I was just complimenting her on how beautiful she is and if it makes you feel any better, I won't touch her again," Ashley told Precious.

"Please and thank you," Precious said stubbornly.

"That's that lil girl shit again," I chimed in. "What if something bad happened to me, would y'all be able to forget about competing with each other to hold me down or what?" I asked them both.

"What kind of question is that?" Precious asked.

"Both of y'all know how I move in the streets so y'all both know that any minute could be my last minute. I could die or go to jail any day and if that day came I don't need y'all fussing and fighting each other. I'ma need y'all to both have my best interest in mind. I'm saying this because tomorrow I got something big lined up and I don't know how that shit gon' play out to be honest. I got a funny feeling about that shit, but I need to know that if the worst were to happen y'all gon' hold me down like I need y'all too and secondly, I just want the rest of this night to be as peaceful as possible," I said looking back and forth from Ashley to Precious.

"What are you supposed to be doing tomorrow?" Ashley asked.

"It really don't even matter what I'm doing. Just know I'm doing it but Bone gon' stay here with y'all while I handle that shit. If shit don't go right, I left almost a hundred thousand dollars at my OG crib. It's in my room, inside my mattress. My goal is to make it back here but if I don't, y'all split that bread and anything else you ever need just call Bone," I explained.

"Why are you talking like you're going to get yourself killed or something?" Precious asked with worry written all over her pretty face.

"I'm just preparing for the worst," I said handing her our daughter before stretching my small frame. "I'm about to go see what Moe nem on. I'll be back," I said before heading to the other room where Nutso ,Bone, T Stone and Breezy were smoking Kush, drinking Hennessy, and watching Juice.

"What's the demo, law?" Bone slurred dropping a gang sign with me.

"Shit, what you on lil bro?" I asked grabbing the smoldering blunt that Nut was tryna hand him.

"Shit, ready for tomorrow."

"You and Breezy not going with us. Y'all staying here."

"No, the fuck I'm not! You can't keep me outta this one, Moe," he said cutting me off.

"Bro, I can't put you in that type of danger. It's already bad enough I'm letting my lil cousin go but I can't let you ride," I told him shaking my head.

"He right lil bro. Let the big Moes handle this shit," Nutso said with a smirk.

"Shut yo' bitch ass up," Bone growled angrily.

"See, you a kid. You can't control yo' emotions and that's why you can't come now," Nut shot back causing the rest of us to laugh.

"At least I can control my bladder," Bone shot back making Nutso shoot him a funny look.

"Yeah, keep talking crazy," Bone threatened.

"Let me see the pipes you brought with you," I told T Stone. He got up from his seat, grabbed a Nike backpack and emptied its contents on the bed. "Now this what the fuck I'm talking about, Law!" I said rubbing my hands together while I admired the small arsenal of weapons he had.

"When we go in this bitch, we gotta be on point. Anything fishy and we fucking everybody up, even Killa. Nut, I want you to carry the bricks. They want ten. T Stone you gon' grab the money and make sure everything is everything. That's when we gon' give them the work. After that, we getting straight the fuck up outta there, ya hear me?" I asked.

When nobody replied I said, "Bone, let me holla at you real quick." I led him into the bathroom before closing the door and turning on the sink. "Bro, if some Fu shit happen tomorrow, it's gon' be all on you to keep this shit going. You, Tippu, Breezy, Binky, Von D and Lil C gon' have to step up for us. I told Lopez if you ever came to him alone to serve you. Here." I passed him a prepaid flip phone. "This the only phone you use to contact him. He one of them paranoid ass niggas so don't call him unless it's business and don't ever play with that nigga money. Them Mexican mufuckas will try to kill everybody close to us behind they bread. And one more thing lil bro, make sure you always come through for Ashley and Precious for me," I told him.

"How much work y'all taking again?"

"Ten bricks. It's fifteen in the trap on Prairie. Keep six for yourself and let the guys eat with you. Don't get big headed gang. I want you to run yo' bag to the fuckin ceiling and remember that just because a nigga yo' friend today, don't mean he gon' be yo' man tomorrow. Shit change bro. Believe it or not, it a be a nigga like Von that will trade on you in the long run. You never a know so watch everybody," I said trying to school him even though I was still learning myself.

"All well, even doe I know y'all gon' be good. Do you think y'all should trust T Stone?"

"Hell yeah, we brothers and brothers fight from time to time but we don't hold grudges. I know where Moe stands. He one of the most solid niggas I ever met," I said truthfully before giving him a brotherly hug. For some reason, I was in my feelings. I was the one who brought him into this shit just like the big bros like Henno, Wooski D, Baby, Brutis, Rego and Ray Real brought me in. I wondered if our bond would ever deteriorate or would our bond be able to get tested to the point where we stopped trusting each other. I hoped not. Bone was my best friend. He was like my little brother. Blood couldn't make us any closer than we were. It was no amount of money, no bitch or nothing else that I could think of that was worth our bond.

The rest of the night dragged by. I chilled and kicked it with Ashley and Precious all night. When it was finally time to lay it down, I couldn't get any sleep. I tossed and turned all night. It seemed like I had just dozed off when Killa called me.

"They ready," he said.

"Right now?" I asked sleepily. Something told me to hang up and go back to sleep. A part of me wanted to hang up so bad but I couldn't.

"Yeah."

"Bro, it's nine in the fuckin morning. Them weird ass niggas can't wait?"

"Money don't wait for nobody," Killa shot back.

"Where they tryna meet at?"

"On 62 and St. Lawrence."

I was quiet for a moment. My mind flashed back to when I met Mieysha's cousin at a location he chose. I walked out of that situation robbed with a dead friend. I wasn't going for that shit for a second time.

"Hell naw, tell them to meet us on the block."

"What block?"

"The building. Tell them on Maryland doe. We gon' do that shit in Law old trap."

"You wanna do a four hundred thousand dollar drug deal in a fuckin bando?"

"Yeah, and I won't be there until about 10:30," I told him hanging up before he could protest. I wanted to meet them in the hood just in case we had to kill they ass.

I rolled over and flamed up a pre rolled Kush blunt. I laid there smoking while getting my thoughts together. I really wanted to pass the deal up. That thought kept running through my mind but if I passed the deal up, what type of hustler would I be? I had to secure the bag.

"I'm about to go bust this move," I said nudging Ashley in the ribs, waking her up. She didn't respond. She only stirred in her sleep. "Wake yo' lil ostrich-looking ass up," I said loudly.

"I hear you," she said turning towards me. "I Love you, Baby Dre and I always will but you might always be the dumbest man I ever loved," she said frowning at me. She had tried her best to convince me not to go and was mad that she couldn't.

"I know Ashley, baby, and I love you too," I said before getting up and going to the room where Precious was.

"Precious, I'm about to slide. I just wanted to come give you and Paradise a kiss before I left," I said waking her up. "Daddy loves you," I whispered to Paradise before kissing her forehead. "I love you too, Precious. I'ma see you later, aight?" I said before giving her a passionate tongue kiss.

"I love you more. Be safe."

"I got you," I promised before leaving out.

"YOOOO!" I shouted entering the room where the guys were. "It's that time," I said. Nutso and T Stone were already up, sitting on the bed talking and smoking. Bone was knocked out, but my yelling woke him up. "Killa just called me. We meeting dude nem on Maryland."

"Who the fuck picked that spot?" T Stone cut me off to ask.

"Me. Now what pipes y'all toting?" I asked.

"I got my Tech and a sawed off shotgun," Nutso stated proudly.

"Man, if you don't put that dumb ass shit down and grab some handguns," I told him walking to where he had all the guns laid out at. "What you got?" I asked T Stone.

"Two D.E.'s," he replied with a smile.

"You better blow them bitches too," I joked. He was the last person I worried about not shooting. I should've reminded him *not* to shoot someone if he didn't have to.

"I'ma take both of these Glocks," Nutso said showing me a Glock 27 and a Glock: 19. The Glock 27 had a stick in it.

I decided to carry a XD .45 with a stick in it and a .357 Sig Sauer. "Nut, you got them bricks?" I asked as we prepared to leave.

"Duh!" He huffed grabbing my daughter's *Hello Kitty* suitcase. "What?" he asked when he saw the look that I was giving him. "I thought we would look lowkey like this. Don't judge me," he said, making a goofy face that made everybody laugh as we left out. We were all on edge and needed that laugh desperately.

Ashley and Precious, who had Paradise in her arms, were in the hallway posted by the door.

"We just wanted to see you before you left and tell you to be safe and we love you," Precious said flashing me a warm smile.

"You really should consider cutting that shit off your head. Who goes to handle business with a ponytail?" Ashley asked with a giggle while grabbing my puffy ponytail and yanking it softly.

"Shut the fuck up," I said playfully smacking her hand away. "See y'all in a minute. Make sure y'all be ready for that threesome we talked about," I joked.

"You wish!" Precious said as we got on the elevator.

I was laughing but deep down I was nervous as hell for some reason. I thought about turning around for the hundredth time. I wanted to grab Paradise and run away from reality with her, but I knew that that wasn't an option. I prepared myself for what was ahead of me.

The ride to the hood was a silent, eerie one. Nobody spoke. We just smoked blunt after blunt. When we pulled up on 104th and Maryland, Killa was sitting in his Infiniti bobbing his head to a MMG Rome song.

"It took you niggas long enough," he gruffed climbing out of his truck.

"What time dude nem supposed to be pulling up?" I asked scanning the block looking for anything suspicious. I was also looking out for signs of Reesie or one of the Foes. Killa was dressed in all black like he was ready to go slide or something.

"They already in the trap."

"What the fuck they doing inside without you?" T Stone asked as if he could read my mind. The fact that dude nem were sitting in an abandoned house waiting for us was a red flag but I ignored it.

"On the G, what the fuck I look like sitting in a muthafucking trap?" Killa asked with an attitude.

As we entered the trap, I got washed over by the feeling of déjà vu. I played the back, looking around with my gun clutched in my hand. I was expecting for twelve to pop out at any moment.

"Where the fuck they at?" Nutso asked as we entered the living room of the trap. I could hear the nervous edge in his voice.

"They upstairs man. You niggas actin scary as hell. What the fuck wrong with y'all?" Killa replied, leading the way. You could look at Nut, T Stone or myself and tell that we were all on edge. We were all clutching, looking all over for any signs of danger.

When we made it to the second story of the house, two men were waiting inside the master bedroom. The taller one was dark skinned with long, thick dreadlocks and big pink lips. The other guy was shorter, about 5'9 with wavy hair and light brown skin. They were both dressed in designer from head to toe. They didn't look like they were the police but looks could be deceiving.

"Where's the shit?" The dread head asked. He had an accent like he was Haitian or Jamaican.

"We got it. Where that bread at, doe?" Nutso asked.

"Four-hundred-thousand dollars," the shorter guy said lifting a grey duffle bag in the air.

"I gotta piss," Killa said as the shorter guy opened the duffle bag, showing us bricks of fifty and hundred dollar bills.

"Let us see the work," the dread head said, pulling out a small pocket knife. Nutso unzipped the suitcase he was carrying, pulled out a brick and handed it to the dread head who poked it with the pocket knife and used his index finger to rub a little coke on his gums.

"Count that bread out," Nutso demanded.

"You count it," the shorter guy said tossing the duffle bag towards him. T Stone grabbed it, unzipped it, and immediately started flipping through a brick of bills just trying to make sure that they were all hundreds and fifties and that they felt real.

I was so wrapped up in watching the two men that when I heard a *click* in my ear, I damn near jumped out of my skin. I turned around to see Killa aiming his .40 at my head. He was squeezing the trigger but the gun wasn't going off. For a moment, I was stuck. I know I had to look like a deer caught in a pair of headlights. I had frozen up but I quickly snapped out of it as Killa tried chambering a round in his gun and T Stone sent multiple slugs ripping through his chest and neck. Nutso quickly upped his Glock 27 and started unloading on the two dudes who were supposed to be buying the bricks from us. Surprisingly, they both seemed as surprised as us and if they did have guns on them, they didn't even reach for them before Nut dropped them.

A thunderous boom went off from someone blowing a hole through the wall with a shotgun. "Shit!" I jumped behind an old wooden dresser as the shotgun and another gun went off.

"That bitch ass nigga backdoored us bro!" T Stone growled with thick veins coming out of his forehead. I bounced up from where I was at and ran to the bedroom door, kicking it open. Another blast went off before I popped out shooting wildly. Nut was right behind me. He caught the guy with the shotgun with a bullet to his chin, dropping him. Another guy who was shooting a .45 while running almost made it to the stairs that led to the first story of the house but T Stone's D.E. caught his upper back, sending him crashing to the ground.

"We gone!" Nutso shouted running back in the room to grab the suitcase with the bricks.

I heard movement downstairs, so I knew it was more people in the house. The guy on the floor was still breathing so I walked up and shot him in the back of the head. I slowly moved down the stairs with my gun aimed and my finger curled around the trigger.

Before I could make it all the way down the stairs, shots went off. I returned fire trying to see if I could make it to the front door of the home without getting shot. T Stone swung a arm around me and shot his D.E. about four times before almost pushing me down the stairs which led to the dining room. I could've bolted through the dining room to the front room and out of the front door but seeing Reesie crouched behind the island in the kitchen changed my whole gameplan. I wanted to end this shit today and I could only do that by killing him.

"Reesie in the kitchen!" I said before Lil 4 sent a flurry of shots towards me. One grazed my thigh. Nutso sent a barrage of shots at Lil 4 causing him to retreat in the basement. Reesie popped up from behind the island shooting his Glock with both hands.

"I think I hear sirens!" T Stone yelled just as the front door flew open and Bands came through shooting a Smith and Wesson .9mm. Nutso dropped the suitcase with the bricks in it as he ran through the door that led to the basement of the house. I saw Reesie bolt for the backdoor and I started to pursue him. I thought about grabbing the work, but I was so blinded by revenge that all I could think of was chasing Reesie. I ran through the kitchen and out the backdoor that was wide open. Reesie was moving through the backyard of the trap headed for the alley. I ran behind him shooting my XD with both hands. A bullet hit him in the back of his knee causing him to trip over his own feet and go tumbling to the ground. His gun flew out his hand and landed near a garbage can. I slowly crept up on him with my gun pointed ready to shoot if he made any sudden movement. He was laying there clutching his side where another bullet had caught him. His Moncler coat was soaked with blood.

"I'm hit, bro," he groaned as I stepped closer.

I chuckled and shot him again. This time in his thigh.

"I'm not yo' bro, you bitch ass nigga. I been waiting for this moment for so long," I said with venom in my tone.

Reesie went into a coughing fit before spitting a glob of blood out. "You don't really wanna kill me nigga. If the shoe was on the other foot, you would have been dead on the Foe," he said before flashing me a bloody smile.

This nigga was staring death in the face and he was still talking crazy. I had to respect his gangster. I actually wouldn't have expected anything less from him. He lived as a G and now he was about to die a G. I thought to myself as I lifted my gun and squeezed the trigger. Before I could get off more than three shots, another gun went off and I felt a hot bullet rip through my lower back and out my stomach.

"POLICE! DROP YOUR WEAPON!" a plain clothes detective yelled from behind me after he shot me. Before I could attempt to run or drop my weapon, the detective sent another bullet ripping through my upper shoulder and another one through my thigh. I dropped my gun and fell in the cold snow right next to Reesie, my brother turned enemy. Both of us were shot multiple times, bleeding to death. My mind raced back to the times when we used to talk about dying in the field by each other's side, only difference was back then it was us against them and we promised to go out together against the other side. Who would've thought we would take each other out?

My body started burning up and breathing got hard. My whole life started flashing before my eyes as I faded into thoughts of the good, the bad, the fun and the sad times. To be 19, I thought I did a lot of living but I really hadn't lived enough. I had a small share of the money and hoes. I learned how Risky the road of life was by walking each mile without taking a shortcut. They say the bigger, the risk, the bigger the reward. I'm from Risky Road where we risked it all. I just hate it had to end like this. I thought before the burning and darkness consumed me.

TO BE CONTINUED...

CITY OF SMOKE 2
Coming Soon

Lock Down Publications and Ca$h Presents
Assisted Publishing Packages

BASIC PACKAGE	UPGRADED PACKAGE
$499 Editing Cover Design Formatting	$800 Typing Editing Cover Design Formatting
ADVANCE PACKAGE $1,200 Typing Editing Cover Design Formatting Copyright registration Proofreading Upload book to Amazon	**LDP SUPREME PACKAGE** $1,500 Typing Editing Cover Design Formatting Copyright registration Proofreading Set up Amazon account Upload book to Amazon Advertise on LDP, Amazon and Facebook Page

***Other services available upon request.
Additional charges may apply

Lock Down Publications
P.O. Box 944
Stockbridge, GA 30281-9998
Phone: 470 303-9761

Submission Guideline

Submit the first three chapters of your completed manuscript to ldpsubmissions@gmail.com. In the subject line add **Your Book's Title**. The manuscript must be in a Word Doc file and sent as an attachment. Document should be in Times New Roman, double spaced, and in size 12 font. Also, provide your synopsis and full contact information. If sending multiple submissions, they must each be in a separate email.

Have a story but no way to send it electronically? You can still submit to LDP/Ca$h Presents. Send in the first three chapters, written or typed, of your completed manuscript to:

LDP: Submissions Dept
P.O. Box 944
Stockbridge, GA 30281-9998

DO NOT send original manuscript. Must be a duplicate. Provide your synopsis and a cover letter containing your full contact information.

Thanks for considering LDP and Ca$h Presents.

NEW RELEASES

SOSA GANG 2 by ROMELL TUKES

KINGZ OF THE GAME 7 by PLAYA RAY

SKI MASK MONEY 2 by RENTA

BORN IN THE GRAVE 3 by SELF MADE TAY

LOYALTY IS EVERYTHING 3 by MOLOTTI

Coming Soon from Lock Down Publications/Ca$h Presents

BLOOD OF A BOSS VI
SHADOWS OF THE GAME II
TRAP BASTARD II
By **Askari**

LOYAL TO THE GAME IV
By **T.J. & Jelissa**

TRUE SAVAGE VIII
MIDNIGHT CARTEL IV
DOPE BOY MAGIC IV
CITY OF KINGZ III
NIGHTMARE ON SILENT AVE II
THE PLUG OF LIL MEXICO II
CLASSIC CITY II
By **Chris Green**

BLAST FOR ME III
A SAVAGE DOPEBOY III
CUTTHROAT MAFIA III
DUFFLE BAG CARTEL VII
HEARTLESS GOON VI
By **Ghost**

A HUSTLER'S DECEIT III
KILL ZONE II
BAE BELONGS TO ME III
TIL DEATH II
By **Aryanna**

KING OF THE TRAP III
By **T.J. Edwards**

GORILLAZ IN THE BAY V
3X KRAZY III
STRAIGHT BEAST MODE III
By **De'Kari**

KINGPIN KILLAZ IV
STREET KINGS III
PAID IN BLOOD III
CARTEL KILLAZ IV
DOPE GODS III
By **Hood Rich**

SINS OF A HUSTLA II
By **ASAD**

YAYO V
BRED IN THE GAME 2
By **S. Allen**

THE STREETS WILL TALK II
By **Yolanda Moore**

SON OF A DOPE FIEND III
HEAVEN GOT A GHETTO III
SKI MASK MONEY III
By **Renta**

LOYALTY AIN'T PROMISED III
By **Keith Williams**

I'M NOTHING WITHOUT HIS LOVE II
SINS OF A THUG II
TO THE THUG I LOVED BEFORE II
IN A HUSTLER I TRUST II
By **Monet Dragun**

QUIET MONEY IV
EXTENDED CLIP III
THUG LIFE IV
By **Trai'Quan**

THE STREETS MADE ME IV
By **Larry D. Wright**

IF YOU CROSS ME ONCE III
ANGEL V
By **Anthony Fields**

THE STREETS WILL NEVER CLOSE IV
By **K'ajji**

HARD AND RUTHLESS III
KILLA KOUNTY IV
By **Khufu**

MONEY GAME III
By **Smoove Dolla**

MURDA WAS THE CASE III
Elijah R. Freeman

AN UNFORESEEN LOVE IV
BABY, I'M WINTERTIME COLD III
By **Meesha**

QUEEN OF THE ZOO III
By **Black Migo**

CONFESSIONS OF A JACKBOY III
By **Nicholas Lock**

JACK BOYS VS DOPE BOYS IV
A GANGSTA'S QUR'AN V
COKE GIRLZ II
COKE BOYS II
LIFE OF A SAVAGE V
CHI'RAQ GANGSTAS V
SOSA GANG III
BRONX SAVAGES II
BODYMORE KINGPINS II
By **Romell Tukes**

KING KILLA II
By **Vincent "Vitto" Holloway**

BETRAYAL OF A THUG III
By **Fre$h**

THE MURDER QUEENS III
By **Michael Gallon**

THE BIRTH OF A GANGSTER III
By **Delmont Player**

TREAL LOVE II
By **Le'Monica Jackson**

FOR THE LOVE OF BLOOD III
By **Jamel Mitchell**

RAN OFF ON DA PLUG II
By **Paper Boi Rari**

HOOD CONSIGLIERE III
By **Keese**

PRETTY GIRLS DO NASTY THINGS II
By **Nicole Goosby**

PROTÉGÉ OF A LEGEND III
LOVE IN THE TRENCHES II
By **Corey Robinson**

IT'S JUST ME AND YOU II
By **Ah'Million**

FOREVER GANGSTA III
By **Adrian Dulan**

GORILLAZ IN THE TRENCHES II
By **SayNoMore**

THE COCAINE PRINCESS VIII
By **King Rio**

CRIME BOSS II
By **Playa Ray**

LOYALTY IS EVERYTHING III
By **Molotti**

HERE TODAY GONE TOMORROW II
By **Fly Rock**

REAL G'S MOVE IN SILENCE II
By **Von Diesel**

GRIMEY WAYS IV
By **Ray Vinci**

Available Now

RESTRAINING ORDER I & II
By **CA$H & Coffee**

LOVE KNOWS NO BOUNDARIES I II & III
By **Coffee**

RAISED AS A GOON I, II, III & IV
BRED BY THE SLUMS I, II, III
BLAST FOR ME I & II
ROTTEN TO THE CORE I II III
A BRONX TALE I, II, III
DUFFLE BAG CARTEL I II III IV V VI
HEARTLESS GOON I II III IV V
A SAVAGE DOPEBOY I II
DRUG LORDS I II III
CUTTHROAT MAFIA I II
KING OF THE TRENCHES
By **Ghost**

LAY IT DOWN I & II
LAST OF A DYING BREED I II
BLOOD STAINS OF A SHOTTA I & II III
By **Jamaica**

LOYAL TO THE GAME I II III
LIFE OF SIN I, II III
By **TJ & Jelissa**

IF LOVING HIM IS WRONG...I & II
LOVE ME EVEN WHEN IT HURTS I II III
By **Jelissa**

BLOODY COMMAS I & II
SKI MASK CARTEL I, II & III
KING OF NEW YORK I II, III IV V
RISE TO POWER I II III
COKE KINGS I II III IV V
BORN HEARTLESS I II III IV
KING OF THE TRAP I II
By **T.J. Edwards**

WHEN THE STREETS CLAP BACK I & II III
THE HEART OF A SAVAGE I II III IV
MONEY MAFIA I II
LOYAL TO THE SOIL I II III
By **Jibril Williams**

A DISTINGUISHED THUG STOLE MY HEART I II & III
LOVE SHOULDN'T HURT I II III IV
RENEGADE BOYS I II III IV
PAID IN KARMA I II III
SAVAGE STORMS I II III
AN UNFORESEEN LOVE I II III
BABY, I'M WINTERTIME COLD I II
By **Meesha**

A GANGSTER'S CODE I &, II III
A GANGSTER'S SYN I II III
THE SAVAGE LIFE I II III
CHAINED TO THE STREETS I II III
BLOOD ON THE MONEY I II III
A GANGSTA'S PAIN I II III
By **J-Blunt**

PUSH IT TO THE LIMIT
By **Bre' Hayes**

BLOOD OF A BOSS I, II, III, IV, V
SHADOWS OF THE GAME
TRAP BASTARD
By **Askari**

THE STREETS BLEED MURDER I, II & III
THE HEART OF A GANGSTA I II& III
By **Jerry Jackson**

CUM FOR ME I II III IV V VI VII VIII
An **LDP Erotica Collaboration**

BRIDE OF A HUSTLA I II & II
THE FETTI GIRLS I, II& III
CORRUPTED BY A GANGSTA I, II III, IV
BLINDED BY HIS LOVE
THE PRICE YOU PAY FOR LOVE I, II ,III
DOPE GIRL MAGIC I II III
By **Destiny Skai**

WHEN A GOOD GIRL GOES BAD
By **Adrienne**

A GANGSTER'S REVENGE I II III & IV
THE BOSS MAN'S DAUGHTERS I II III IV V
A SAVAGE LOVE I & II
BAE BELONGS TO ME I II
A HUSTLER'S DECEIT I, II, III
WHAT BAD BITCHES DO I, II, III
SOUL OF A MONSTER I II III
KILL ZONE
A DOPE BOY'S QUEEN I II III
TIL DEATH
By **Aryanna**

THE COST OF LOYALTY I II III
By Kweli

A KINGPIN'S AMBITION
A KINGPIN'S AMBITION **II**
I MURDER FOR THE DOUGH
By **Ambitious**

TRUE SAVAGE I II III IV V VI VII
DOPE BOY MAGIC I, II, III
MIDNIGHT CARTEL I II III
CITY OF KINGZ I II
NIGHTMARE ON SILENT AVE
THE PLUG OF LIL MEXICO II
CLASSIC CITY
By **Chris Green**

A DOPEBOY'S PRAYER
By **Eddie "Wolf" Lee**

THE KING CARTEL I, II & III
By **Frank Gresham**

THESE NIGGAS AIN'T LOYAL I, II & III
By **Nikki Tee**

GANGSTA SHYT I II &III
By **CATO**

THE ULTIMATE BETRAYAL
By **Phoenix**

BOSS'N UP I, II & III
By **Royal Nicole**

I LOVE YOU TO DEATH
By **Destiny J**

I RIDE FOR MY HITTA
I STILL RIDE FOR MY HITTA
By **Misty Holt**

LOVE & CHASIN' PAPER
By **Qay Crockett**

TO DIE IN VAIN
SINS OF A HUSTLA
By **ASAD**

BROOKLYN HUSTLAZ
By **Boogsy Morina**

BROOKLYN ON LOCK I & II
By **Sonovia**

GANGSTA CITY
By **Teddy Duke**

A DRUG KING AND HIS DIAMOND I & II III
A DOPEMAN'S RICHES
HER MAN, MINE'S TOO I, II
CASH MONEY HO'S
THE WIFEY I USED TO BE I II
PRETTY GIRLS DO NASTY THINGS
By Nicole Goosby

LIPSTICK KILLAH I, II, III
CRIME OF PASSION I II & III
FRIEND OR FOE I II III
By **Mimi**

TRAPHOUSE KING I II & III
KINGPIN KILLAZ I II III
STREET KINGS I II
PAID IN BLOOD I II
CARTEL KILLAZ I II III
DOPE GODS I II
By **Hood Rich**

STEADY MOBBN' I, II, III
THE STREETS STAINED MY SOUL I II III
By **Marcellus Allen**

WHO SHOT YA I, II, III
SON OF A DOPE FIEND I II
HEAVEN GOT A GHETTO I II
SKI MASK MONEY I II
By **Renta**

GORILLAZ IN THE BAY I II III IV
TEARS OF A GANGSTA I II
3X KRAZY I II
STRAIGHT BEAST MODE I II
By **DE'KARI**

TRIGGADALE I II III
MURDA WAS THE CASE I II
By **Elijah R. Freeman**

THE STREETS ARE CALLING
By **Duquie Wilson**

SLAUGHTER GANG I II III
RUTHLESS HEART I II III
By **Willie Slaughter**

GOD BLESS THE TRAPPERS I, II, III
THESE SCANDALOUS STREETS I, II, III
FEAR MY GANGSTA I, II, III IV, V
THESE STREETS DON'T LOVE NOBODY I, II
BURY ME A G I, II, III, IV, V
A GANGSTA'S EMPIRE I, II, III, IV
THE DOPEMAN'S BODYGAURD I II
THE REALEST KILLAZ I II III
THE LAST OF THE OGS I II III
By **Tranay Adams**

MARRIED TO A BOSS I II III
By **Destiny Skai & Chris Green**

KINGZ OF THE GAME I II III IV V VI VII
CRIME BOSS
By **Playa Ray**

FUK SHYT
By **Blakk Diamond**

DON'T F#CK WITH MY HEART I II
By **Linnea**

ADDICTED TO THE DRAMA I II III
IN THE ARM OF HIS BOSS II
By **Jamila**

YAYO I II III IV
A SHOOTER'S AMBITION I II
BRED IN THE GAME
By **S. Allen**

LOYALTY AIN'T PROMISED I II
By **Keith Williams**

243

TRAP GOD I II III
RICH $AVAGE I II III
MONEY IN THE GRAVE I II III
By **Martell Troublesome Bolden**

FOREVER GANGSTA I II
GLOCKS ON SATIN SHEETS I II
By **Adrian Dulan**

TOE TAGZ I II III IV
LEVELS TO THIS SHYT I II
IT'S JUST ME AND YOU
By **Ah'Million**

KINGPIN DREAMS I II III
RAN OFF ON DA PLUG
By **Paper Boi Rari**

CONFESSIONS OF A GANGSTA I II III IV
CONFESSIONS OF A JACKBOY I II
By **Nicholas Lock**

I'M NOTHING WITHOUT HIS LOVE
SINS OF A THUG
TO THE THUG I LOVED BEFORE
A GANGSTA SAVED XMAS
IN A HUSTLER I TRUST
By **Monet Dragun**

CAUGHT UP IN THE LIFE I II III
THE STREETS NEVER LET GO I II III
By **Robert Baptiste**

NEW TO THE GAME I II III
MONEY, MURDER & MEMORIES I II III
By **Malik D. Rice**

CREAM I II III
THE STREETS WILL TALK
By **Yolanda Moore**

LIFE OF A SAVAGE I II III IV
A GANGSTA'S QUR'AN I II III IV
MURDA SEASON I II III
GANGLAND CARTEL I II III
CHI'RAQ GANGSTAS I II III IV
KILLERS ON ELM STREET I II III
JACK BOYZ N DA BRONX I II III
A DOPEBOY'S DREAM I II III
JACK BOYS VS DOPE BOYS I II III
COKE GIRLZ
COKE BOYS
SOSA GANG I II
BRONX SAVAGES
BODYMORE KINGPINS
By **Romell Tukes**

QUIET MONEY I II III
THUG LIFE I II III
EXTENDED CLIP I II
A GANGSTA'S PARADISE
By **Trai'Quan**

THE STREETS MADE ME I II III
By **Larry D. Wright**

THE ULTIMATE SACRIFICE I, II, III, IV, V, VI
KHADIFI
IF YOU CROSS ME ONCE I II
ANGEL I II III IV
IN THE BLINK OF AN EYE
By **Anthony Fields**

CITY OF SMOKE | MOLOTTI

THE LIFE OF A HOOD STAR
By **Ca$h & Rashia Wilson**

THE STREETS WILL NEVER CLOSE I II III
By **K'ajji**

NIGHTMARES OF A HUSTLA I II III
By **King Dream**

CONCRETE KILLA I II III
VICIOUS LOYALTY I II III
By **Kingpen**

HARD AND RUTHLESS I II
MOB TOWN 251
THE BILLIONAIRE BENTLEYS I II III
REAL G'S MOVE IN SILENCE
By **Von Diesel**

GHOST MOB
By **Stilloan Robinson**

MOB TIES I II III IV V VI
SOUL OF A HUSTLER, HEART OF A KILLER I II
GORILLAZ IN THE TRENCHES
By **SayNoMore**

BODYMORE MURDERLAND I II III
THE BIRTH OF A GANGSTER I II
By **Delmont Player**

FOR THE LOVE OF A BOSS
By **C. D. Blue**

KILLA KOUNTY I II III IV
By **Khufu**

MOBBED UP I II III IV
THE BRICK MAN I II III IV V
THE COCAINE PRINCESS I II III IV V VI VII
By **King Rio**

MONEY GAME I II
By **Smoove Dolla**

A GANGSTA'S KARMA I II III
By **FLAME**

KING OF THE TRENCHES I II III
By **GHOST & TRANAY ADAMS**

QUEEN OF THE ZOO I II
By **Black Migo**

GRIMEY WAYS I II III
By **Ray Vinci**

XMAS WITH AN ATL SHOOTER
By **Ca$h & Destiny Skai**

KING KILLA
By **Vincent "Vitto" Holloway**

BETRAYAL OF A THUG I II
By **Fre$h**

THE MURDER QUEENS I II
By **Michael Gallon**

TREAL LOVE
By **Le'Monica Jackson**

FOR THE LOVE OF BLOOD I II
By **Jamel Mitchell**

HOOD CONSIGLIERE I II
By **Keese**

PROTÉGÉ OF A LEGEND I II
LOVE IN THE TRENCHES
By **Corey Robinson**

BORN IN THE GRAVE I II III
By **Self Made Tay**

MOAN IN MY MOUTH
By **XTASY**

TORN BETWEEN A GANGSTER AND A
GENTLEMAN
By **J-BLUNT & Miss Kim**

LOYALTY IS EVERYTHING I II
By **Molotti**

HERE TODAY GONE TOMORROW
By **Fly Rock**

PILLOW PRINCESS
By **S. Hawkins**

BOOKS BY LDP'S CEO, CA$H

TRUST IN NO MAN
TRUST IN NO MAN 2
TRUST IN NO MAN 3
BONDED BY BLOOD
SHORTY GOT A THUG
THUGS CRY
THUGS CRY 2
THUGS CRY 3
TRUST NO BITCH
TRUST NO BITCH 2
TRUST NO BITCH 3
TIL MY CASKET DROPS
RESTRAINING ORDER
RESTRAINING ORDER 2
IN LOVE WITH A CONVICT
LIFE OF A HOOD STAR
XMAS WITH AN ATL SHOOTER

Printed in the USA
CPSIA information can be obtained
at www.ICGtesting.com
LVHW021819290923
759666LV00002B/115